King Killa

Lock Down Publications and Ca$h
Presents

King Killa

A Novel by *Vincent "Vito" Holloway*

King Killa

Lock Down Publications
P.O. Box 944
Stockbridge, Ga 30281
www.lockdownpublications.com

Lock Down Publications
Like our page on Facebook: Lock Down Publications @
www.facebook.com/lockdownpublications.ldp

Book interior design by: **Shawn Walker**
Edited by: **Lashonda Johnson**

Vincent "Vito" Holloway

Stay Connected with Us!

Text **LOCKDOWN** to 22828 to stay up-to-date with new releases, sneak peaks, contests and more...

Thank you!

Submission Guideline.

Submit the first three chapters of your completed manuscript to ldpsubmissions@gmail.com, subject line: Your book's title. The manuscript must be in a .doc file and sent as an attachment. Document should be in Times New Roman, double spaced and in size 12 font. Also, provide your synopsis and full contact information. If sending multiple submissions, they must each be in a separate email.

Have a story but no way to send it electronically? You can still submit to LDP/Ca$h Presents. Send in the first three chapters, written or typed, of your completed manuscript to:

LDP: Submissions Dept
P.O. Box 944
Stockbridge, Ga 30281

DO NOT send original manuscript. Must be a duplicate.

Provide your synopsis and a cover letter containing your full contact information.

Thanks for considering LDP and Ca$h Presents.

Vincent "Vito" Holloway

King Killa

Prologue

"Mem gwan kill dem fada!" Majestic spat vehemently as he watched his backbone, his father, grow weaker by the minute as the cancer ravishing his body took his soul. "Mem no run from Nearia, mon. Mem 'ave 'eart of de lion," he said through clenched teeth as he thumped his chest with his fist over his heart.

"No," Buju said as he forcefully grabbed his son by the arm. He glared at his boy before falling back into his pillows and closing his eyes again. He hated that the simplest acts now seemed to take so much out of him when before he accomplished them with ease. But now he was faced with an enemy he couldn't defeat with sheer force or mental manipulation, and it was killing him. "Ye will do wat mem tell ye at do. Wen mem pass, mem enemies will smell de blood in de water…"

Majestic blew out a frustrated breath and did something he would never do under normal circumstances: interrupt his father. "But fada, mem gwan do wat must be done. Mem will 'old down de f——"

Buju held up a hand, cutting his son's rant short. He understood perfectly where Majestic was coming from, but he needed him to follow his instructions to the letter. He smiled at his lessons coming out of his son's mouth, but he hadn't had nearly enough time to teach him all that he needed to know and he was getting angry because time was short and he could feel it slipping away. The angrier he became, the more energy he used, which wasn't a lot these days.

"Ye friends are not ye friends. De only ting keeping dem from revealing de face of de snake is de air mem still drawing. As soon as mem soul leave mem body, de face's ye grew up loving and admiring will become foes."

"Well, let mem clean de bomba clot snakes up now before ye close ye eyes. Admit mem…" Majestic had to stop and compose himself because talking about his father dying made his chest tight and his breath short. "…admit mem ta protect ye legacy, fada," he added quietly out of respect for the way his father was looking at him.

"No," Buju said quietly. He looked at his only son. He hated the fact that he wouldn't be around to finish teaching him the lessons of becoming a man, a king who ruled. So sometimes one had to be the example instead of showing an example, and it was his son's time now, no matter how much he might not be ready. "Listen," he growled when he saw that his son was about to interrupt again. Majestic immediately closed his mouth. "Listen, go ta de States wit' ye mudda and sistas and build ye a loyal team. Trust Nearia, mon, but recognize de strength and de weakness in each mon ye use. Ye foundation 'ave ta be strong before ye come reclaim wat mem 'ave built and wat belongs ta ye and ye sistas, because as of now it is lost. De moment mem take mem last air, Jacques de 'ouse servant will spread de word ta 'is new master, de pussy boy 'e's now working fa. More than likely it's Terror." He spat when he spoke that name. It was no secret they were bitter enemies, and only three people on earth knew why: him, his wife and Terror. "Ye already know wat ta do. So don't waste time and do mem bidding. Me love ye wit' mem very soul. Ye are a Livingston true and true and mem know ye will do mem proud." He smiled wanly as he opened his eyes again to look at his son, whose shoulders now carried the weight of the world upon them. Oh, how he wished he could live to witness the rise his heir would accomplish by any means necessary! But his time was up, and death would not be cheated. "Tell ye mudda mem love 'er. Tell 'er that mem couldn't ask fa a betta rib. Tell 'er mem sorry. Tell ye sistas mem said do wat must be done. Admire de strength in de women around ye. They are de foundation, son." He grabbed his son's hand and closed his eyes for the last time.

It took Majestic a minute before he realized that his father had gone to the other side. He wanted to cry, but he knew how his father would feel about that, so he laid his father's hand onto his chest and kissed him on his forehead. He didn't want to leave his body because he knew what their enemies would do to it once they got their hands on it, but he had to do what his father instructed him to do: leave him be. He got up and was about depart when he remembered the wooden lion's head his father wore around his neck. He turned back towards his father and gently lifted the wooden necklace from his body. When he put it on, he could've sworn that a piece of his father's spirit entered his body. It was like his voice was now in his ear. He knew what he had to do. He pulled his Beretta from his waist, stalked to the door like he was a lion after a gazelle, and snatched it open.

The house servant Jacques fell onto his backside as he tried to scramble away from listening at the keyhole.

"Mas...Master Majestic, mem just wanta know if ye and ye fada..." His voice trailed off at the look on Majestic's face.

Majestic felt his face tighten up at the mention of his father coming out of this snake's mouth. He tightened his grip around the handle of his pistol.

"Which mon ye work fa now?" he asked the quivering servant on the floor in front of him.

"Mem...mem don't know wat ye mean, Master Majestic." Jacques started sliding away from him as he tried to explain. "Mem loyalties are wit' de Livingstons." He was trying to appear confident, but was failing miserably. He came across as a man who was guilty of something.

"Which mon ye work fa, now?" Majestic asked again as he raised the Beretta and pointed it at the chest of the man who was willing to sell his father out to his enemies.

Jacques's eyes grew wider as he spotted the gun for the first time. He closed them quickly as if he could make the scene disappear and started mumbling like he was praying.

"Mem not gwan ask ye again, pussy boy," Majestic growled. He was running out of patience.

Jacques swallowed his panic and took a deep breath to try and calm down before he spoke. "Mr. Colston paid mem ta tell 'im wen Master Buju took 'is last breath. Mem sorry, sir." Tears started cascading down his cheeks as he prepared for death. His heart hurt with his betrayal, and now he would pay the ultimate price.

"Turn over on your stomach, pussy boy," Majestic ordered. Jacques started screaming and begging for mercy. "Shut ye mouth, pussy boy. Mem not gon' kill ye. Death will be too easy fa ye," Majestic said, tired of the displays of weakness. Jacques calmed down and did what he was told. He was eager to comply with whatever he was told to do if it meant living.

"Tell Terror de lion will rise again," Majestic said before putting the gun against his spine and pulling the trigger. "Now de snake will slither like de snake is s'posed to." He laughed maniacally before stepping over the screaming man and disappearing into the night.

****

Correctional Officer Tammy Sanchez was one of the most beautiful women to walk the yard and she knew it. She was of Dominican descent with a body only God could have created. Men on the compound inmates and officers alike wanted to taste, but she only had eyes for one man: King Domingez.

"King, you have to report to the sergeant's office to sign for your legal mail," she said when she arrived at the weight pile, where a group of convicts was working out. She stood there watching the muscles ripple and flex in King's arms and chest as he lifted the bar repeatedly. Her attraction was evident - a fact that didn't go unnoticed.

"Damn 'chez, you staring at my man like you want to eat him or something," Tango joked when he caught her staring. His remark drew chuckles from those around the weight pile.

"Whatever, nigga." She rolled her eyes and smacked her lips. She waved him off as she kept her attention on King. "Did you hear me?" she asked when he kept lifting weights.

King heard her, but didn't bother to respond because there wasn't any need to. He finished his set, grabbed his shirt, and dapped up Tango before walking right past her on his way to the sergeant's office without saying a single word.

Officer Sanchez looked at his retreating back and sucked her teeth. He frustrated her no end.

"Looks like you need to step your game up Ms. 'chez." Tango tried to keep a straight face, but he couldn't because the weight pile burst out laughing again.

She gave him the finger as she stalked off after King.

"Why are you ignoring me?" she asked when she caught up to King.

"You know why," he replied as he cut his eyes at her. He had to admit that she was sexy, but he had a rider on his team and word traveled.

"She doesn't have to know," she said seriously.

"I would know," he replied, just as serious. "I wouldn't go against my own character because a man who doesn't stand for something will fall for anything." He was now speaking in English because he didn't want any misunderstandings.

Officer Sanchez was amazed at how faithful he was to his girl. She didn't want for attention, but she couldn't get any from him. Other inmates would try and holla at her all during the week, masturbating to her, giving her love letters, then they would go to visitation with their wives and girlfriends and profess their undying love. But King wouldn't even give her conversation unless she forced him to, like now. He was so young, but so serious, and she liked the fact that he didn't see her like the rest of the thirsty niggas on the yard. She wanted him and she was rarely denied what she wanted. "You think she is faithful to you?" she asked slyly. She knew with the time he was serving, no woman would be faithful - not even her.

"No, she is faithful to my money." King was watching her study him. He knew what she wanted but she was simple, unoriginal, and messy. The potential was there though.

"I'ma make you forget about your girl," she said with a smirk gracing her plump lips.

King stopped before they entered the building and turned to fully look at her. He snorted a laugh at how she was blushing and trying to act all shy. "What can you do for me?" he asked, just to see how she would respond. He didn't need her to do anything for him, but maybe she could be useful eventually.

"I can make your time easier," she said, letting it be known that she was down for whatever.

"Money can arrange that." King dismissed her clumsy attempt to seduce him. She would have to come better than that.

"Yes, you are correct. But why spend money when you can get it for free?" she responded.

"Because when you pay for it, you don't have to worry about emotional involvement," King said before he turned and walked into the building, leaving her looking silly.

"He acts like he is King for real." She rolled her eyes as he gave her his back to stare at for the second time that day. She had to keep it real with herself, though he had her panties soaking wet. There was just something about him that intrigued her. She had never chased after a man before, but she was up to the challenge. She was used to getting whatever man she wanted and she would get this one.

King walked towards the sergeant's office, wondering if this was another letter informing him that another appeal got turned down. He couldn't deal with too many more rejections. If it wasn't for his best friend Marco and his wifey Sophia, he would've given up hope a long time ago, but he knew that they were holding him down in every way, so he had to remain strong. He rounded the corner to find a line of other inmates waiting to sign for their own mail also. He hopped onto the end of the line to await his turn. When he reached the office, Sergeant Harris was waiting for him.

"I kind of figured you would be the last one in here, King," she said, smirking at him.

"They say you save the best for last," he said, smiling. He closed the door behind him.

"Whatever, nigga. You have a girl, remember?" she said, arching her eyebrow as she looked at him. King didn't reply to that statement. "Just like I thought. You don't have anything to say. Sign the book and open your mail," she added, pointing to where he needed to sign. When that was completed, she handed him his mail.

"This is probably another rejection from the justice system," he said before stuffing the letter into his pocket unopened.

"Ye of little faith." She frowned at him. "Boy, open that letter and find out what's up," she told him, hoping that he finally got some good news because she had grown attached to him since he had been there and she thought he had so much to offer the world.

King pulled the letter from his pocket and stared at it for a few seconds before tearing it open. He scanned the letter quickly, not really reading it until something caught his attention. He stood up abruptly, ready to leave. "Yo, you got me tonight when I clean up?" he asked.

"You know I do," she answered as she looked at him curiously. "What up? Good news?" she asked, wondering what had him anxious.

"I don't know yet, but I'll talk to you tonight," he replied over his shoulder as he rushed out of her office. He made it back to his block in record time and made a beeline straight to his room. He found his bunk mate Tango lying across his bottom bunk. He looked up when King rushed into their room, saw the look on his face, and asked what was wrong.

"Read this, son," King said as he handed him the legal mail he just received."

Tango took he letter and quickly read it. After he finished, he looked up to find King smiling at him. "You did it, my nigga. You beat them crackers," he said, smiling right along with him. "It's time to go, dog. We hit the bricks a couple of months apart now," he added, getting hyped up.

King smiled at his home boy's excitement. He was excited also, but he needed to make a few calls first before he got carried away. "I need to hop on the line and get at a few people. Keep a lookout for me, dog." He pulled the cell phone out of his pants where he had it tied to his boxers.

"I got you, son," Tango said, hopping up and leaving the room.

King put the blind up on the door window and called his lawyer.

"Hello?" a female voice answered the phone.

"Is that how Latoya Watkins, attorney at law, is supposed to answer her phone?" he asked, teasing her.

"Boy, whatever," she said, laughing when she recognized his voice. "My secretary had to leave early and I'm tired of answering this damn phone, but I've been waiting on your call. You got my letter yet?" She tried hard to keep the excitement out of her voice, but it was damn near impossible because King wasn't just a client to her.

"So it's official?" he asked her in Spanish, needing to hear it from her directly.

"Of course it's official, King," she answered in Spanish. "I told you that the murder charge was bogus anyway. You read the letter, right?"

"Yeah, I got it, T, but did you get the rest of the money from Marcos and Sophia yet?" he asked. Everything had changed now that he had won his appeal.

"I got the fifty stacks they dropped off a couple of months ago, but they have been avoiding me ever since. They won't return calls. They've moved from the address you gave me. I'm telling you, King, I think they are fu——"

"Let me call you back," he said, cutting her off. He was tired of hearing her suspicions about his wifey and best friend. They had history and he trusted her, but nothing compared to his heart and his right hand. He never questioned their loyalty and he wasn't about to let anyone else do it either.

"Alright, but call me on my cell 'cause I was only waiting on you to call before I left for the day," she said quietly. She expected him to cut her off because he never allowed her to tell him about her suspicions, but she knew in her heart that she was right. She just hoped he didn't catch another murder charge when the truth finally came out.

"I will call you later on tonight."

"Thank you. I appreciate you." She was a trooper and he was lucky to have her on his team.

Latoya was quiet for a few minutes as she gathered her thoughts. Every time he talked to her in Spanish, it brought back memories of all the nights they spent in her office with him teaching her to speak the language. During those long nights, she fell in love with the young, silent King, but he let it be known that he had a girl and so she played the position of his lawyer. She knew his bitch was a sack-chasing gold digger and was cheating on him. She just waited until her house of cards fell down and the lies came to the light because she would be there to help King put it all back together again. "You know that it was nothing, King," she said quietly before hanging up.

King knew what she was feeling and thinking, but at the moment, he had no time for dealing with emotions, no matter how strong they were. He dialed Sophia's number and waited for her to answer.

"Hello?" a male voice answered aggressively.

King paused for a second when he heard the tone of voice, but let it go when he recognized his friend's voice. "Marco, what's up?"

"What's up, King?" Marco replied coolly when he recognized the voice.

"Let me speak with Sophia and then I will talk to you," King said, ready to tell his baby the good news.

"Before I put her on the phone, let me tell you something, kid," Marco said arrogantly. He was starting to gain confidence and it was coming through the phone.

King heard rage in the tone of his voice and felt his gut clench. He thought back to all of the warnings Latoya tried to give him, but he had ignored them and hoped she wrong. In his heart, though, he knew she wasn't. He kept his silence because he didn't trust his voice at that moment. The arrogance in Marco's voice was starting to get to him, but he kept that to himself.

When King didn't respond, Marco gained even more confidence and continued. "Everything you built out here now belongs to me."

"Everything?" King asked softly.

"*Everything*," Marco replied mockingly. "For a long time, you really thought you were a King out here. Well, pussy, it's over for you. Hope you don't drop the soap."

"Let me talk to Sophia," King said so coldly that Marco felt the ice through the phone.

"Baby, tell this lame what it is," Marco bragged before handing phone to Sophia.

Sophia put the phone to her ear and spoke directly. "King, you will always have a place in my heart but you have twenty-five years, my love. Life goes on. This thing with Marco just happened. Sorry, but shit happens," she said with fake regret.

"Put me on speakerphone," King said calmly. "You both are right. Life goes on. Y'all betrayed me and for that, I will repay you both. Marco, you have the top spot. I hope you can keep it, kid." He said his piece and hung up before either of them could respond. He had nothing else to say to them, and besides, he didn't understand snake anyway. He dialed another number and waited for it to be answered.

"What's up?"

"Trey, what's up?" King asked when he heard the voice of his little homie.

"King, what's up, big homie?" Trey asked excitedly.

"I'm about to come back to the streets in less than a year," King told him.

"Word up?" Trey asked excitedly. "Word up. That's what's up." This was the news he had been waiting to hear.

"Listen, Marco has the top spot," King said and waited on the explosion.

"What!" Trey said loudly through the phone. "Shit. He is a fucking pussy."

"Just listen, and do as I say," King instructed, smiling a little. He needed Trey to focus and pay attention because he was now losing the race and had to catch up. "Take that money to my lawyer for me."

"I got you," Trey said, listening closely despite his ringing emotions.

"Be my eyes and ears. Become his right hand and get in his pocket."

"I got you, big homie," Trey said, smirking at the plan that was being set in motion. Marco wouldn't see it coming from a mile away. He hoped he was the one who got to kill that bitch nigga.

"Be easy and I'll be in contact," King said before hanging up. He sat on the bed for a few minutes trying to fully process everything that had just transpired. He got up and left the room after hearing the call for chow.

****

Czar was on the phone trying to get in contact with his connect. He was watching the ass of his shorty as she tore through the boutique they were shopping in. She wasn't paying attention to any price tags because he told her just throw it in the bag, like Fabolous said.

Even though he appeared to be focusing solely on her and her ass, his eyes old a different story. They were moving in all directions, trying to spot anything out of the ordinary. He was kind of a big deal in the streets of New Orleans, the place where he was raised into a man and where his earliest memories were of catching crawfish at the creek. Niggas hated him because of his brash, cocky, and arrogant attitude, but what could he say? Money made him feel like he was the king of the hill. His mother did right in naming him Czar because he felt like royalty. His name was on people's lips almost as much as Lil Wayne's and Boosie's in New Orleans because he was the man to see for just about anything you wanted: coke, heroin, pills and guns. He had the connect, and to the streets he was the gateway to a better way of living because his prices beat everyone else's three states in any direction.

Vincent "Vito" Holloway

After Hurricane Katrina, New Orleans became a cesspool to those who thrived off of the chaos, but it also became a hustler's paradise for those who were strong enough to take their piece of the pie. He recognized the potential, even as a youngster, but he was only a petty hustler at the time. So he got his where he could - that is, until he stumbled across his pot of gold. Only difference was his wasn't at the end of the rainbow, but on a corner in the Ninth Ward getting jumped by some roughnecks. He didn't like the cowardly tactic of a group of men jumping a solitary individual, so he stepped in and put a stop to it. Niggas were feeling some type of way because they felt like he stopped a quick come-up, but Czar was raised right there in the Ninth Ward and his hammer game was well documented. He had two 44 bulldogs, revolvers he called grave diggers. He kept them on him at all times and they had saved his life more than once. So them niggas kept their feelings to themselves.

The guy getting jumped was a Mexican named Raúl who was in love with a hood rat and driving a hundred thousand dollar car, but he didn't know niggas in the hood smelled easy money like a shark with blood in the water. He learned his lesson the hard way and never made that mistake again. Raúl was so grateful that he introduced Czar to his father, who was the connect and vouched for his thoroughness despite his young age. It'd been popping ever since. Raúl became one homie he trusted and their bond was tight til this day.

After securing the connect, Czar put a ruthless team together and took over New Orleans in a way that was unprecedented for one his age. He served up the city faster than people could say F.E.M.A. He was bumping in parts of Texas, Alabama, Georgia, Florida, and parts of the Midwest. Nobody could beat his prices and if they did, it was because the product had been stepped on so many times it was inferior and no good. His mother, who was a voodoo priestess, always told him she foresaw his rise to power, but he didn't think even she knew how far he would rise. He was making so much money he didn't know what to do with it all, but he wasn't greedy, so he brought his best friend, his right hand, his brother from another mother, Jimmy Slim, along for the ride. He trusted Jimmy with everything except his connect, and it was a point of contention between them, but some things you just didn't share. He thought about telling him who his connect was in case something ever happened to him, but every time he came close to doing so, Jimmy would do something to remind him that not everyone could be the chief. Someone had to be Indians. Czar knew that as long as he had the connect, he was untouchable—or so he thought.

Czar and his team were at the top of every jackboy's fantasy lists of desired targets, but no one was stupid enough to try them. For one, their exploits with gunplay were well known, and for two, his team of young wolves was ready to put on a newsworthy show anytime, anyplace. And lastly, he didn't trust a lot so he was always on point and vowed to never get caught slipping. His mother made sure he was raised with the right amount of paranoia, and that's why he was able to spot the two men who had been tailing them all day as they shopped. He was confident in his own abilities, but it was at times like this he wished he had let some of his young boys become his shadow. The men following them were not too discreet. It was like they wanted him to see them, or maybe they thought he was just a dumb dopeboy and wasn't smart enough to spot them.

Their mistake, he thought as he waited for his connect to pick up. "What the fuck," he mumbled to himself when the call went straight to voicemail again. He had been trying all day to get in contact with his connect because it was time to re-up, but something wasn't right. He dialed Jimmy's number and waited for him to pick up. His phone rang about five times before he hung up and dialed Raúl's number. He turned to look out of the storefront window to see if he could spot his two tails. He couldn't see them and figured they were waiting for them to come out of the store, but as he turned back from the window, he caught a reflection that he didn't expect to see. His two shadows were inside of the store with guns oriented directly at them. But before he could react, they started shooting. His girl's head exploded like a ripe melon. Brain matter and pieces of her skull showered his body, but he didn't have time to worry about that now because he wanted to live.

Czar dropped his phone and reached for his gravediggers. He turned and let go with his angels of death. He saw one of the men go down immediately with his face missing, but he missed his partner - to his detriment because the bullets from his return fire hit him in the chest, tossing him back into a clothes rack. Even though the bulletproof vest he wore religiously stopped the shots from penetrating, it still felt like he had been kicked in the chest by a mule. He didn't have time to check the damage since he knew the remaining assassin was moving in to finish him off. He gripped his bulldogs and took a deep breath, grimacing. It felt like he had at least some fractured ribs.

Czar looked through the clothes racks and tried to locate the man trying to kill him. It was hard because people were running everywhere, screaming and trying to get away, but he finally spotted the man's legs and despite the pain he felt every time he took a breath, he made his move. He raised his guns and sent slugs into the man's thighs and legs, knocking him off of his feet. He rolled over and sat up. He knew that the police would be converging at the scene and he couldn't afford to get locked up, especially with two bodies lying a few feet away. He got up and shot out the storefront window to create more chaos, grabbed his phone where he dropped it, and headed for the exit at the back of the store. He was about to vault the counter when he was shot in his left arm, causing him to drop one of his guns. He turned and saw the man who would never walk again trying to sit up as he pointed his pistol in his direction. Czar grew angry all over again as he raised his remaining bulldog and put the man to sleep forever. He tucked his gun into his waist, retrieved his other pistol, and escaped out the back of the store. He looked both ways down the alley and saw that it was congested with pedestrians. Moving with purpose, he tried to blend in with them as best he could. He knew the streets of New Orleans like the back of his hand and he put that knowledge to use. He felt his wound dripping steadily down his side and knew that he had to get off of the streets quickly or he would lose consciousness due to blood loss, something he couldn't afford to happen. Getting back to his car was out of the question because he didn't know if they had somebody watching it, waiting on him to show. So he had to come up with a different plan, and fast. His mind kept trying to figure out who had the balls to send shooters at him, but it was hard to focus at the moment. He needed a spot to lay up in until he got his shit together.

Suddenly he remembered a family friend named Annie who stayed a few blocks away from where he was currently standing. He made his way straight to her spot. He used every shortcut he knew and hoped she was home. When he got there, he was happy to find her block relatively deserted. He walked around to the back of her house and pounded on the back door. He hoped that she was home because he could feel himself growing weaker.

"Hold on and let me get to the damn door!" an older voice yelled out.

Czar heard the voice and blew out the breath he had been holding in. He grimaced as he was reminded of his injured ribs.

The door opened and the wizened face of Annie peered out at him. "St. Pierre, you're bleeding. Get in here so I can fix you up," she said frantically as she ushered him into her house.

"What the fuck is going on, Ms. Annie?" he growled as he hurried into the house.

"Shhh, boy. Let me get you fixed up, then all will be revealed," she said, closing the door behind him. "Take off your hoody," she ordered him.

"I'ma need some help," he said with a grimace on his face as he tried to lift his arm.

Ms. Annie grabbed a pair of scissors and cut the hoody off. She frowned when she saw the bulletproof vest with fresh indentions in it. She loosened the straps and gently lifted it from his body.

Czar tried not to make a sound as she cleaned his gunshot wound and wrapped it with gauze, but when she started wrapping his upper body in an Ace bandage to keep his ribs stabilized, he almost passed out from the pain. He clenched his jaw until she finished.

"Martinez thinks you set up his son Raúl to get knocked by the D.E.A.," she told him matter-of-factly.

"What!" he shouted as he tried to wrap his mind around what she had just told him. "Raúl is locked up?" he asked to be sure he heard her right.

"As of this morning," she said, watching his reactions. She could read anybody, especially someone she helped raise.

"That's why I couldn't get in contact with Raúl this morning," he said to himself. He looked up at Ms. Annie suspiciously as he gripped his guns. "And how the fuck do you know all of this?" he asked seriously. Despite the affections and love he felt from Ms. Annie, now was not the time to let that blind him.

"Jimmy Slim came by and told me," she replied calmly, showing no fear for the guns he now held.

"When?" Czar shouted. "Where my nigga at?" he asked, needing his closest comrade to get at him immediately.

Ms. Annie looked at Czar silently for a few minutes, wondering if he was suffering from post-traumatic stress disorder because it was obvious that nothing she was saying was getting through to him. "Jimmy Slim came by this morning early with some dope for me to cook up and test. Then he told me what I've told you, then left," she said, lighting up a cigarette. "It was almost like he was gloating. Like he thought he had finally won," she added distastefully.

"He brought you some dope and told you about Raúl?" Czar asked, confused. "Where the fuck he get some dope from?" he mumbled to himself. "I've been calling him all day, but all I've been getting is voicemail."

"He has a lot of dope too," she threw out there, rolling her eyes.

"Word up?" Czar asked as he hopped up off the table he had been sitting on. "I need to find him so we can find out who gunning for our spot and tried to get me hit. We need to clear this snitch shit up before it spreads in the streets and find out who is trying to dead me and my character. When I do, it's lights out for that pussy," he said seriously as he tucked his two bulldogs into his waist and pulled on an old hoody he had left over at Ms. Annie's house before. His anger was so great that it was masking his pain. "All of this connected somehow. Somebody trying to take me off the board," he mumbled to himself.

Ms. Annie looked at the man she considered family and shook her head at this obstinacy. "Boy, I promised your mother I would watch over you when they locked her up, but you are really making this hard, St. Pierre," she said with a sigh. "Jimmy Slim has a lot of dope because he's preparing to take over your territory. He's not your friend. He's been jealous of you since y'all were little and he's been looking for a way to get from up under your shadow forever. I've been telling you this for too long, and now he's trying to wipe you out. He's the one spreading the snitch rumor because that's the only way people will side with him. He's played his hand right and you're too stupid to see that you've been played. You let your judgment cloud your common sense. How many snake tendencies have you overlooked in him over the years?" She was spitting fire and every dagger was straight to the heart. "He has the connect now. Martinez is supplying him now." She prayed that he took heed to her words.

"Motherfuckas not going for this shit!" he shouted, incensed. "My name and rep speaks for itself," he added, pounding his chest for added emphasis. His ire had overtaken the pain from his wounds.

"Boy, this is no time for arrogance," Ms. Annie said loudly, her own anger showing its head. "Who else do you think would send two trained killers at you in broad daylight? Martinez, that's who. Jimmy Slim played you. He's been setting you up for a while now, but your arrogance blinded you. You've been getting warnings about him most of your life but you never heeded them and now it may be too late. The attacks were too coordinated to be a spur of the moment thing. Someone has been planning this for a long while now." She pointed her cigarette at him in warning.

"Jimmy Slim got to the connect and convinced him you're the rat. Figure out how and you fix the problem."

"My little niggas in the streets not gonna go for it," he said stubbornly, not wanting to believe what she was saying even though it made sense. He didn't tell her that Jimmy Slim didn't know who the connect was. That was something he had kept from him. "They are loyal to me."

Ms. Annie looked at him like he had grown two hands. "Are you deaf, dumb, and blind?" she asked incredulously. "Your little niggas..." She made air quotes with her fingers with a look of distaste on her face. "...as you so aptly call them weren't loyal to them pretty dimples on your face, boy. They were loyal to the connect, and you're no longer plugged in. Jimmy Slim is. Keep thinking like that and you'll be dead by tomorrow morning and I would have to travel up to that prison to inform your mother you were dead because you were too stupid to listen to me," she added, stubbing her cigarette out and lighting up another one.

Czar wanted to further protest, but he knew it was useless. What she was saying was making too much sense. Who else could it be other than Jimmy Slim? But the question he needed answered the most was how Jimmy found out who the connect was. Like she said, if he found that out, he could fix his problems. It was all too much to think about right then and he needed time to heal and figure out his next move.

Niggas thought the game was over, but he still had a few tricks up his sleeve. Regardless of what Ms. Annie said, he knew everybody wouldn't go for the bullshit. He would just have to wait and see who didn't believe the hype. Loyalty was out there. He just had to find it. In chess and in life, superior pieces meant nothing when your opponent had superior positions. His enemies would find that out soon enough.

****

Pharaoh Carter looked around the auditorium and for the first time in a long time, he felt a sense of accomplishment. He had done something his father didn't pay for or pull any strings to get done. He looked out at all of the parents and felt a surge of gratitude towards his mother. Somehow, someway, she had convinced his father to show up without his usual bodyguards. He knew his father was a very important and powerful man, but for one day in his life, he wanted to feel normal and his mother knew that, so she had made it happen for her only child.

Maybe Mother really wore the pants in the family, he thought, silently laughing to himself.

As far back as he could remember, everywhere they traveled they were accompanied by bodyguards. Even when he went to school he had two armed guards. In the first grade he had men in black like he was the president's son. All through school he had received preferential treatment. Even when he knew that he had failed on a test or exam, the teachers still gave a passing grade, trying to garner attention or favor with his father. He guessed being a Carter had its benefits. One day when he was in middle school he finally worked up the nerve to ask his father why people were afraid of him. He remembered his answer vividly.

"Be happy people are afraid of me, boy," he said with a snort before he went back to reading the newspaper.

He finally asked his mother one day and she was evasive, as was her custom. "Be proud of your father. He is a very important man."

Eventually he became used to getting through life on his father's name but it wreaked havoc on his self-confidence. So today was a monumental moment in his life. He was about to graduate from Columbia University with a Master's degree in computer engineering. This was something he accomplished without his father's power or money. He even had the student loans to prove it. He looked at the sea of people again and caught his mother's eye. She smiled, waved vigorously, and went to work again with her digital camera like she was at a photo shoot. Anyone who knew his mother would say she was acting out of character because she was usually more reserved in public and always dignified with a touch of arrogance, but today her whole body radiated with joy. He even thought he caught a wink and a smile from his father. It was gone so fast he might've imagined it. He continued to scan the crowd and caught the eye of his father's most trusted and deadliest bodyguard, Bear. He gave him a nod and continued doing what he did best —looking for and neutralizing danger. He couldn't expect his father to show up naked. At least there wasn't the usual ten bodyguards though. For one day, he wanted to feel like a normal student with his classmates.

The master of ceremonies stepped up to the podium ad cleared his throat to get everyone's attention.

"I would like to thank everyone for attending the graduating class of Columbia University's best and brightest..." He waited for all of the applause and whistling to subside before continuing. "To start things off, I would like to say that the young man I'm about to introduce is one of the most enjoyable and brightest students I've ever had the pleasure to teach. He's number one in his class of over a hundred students and he's ready to set the world on fire..."

Pharaoh could hardly contain himself. He didn't want to start smiling and give it away. This was the surprise he had told his parents about. He wanted them to know that their son could stand on his own two feet.

"Graduating summa cum laude with a Master's degree in computer engineering, Mr. Pharaoh Carter. Everybody stand up and give this man a round of applause."

Pharaoh stood up, smiling and waving at the crowd. He walked up to receive his diploma and take pictures with the dean of the university. He turned to find his parents and was blinded by the flash of what seemed like a thousand cameras. When his vision cleared and he looked towards his parents, his heart skipped a beat. Walking into the auditorium unnoticed were men dressed in business suits. The suits weren't what cast a pall over his heart. It was the automatic weapons they were carrying in their hands like briefcases. He started panicking and waving his arms to get his parents' attention because he knew without a doubt that his father was the target, but he was too late. He noticed that Bear recog-

King Killa

nized his distress, but as he turned to react to what he knew was a hit, he swallowed a bullet that exploded out of the back of his head. No one reacted at first because they were using silencers, but then there was pandemonium as people finally noticed the mangled head of his father's dead bodyguard. His father tried to get to his gun, but his body was riddled with so many holes you could play connect the dots. All of this happened in the span of a few seconds. Pharaoh looked at everyone cowering, trying to not be noticed, and vaulted off of the stage with only one thought on his mind: get to his mother. Now he was feeling guilty for begging his mother to make his father leave his bodyguards at home and he was dead because of it. He tried to get through the crowd, but since he was the only person moving towards the chaos, it was almost impossible. He was finally able to break through and saw that his father's body had fallen on top of his mother, partially blocking her from the shooters. Even in death, he was still protecting her. He saw that she was struggling to get up and ran to help her, relief flooding his body at the sight of her unhurt. Before he could reach her, she succeeded in getting from up under his father's body. They locked eyes and she broke down at the sight of him. She tried to get up and stumbled. He tried to help her up and almost slipped in his father's blood. His mother was covered in it. His thoughts threatened to overwhelm him, but he locked his mind down and focused on helping his mother. When he finally had her in his arms, he felt her shudder and heard her gasp like she was struggling for breath. At first he was confused as to what was happening until he felt her blood leaking out her back. He looked up in horror to find one of the gunmen standing there with his pistol pointing at his mother's back. A rage unlike anything he had ever felt before coursed through his body as he and the gunmen stood there, gazes locked, memorizing each other's features. The gunmen finally decided he was of no significance, smirked at him, and hit him with a mock salute before disappearing with the rest of his hit squad. His mother gasped again and grasped his shirt, drawing his attention back to her and what was most important: saving her life. He scooped her up into his arms and raced to find help.

"Hold on, Mother. Please don't die on me," he pleaded in her ear as he raced for the approaching sirens. "Please, I need you," he added as he choked back a sob.

He made a vow to avenge his family if it was the last thing he did. He would personally kill the man who made the fatal mistake of underestimating him and leaving him alive.

Chapter 1

Shinah couldn't believe that she was actually doing this. She looked around at the dilapidated houses and abandoned cars and knew that she was in the right place. She cast worried glanced at the dirty, smelly, and emaciated people she considered crackheads, junkies, and fiends and knew that she wasn't one of them. She was also smart enough to know that if she didn't turn around and go home, she would eventually end up like them. As great as the idea of leaving sounded, getting high sounded even better. Even though she hated herself for being weak, that didn't stop her from getting to the back of the line to wait for her turn to touch heaven.

It was springtime 1985 and SL was on the come-up. He finally had his own dope house, his own workers, and he was doing his numbers. It was a long time in the making, but he was now making moves instead of moving to make it. He started from the bottom, so he appreciated everyone on his team despite their job description, from the lookouts to the shooters to the lieutenants who oversaw his dope houses. He understood what every job entailed because he came up performing each one until his stash was where he needed it to be. He played the long game because he knew he was destined for greatness, so most of his earnings went back into his re-up. He went from buying double-ups to eights balls, to ounces, to half birds, to whole bricks. He had a prime dope spot off of Angier Avenue with a team of workers playing their positions from point guard to center, and he was roaming the sideline watching his money stack like Pat Riley.

He pulled up to the block in a brand new midnight blue Acura and smiled when he spotted the long line of fiends waiting to get served. He pulled his phone out to make some calls while he watched his team in action, getting to the money. He was about to hit up some new pussy he had met at the mall earlier that week when he saw a ray of sunshine standing in his line of darkness. He leaned forward in his seat to make sure that his eyes weren't playing tricks on him. The woman he saw standing in his line waiting to get served didn't belong there - or at least, at first glance she didn't. He could see from where he was parked that she was well-dressed and had her hair done. He figured she was either copping for somebody she knew, or somebody had turned her out and she couldn't fight the temptation any longer. Either way, she was money and he planned to get it. He used his phone to call Jay Jay, one of his workers.

"What's up, boss?" he answered.

"You see shorty standing in line?" SL asked, deliberately leaving out details just to see how on point he was.

"Yeah, nice clothes, hair done. She look like money," Jay Jay replied sarcastically, hip to SL's little tests.

My thoughts exactly, SL thought as he kept his eyes on the girl. "I'ma handle her," he said, knowing he had something other than money on his mind.

"A'ight, boss," Jay Jay said, signing off.

Since he never left anything to chance, he tossed a bag of rocks in his pocket before getting out of the car. He made his way towards the line of hopeless souls with a feeling that he was about to get lucky.

Shinah was starting to get frustrated with the slow-moving line because she was ready to get high. She was so used to getting what she wanted when she wanted it that she was becoming angry. She was already having doubts about being there so she was on the verge of leaving when the people around her in the line started calling out to somebody named SL like he was the president about to hand out free health care. She turned her head and saw a man walking towards them with a cocky gait that screamed arrogance. She took notice of his attire because she felt that you could tell a lot about a person by how they dressed, and she had to admit that he was fly in a street hustler kind of way. He had on an all-white velour troop suit with a pair of black and white British Knights. He was brown skin, about 6 feet tall, with pretty eyelashes that framed penetrating eyes and a brush cut with waves that were so deep it was like they were moving. Even from where she was standing she could tell he was well-built under his clothes like he regularly worked out. She also noticed how his jewelry cast rainbows whenever the sun hit them. All she could see was herself getting to know him, but since she wasn't there for that, she turned back around and minded her business.

SL maneuvered his way through the crowd, ignoring the pleas for free rocks or a couple of dollars, and kept his focus on the enigma standing in his line. He saw her look at him with what he thought was an appraising eye before she turned away, apparently not impressed. When he drew close, he was surprised to see that she was even more beautiful than he originally thought. She was straight up gorgeous. She had mahogany skin that reminded him of burnt bronze and light brown eyes. Her hair was bone straight and it framed her face, giving her the appearance of wearing some type of veil. His eyes traveled down to her body and he found himself getting even more turned on. The jeans she had on could hardly contain her hips and ass. The button-up shirt that she was wearing was tailored to accentuate her flat stomach and firm breasts. He finally ended up at her designer sneakers and knew that he had a winner.

"Shorty, let me talk to you for a minute," he said, grabbing her by her arm to lead her to his car. Her refusing him never entered his mind.

"You need to let me go," Shinah said as she yanked her arm out of his grasp. She gave him a look that made him feel like a creep for touching her arm.

"Look, ma, you're standing out here drawing attention to yourself with meaningless theatrics. We both know I don't mean you any harm, so you can kill the damsel in distress routine." He returned her look coldly. "You're in a crack line looking like money, wearing a pair of sneakers that cost more than these people see in months. You're a sheep standing with a bunch of wolves," he added, putting it together for her.

Shinah looked at him for a few seconds, pondering what he just said to her. She chewed her bottom lip as she looked around and realized that he was right. The people around her were staring at her like she was an ATM machine. Suddenly she felt vulnerable and wanted to leave. She looked back at him, lost.

SL saw the indecision in her eyes and played on it. "Look, I just want to talk to you. I can tell that you don't know what you are doing out here. I promise I can help."

"How can you be so sure you can help me?" she asked tentatively, unsure if whether she really wanted his kind of help.

"I can help because I own this block," he said, waving his arms around.

Shinah looked at him to see if he was trying to impress her, but realized that he was just stating fact.

"You gonna come talk?" he asked quietly, respecting her space.

"Where we going?" she asked, looking around at how everyone had stopped talking and was paying attention to them. She also noticed that the attention didn't seem to bother the man standing so confidently in front of her, but she was starting to feel creeped out because she hated it. She wanted to leave because she realized that she was out of her element.

"To sit in my car for some privacy," he said, pointing back at his car. "Too many ears out here," he added helpfully.

Shinah looked at the car and recognized it as the same model that she drove. For some reason that fact calmed her enough for her to nod her assent

SL let go of the breath he didn't realize he was holding in and led the way through the crowd. When they arrived at his car, he opened the passenger door like a gentleman before getting in himself. The act of chivalry surprised her, but she didn't let it show. It did make her look at him in a different light. She looked around the interior of the car and could tell that it was new. Even though she was hyper aware of his presence, she ignored him as he started the car and pulled off.

"What are you doing standing in a crack line?" he finally asked after a few minutes of awkward silence. "Miss…" he started again before she interrupted him.

"My name is Shinah and I'm here for a friend," she said, the lie sliding off of her tongue effortlessly.

SL looked over at her with a raised eyebrow, letting her know that he wasn't going for it.

"What?" she asked defensively when she noticed his look. For reasons unknown, she felt the need to defend herself to him. *That's ridiculous. I don't even know him,* she thought. "Why are you looking at me like that?" she asked with an attitude.

"You want to tell me the real reason you are out this early?" he asked quietly. He knew that she was headed down a bad path and he wanted to stop her before it became too late.

"The reason I told you before. I didn't come with you to be interrogated," she snapped. "Do I look like I smoke? What are you, a drug dealer with a conscience?" she asked with a sassiness that was sexy to him. She rolled her eyes at him and looked out of the window.

SL pulled to a stop at a red light then turned his head to really study her. She was right. She didn't look like she smoked but if he was right and somebody had turned her out, then it would be only a matter of time before she was a shadow of her present self. He decided to let it go for now. "So how much you want to buy for your friend?" he asked, putting extra emphasis on the word friend.

Shinah caught his sarcasm, but she was so happy to move on from his interrogation that she let it go. "I'm spending a hundred dollars," she said as she pulled the money out of her pocket.

He shook his head sadly, but he reached into his pocket anyway and pulled out the bag containing the crack rocks. He shook five of them into his hand and gave them to her. He saw the light turn green and made a left to get back to his block. He looked over at her and saw the way she was staring at the rocks nestled in the palm of her hand. She could lie to her friends and family all she wanted, but he knew better.

"Here." She handed him the money before putting the dope into her pocket. She wiped her palms across her thighs to dry them because for some reason, they were unreasonably sweaty. Holding the crack in her hands made her body react in ways she didn't want to admit to. She was ready to go home now.

"Where do you want me to drop you off?" he asked as he turned into the block.

"Right there," she said, pointing at the Acura parked a couple of cars away from where he was originally.

SL spotted the sparkling white Acura and looked over at her. He shook his head, wondering where she came from. He also wondered why he didn't spot that car earlier when he pulled onto the block. *I'm slipping*, he thought as he parked nose to nose with her car.

"Hold off," he said before she got out of the car.

"What is it?" she asked, turning to look at him.

"Let me school you to a few things right quick," he told her, answering her question. He saw another emotion in her eyes that she tried to hide: fear. She was scared.

Shinah settled back into her seat and waited for him to speak, despite her anxiousness to leave.

"Listen, if you ever decide to come to this block again, please dress down and don't drive a brand new car to buy drugs, no matter who it's for. You can get yourself in serious trouble out here flashing your wealth. These fiends are greasy and will cut your throat to get a high," he said seriously. He paused for a few seconds to let what he said marinate. "Or you can just call me directly and I'll sell you whatever you need. That will save you a lot of problems you might come across," he added, hoping she took heed to what he said.

Shinah though about what he said, but didn't really see the danger he was trying to portray. "Okay, give me your number," she told him after deliberating for a minute.

SL wrote down his number on a spare napkin he had laying around and gave it to her. He watched her get into her car and drive off. He wondered who the sorry bastard was who turned her out. She was wife material, but if she let King Kong get a toe hold, she wouldn't be for much longer. When her car disappeared off the block, he picked up his phone and dialed Jay Jay.

"Whenever shorty show up on the block again, make sure you call me," he told him when he answered.

"I got you, boss," Jay Jay replied. "That's you, or can the team taste?" he asked with a smile in his voice.

"Nah, dog, that's me," SL joked back, but deep down he wondered if he could save her before it was too late. He also wanted to know how long it would be before she succumbed to temptation again and put in another appearance because he knew without a shadow of doubt that she would be back.

Shinah stopped at the corner store on her way home and bought a box of blunts along with a lot of junk food, then made her way to her parents' house. She would rather go to the house she shared with two other girls who attended college with her, but she knew that those two nosy bitches wouldn't give her any privacy and at the moment, she needed that more than anything. Her parents weren't any better, but they would leave her alone once she went to her room and locked the door. Her father probably wouldn't even be home. He undoubtedly would be on one of his numerous business trips that he frequently took. When she was a little girl, she hated that he was away so much, but now she would take advantage of his absence.

"One less person I would have to deal with," she mumbled to herself as she pulled up to the gated community in which her parents lived and punched in the access code they made sure she remembered. She drove through the open gate with a lot on her mind. She looked around at all of the high-priced homes as she cruised by and wondered how she came to have five crack rocks in her pocket. She thought about her ex-boyfriend Roland and knew exactly who the architect of her new temptation was. Her anger forced her to jerk to a stop in her parent's driveway as the horrible memories swept her away.

She first met Roland her freshman year at North Carolina Central University. He was unlike any man she had ever dated before and that was one of the main reasons she choose to attend a historically black university, instead of Duke like her parents wanted her to: to experience real life blackness. She was tired of her life being white washed. The African Americans she grew up around were so fake and plastic to her that it was almost sickening.

They were oblivious, condescending, and out of touch with reality. They gave off the impression that if you weren't rich, then you were beneath them.

When she first stepped foot on campus, it was like a breath of fresh air to her. The urban vibe was what had been missing from her life and she was attracted to every bit of it. When Roland first introduced himself, he came at her different than any man before him.

"Ay yo, ma, let me holla at you for a minute," he told her one day in between classes.

She didn't know why, but she was instantly smitten with him. He looked ruggedly handsome to her with his dark skin and bald head. He was so unlike the preppy guys she was used to that she gave him a chance. That turned out to be the biggest mistake of her life.

She let him sweep her off her feet and turn her world upside down. She kept him a secret from her parents because she knew without a doubt they wouldn't approve of him. They were still giving her grief for not going to the school they wanted her to go to, so she could only imagine what they would say about him. She was grown, or at least she thought she was, so she would do with her life as she pleased. She was so in love with him that she moved out of the freshman dorms and into his apartment. She even have him her greatest gift: her virginity.

"Damn, ma, I've never fucked virgin pussy before," he said before penetrating her womb.

After the pain subsided, the pleasure blossomed throughout her whole body. When he gave her her first oral orgasm, she was gone. She thought she couldn't be any happier - until she found out that she was pregnant. Even though she knew that her parents would flip out, she was ecstatic. She broke the news to Roland and received the biggest shock of her life.

"Baby, I'm not ready to be a father," he told her seriously. "We both need to finish school and get situated in life. You will be my wife, so there's no need to rush."

"But I want to have your baby, Roland," she pleaded foolishly.

"No, I'm not ready," he stated firmly, cutting her arguments short, and that was that.

So she had an abortion, and after the operation, she felt so bad that she cried for days. She vowed to herself that if she ever got pregnant again, she would have her baby, no matter who the father was or what he had to say about it. She was so ashamed of what she did that she didn't even tell her parents for fear that they would disown her or worse, snatch her out of school and forbid her from ever seeing Roland again. She didn't want to defy her parents, so she kept it a secret from them. Roland was so caring and loving to her while she was recovering that she fell for every dream he was selling her, hook, line, and sinker. What canceled out whatever negative feelings she had about him and the abortion was Roland's sensitivity for her well-being. She was so in love with him that she would blindly follow him anywhere. She felt so comfortable with him and felt that she could trust him with everything. She told him about her parents and her upbringing, about their money, how out of touch and overbearing they were most of the time. It seemed to her everything changed after that. She remembered the first time he asked her for money.

"Baby, I lost my job today and the bills are due. I don't want us to have to move, so I'ma need you to help out until I get back on my feet," he said seriously.

"Why did they fire you?" she asked with concern written all over her face.

He shrugged his shoulders and smirked at her. "They told me that they had to cut back. So they laid a lot of us off."

Shinah didn't like that explanation because she felt that there was more to the story than he was telling her, but her love for him allowed her to let it go and accept his word at face value. So she took care of the bills even though she was apprehensive about it. Before long, she was taking care of more than just the bills. She was buying groceries because if she didn't, they would starve. She was also buying other miscellaneous stuff they needed, even their clothes, while he claimed he was looking for another job. He even stopped going to school, which was a turn-off for her, but when she tried to talk to him about it he snapped at her, so she left it alone. By this time she was starting to become disenchanted with their relationship and started dropping hints that he needed to get it together or she was gone. Whenever he sensed he had pushed her too far, he would sex her up so good that she would forget all of her worries for a few weeks. After a while, she didn't mind taking care of him because he was sexing her right and respecting her. She looked at it like she was contributing to their relationship, holding up her end, but what she didn't know, what she couldn't fathom, was that her carefully laid plans for her life were now dowsed in gasoline and he was about to light them on fire.

King Killa

Chapter 2

Shinah came home from school one day to find Roland smoking weed in front of their television.

"I know you are not smoking weed in here," she said with a frown on her face.

"Chill, baby, it's only weed." He blew a cloud of smoke her way, then extended the blunt to her. "Try it one time. I guarantee you'll like it."

"No, boy, you are crazy," she said, moving away from him with a smile on her face. For some reason, she couldn't stay mad at him.

"Come on, baby," he pleaded. "It will take your orgasm to new levels," he added with a sly grin plastered onto his face.

"No, baby," she said softly. She could feel her resolve weakening. She had never smoked so much as a cigarette and now here she was thinking about getting high.

Roland could feel her weakening and pounced like a lion after a gazelle. "Please, baby, I promise it won't hurt you. Do you think I would do anything to hurt my future wife?"

Those magic words did the trick. She looked into his eyes and saw the love he was professing for her - or so she thought. She couldn't have known that it was the devil staring back at her, waiting for her to accept his personal invitation to visit his sanctuary. She took the blunt from his fingers and took a small pull.

"Don't play with it, baby," Roland said with a smile as he egged her on.

She looked at him for a few seconds before rolling her eyes and taking another pull.

"Hold it in," he coached, wanting her to get really fucked up.

Shinah did as she was told but it soon became too much for her and she started coughing so hard that she dropped the blunt. She turned and ran into the kitchen to get some water. As she drank directly from the faucet, she could hear Roland laughing at her. She was about to go and curse him out when she felt her body start to tingle. It was unlike anything she had ever felt before. She felt like she was floating and she never wanted to touch the ground again.

Roland walked into the kitchen, saw the look on her face, and smiled as he held out the blunt to her. She playfully mugged him as she snatched it out of his hand.

"It's not funny," she said softly as she took the rest of it the head.

After she was done, he showed her just how enhanced the sex was when you were high. After that orgasmic episode, they smoked and fucked every day, three, sometimes four times a day. The weed made her horny and hungry. She also grew an affinity for junk food and she started gaining a lot of weight, but it was as if it was going straight to her ass and thighs, which Roland loved, so she didn't mind it as much. She never thought that she would be a weed head, but she loved it. She smoked every chance she got, and that was often. She smoked so much that she was starting to slip in school, missing days and multiple classes. She smoked whenever and wherever she could because she couldn't get enough of the feeling it gave her. She remembered smoking with two of her girlfriends from school one day and didn't get the same high that she usually got when she smoked with Roland. So from that point on, she only smoked with him because he seemed to have the only weed that could take her to outer space.

She arrived home from school one day ready to smoke and get some good loving from her man when she received a major reality check. She walked into a dark apartment to find Roland, the love of her life, sitting on the couch in his boxers and T-shirt smoking crack. She stood there for a few seconds in shock before she flipped out.

"Are you sitting there doing what I think you're doing?" She asked incredulously. She knew all about crack and what it did to people.

"What the fuck it look like?" he said before he put the flame back to his pipe for another hit.

King Killa

Shinah thought that she knew Roland better than anybody else in her life, but the person sitting in front of her smoking crack was a complete stranger. She looked at the scattered pieces of crack on the coffee table and wondered how long he had been smoking it and how much of it he had already smoked. She also wondered why she didn't pick up on it sooner because now that she was aware, the signs were obvious. She didn't know any crack heads personally, but she thought she would've been able to spot one a mile away. Apparently she was wrong, because the man in front of her had fooled her and fooled her good.

"Why are the lights off?" she asked calmly. She thought using a different tact would garner her the answers she was desperately seeking. Cursing and anger would only make him belligerent and sarcastic.

"The light company cut them off," he replied sarcastically as he stared at her with the evil eye before loading another piece of crack on his pipe.

So much for that rationale, she thought as her anger grew by the second. She wasn't angry with him as much as she was at herself. "What the fuck did you do with the three hundred dollars I gave you for the bill?" she screamed at him.

Roland didn't even bother to respond. He just used the crack pipe to wave at the crack rocks lying on the table.

"You spent my fucking money on some crack instead of the lights?" She looked at him like he was really the devil reincarnate. "I'm so through with you, because there's no way I'm gonna be with a crackhead," she told him as she walked towards the bedroom to pack her shit, because she was out of there.

"Bitch, what the fuck you been smoking?" Roland asked her with a sick grin that she used to think was so sexy, but now it reminded her of a rabid dog. "Those blunts we were smoking all day, every day, was laced with crack, bitch. So who's the crack head now, you stuck up bitch?" he taunted evilly. He saw the look on her face and started laughing hysterically.

Shinah felt like she was rooted in cement. She couldn't move and she was speechless. She didn't want to believe anything he was saying.

"Oh, you don't believe me, you dumb bitch?" he continued to taunt when he saw that the cat, or in this case the crack, had her tongue. "I know you've smoked with other people. That shit didn't get you as high as my weed, did it?" he continued, not giving her a chance to answer. "Because that laced shit had you in its web already. You ever wonder why I stopped smoking with you?" He kept going when she didn't answer. "'Cause that laced shit stopped getting me high a while ago. So I went to straight to the pipe and freebasing. Now the pot needs to stop calling the kettle black, you crack head bitch." He started laughing even harder than before when he noticed the tears falling from her eyes.

Shinah couldn't believe her eyes. Here she was watching the man she used to love load crack into a pipe as he shattered her world with his revelations. As much as she didn't want to believe his words, she didn't see any reason for him to lie when he was sitting in front of her unashamedly revealing his true self. She vividly remembered not getting as high as she was used to when she smoked with other people, so it made sense. But one thing she knew she was not was a crack head.

She ran to the bedroom they shared and started throwing stuff in her suitcases. She only packed things she absolutely needed and couldn't leave. The rest of the stuff he could keep. She just wanted to get away from him as soon as possible. She walked back into the living room, dragging her luggage, to find Roland sitting in the same position still smoking crack. She stared at him and wondered what she ever saw in him. She had never looked down on or hated anyone in her life, but she hated him with every fiber of her being.

"I hope you burn in hell, you piece of shit!" she spat vehemently.

"Bitch, you can't tell? I'm already on fire," he said before putting the flame back to his pipe. After exhaling, he looked over at her and said, "If the devil has a crack rock this good down there, then book me a first class ticket." At the look of disgust on her face, he started laughing so hard he now had tears streaming down his face.

Shinah was at a loss for words, so she just opened the front door and walked out, leaving his repulsive laughter behind. She slammed the door behind her, closing that chapter to her life forever or so she thought.

"Good riddance," Roland mumbled before he went back to smoking.

Shinah moved in where she was wanted, with two of her home girls from school, and set out to get her life back in order. The first thing she did was quit smoking weed cold turkey, and it was hard because she lived with two people who smoked every day. Peer pressure was real, but she remained steadfast. Over the next couple of months, she caught up on all of her school work, on all of the friends she had been neglecting and cutting off because of Roland, on reestablishing her relationship with her parents, which had become strained because of Roland. She didn't realize it until that moment how much Roland had changed her life, and all for the worse, but she couldn't put all of the blame on him. She had to take responsibility for her part in it all. So she tightened up her life and recognized that she was a changed woman. Even though she was back to her routine, what Roland said to her about smoking crack wouldn't leave her thoughts. She came to the conclusion that he was lying to shake her up, but she had to know for herself. So despite her months of sobriety, she started back smoking with her homegirls and knew instantly that the high wasn't the same. For months she smoked and lied to herself about how she was feeling, but the desire is what led her to Angier Avenue to buy crack that morning. That desire is what led to her parents' home, where she was sitting in their driveway with tears streaming down her cheeks. That desire is what had her ready to cross the threshold of hell.

Shinah shook herself out of her reverie and wiped the tears from her face. She looked at her watch and realized that she had been sitting there for over thirty minutes, reliving the hell she had been through. She grabbed her bag of junk food and got out of her car. One way or another, she would find out the truth today.

Chapter 3

SL went about his business, making runs and collecting money. For some reason, he couldn't get the girl from that morning out of his mind. She wasn't his concern, but he couldn't help feeling for her struggle. He sold crack, but only to people who were already gone and lost. She wasn't gone or lost yet, and he felt like he could save her before the train derailed. He knew that she was lying about who she was buying for because he saw the hunger in her eyes when she held the rocks in the palm of her hand. Even though he didn't know her story personally, it was one that was being told for millions of girls in hoods all across America. Some weak-minded man tricked them into smoking laced blunts because it was the only way he could keep her. He thought about trying to find her, but decided against it because he figured he would see her again soon enough. He couldn't even believe he was thinking about a female that he wasn't fucking, one who smoked crack at that, but he couldn't deny that he felt something when he was with her that morning. He planned on finding out exactly what that something was when he saw her again. He felt his pager vibrating on his hip and unclipped it to see who was beeping him.

When he saw the number on the screen, he pulled a quick U-turn and headed to the other side of town. Just that fast, the girl from that morning disappeared from his thoughts. He had an appointment with someone special: the power of the pussy!

****

Shinah looked at the five blunts she had rolled lying in front of her and chuckled grimly. She knew that if her parents knew that she even could roll a blunt, they would have a heart attack. For the last hour she had been sitting there staring at the blunts, wondering if she really wanted to know the truth. She had taken the five rocks and crushed them up into each blunt and now she was waiting. She didn't know if it was the nerves or the fear holding her back as she sat there replaying the words of Roland in her head over and over again. "Now the pot needs to stop calling the kettle black. You crackhead bitch!" But she couldn't seem to make herself reach out and grab one to light up.

Fuck it, she angrily thought as she snatched up a blunt, lit up and took a long pull, holding the smoke into her lungs. She exhaled and almost immediately she felt what she had been dreading she would feel. She felt her best friend calming her down. She felt her savior leading her back to salvation. She felt her high – yes, her high, because she was owning it - and would never relinquish it. She took another pull of the blunt and started crying because she was feeling the high she had gotten addicted to smoking with Roland.

So what? she rationalized with herself. *This still doesn't make me a crackhead because they smoke out of pipes, smell bad, and beg for money. I don't do that and never will degrade myself like that.*

Satisfied with her rationalizing, she proceeded to smoke her blunts and wonder why anyone wouldn't want to feel how she was feeling now.

She was on her last blunt when she heard her mother's voice. Fear gripped her when she realized that she had smoked four whole blunts openly like she was at her own home. She hopped up and opened up all of the windows in her old room, trying to air the pungent smell of weed and crack out. She also grabbed a can of air freshener and started spraying it all around, hoping it would help because she knew her room was funky. She also knew that her mom would flip out if she even suspected her of smoking in her house.

"Shinah, baby, I wish you would've told me you were coming so I could've had something planned. Your father is out..." Her mother opened her room door, which Shinah forgot to lock, and stopped mid-sentence. She sniffed the air and narrowed her eyes at her only child. "Tell me that you haven't lost your damn mind?" she snapped.

"What do you mean, Mother?" she asked as she held the can of air freshener behind her back. She knew her eyes were blood-shot so she looked at the ground to avoid looking at her mother.

"What do I mean?" she said, mimicking her daughter perfect-ly. "Why does it smell like marijuana in my house?" she asked seriously. "And look at me when I'm talking to you," she ordered.

Shinah knew that she was busted but she would deny, deny, deny until she ran out of breath. She looked up at her mother defiantly and saw that she was looking at something behind her. She looked over her shoulder to see what had captured her attention and felt her heart skip a beat when her eyes landed on the lit blunt that she had completely forgotten about as she tried to air her room out. She tried to dive to get it before her mother did, but she didn't make it. Her mother held it up in front of her face with a look of disgust etched onto her features. She put it out in the ashtray, tossed it at Shinah, and pointed at the door.

"Get out of my damn house," she ordered harshly. Her voice was trembling from the pain and anger she was feeling.

Shinah knew that her mother was upset because she had used profanity which she never did. She thought that kind of language was beneath a lady. Shinah took a deep breath and tried to explain what she was going through before she left. "Mother, I——"

She didn't get another word out before her mother cut her off.

"Get out of my damn house and when you find my daughter, you can call me mother, but until them brain cells me and your father gave you start working again, my name is Charlene Lloyd." She stepped to the side so that she could leave.

Shinah had seen enough arguments between her parents to know her mother was deadly serious. She set the can of air freshener down on the desk, grabbed her bag of junk food and her last blunt, and left without another word or glance at her mother.

Charlene waited until she heard her front door shut and her daughter's car crank up before she let the tears fall from her eyes. She cried for the woman who had just left her house because that wasn't her daughter, and until she gave her child back, she had no daughter.

Over the next couple of weeks, Shinah fought temptation. After the embarrassment she experienced with her mother catching her in the act of getting high, she wanted to die. She thought about reaching out to her parents to explain her side of things, but she never picked up the phone to call them. She felt like she was young and deserved the right to experiment, but she knew that they wouldn't understand that. Her father might, but he knew he wouldn't be allowed to take her side because her mother was probably forbidding him from contacting her. Her mother wanted to humble her, but Shinah refused to bow to her pressure. Her father, on the other hand, had always been lenient with her, but she knew that he wouldn't go against her mother. Her stubbornness was something she inherited from the both of them, so she wouldn't break first. She was also fighting to stay away from Angier Avenue. She wanted to get high so badly that she dreamed about it. The craving for a laced blunt was so strong that she sometimes thought that she was an addict, but she knew that wasn't her reality because she had successfully fought the urge to go buy more crack. She couldn't deny that she missed her best friend, her secret lover, her high, but every time she wanted to go back to Angier Avenue, she remembered the look of sadness and disappointment on her mother's face when she caught her getting high. That was enough to help her tamp down the urge to smoke. Her roommates still smoked every day, but regular weed did nothing for her except make her hungry, so she refused their invitations to indulge. She knew they were thinking that she was turning into a prude and looking down on them, but she didn't care. This was about her. The more she thought about her life, the angrier she became because she was denying herself what she wanted the most to appease other people.

Fuck that, she thought as she jumped out of bed and got dressed. *If I want to get high, I will do that, and nothing or nobody will stop me from being with my best friend, my secret lover, my high.*

Her mind was made up and nothing could change it. She looked for the number SL gave her the morning they met, but she couldn't remember where she placed it. She would keep looking because she was determined to get high and she was also determined to show people, mainly her parents, that she could do whatever she wanted and maintain control.

****

SL picked up his phone to call Jay Jay, again but put it down before he dialed one number because he was starting to feel like a lame. He was tripping. He was becoming obsessed with a woman he knew nothing about other than selling her some crack. Over the last couple of weeks he had been calling his team, specifically Jay Jay, to see if shorty made another appearance, but the answer was always the same: no! He also had to fall back because he could tell that his number two Jay Jay was starting to become suspicious of the fact that he was checking for a chick they all knew or thought was a smoker.

Maybe she was telling the truth, he thought as he paced his living room. Maybe she really was buying it for a friend. He tried to convince himself that what he was thinking was true, but he knew it was a lie because he saw the hunger in her eyes when she held those rocks in her hand. So he was sure she was smoking.

So why am I checking for this bitch then? he questioned himself as he mentally chastised himself. He had no answers for his feelings. He just knew that there was something about her that had him intrigued.

"Man, fuck that bitch," he mumbled to himself as he grabbed his coat and car keys before leaving the house. He knew of one thing that could take her off of his mind----new pussy!

****

Shinah was becoming frustrated because she couldn't find SL's number. She knew she had it somewhere, but she couldn't remember where she put it. Tired of searching for it, she gave up. She knew that if she wanted to get high, she would have to make the trip back to Angier Avenue, a place she had been avoiding like the plague, but her desire for her secret lover outweighed any personal feelings she had about the block. She remembered what SL told her about flashing her money, so she dressed with care. She threw on a white T-shirt, some grey sweat pants, and a pair of all white 5411 Reeboks. She also threw her long hair into a sloppy ponytail before looking into the full body mirror hanging on the back of her door. Satisfied with her appearance, she grabbed a hundred dollar bill, her coat, and her car keys before leaving the house. She wanted her secret lover, and no one would stop her from getting his affection.

****

Jay Jay was doing his daily routine, getting money, when he noticed the white Acura turn onto the block and park a half a block away from where he was serving work. He knew who was driving instantly because SL had the team on the lookout for the pretty smoker like he was falling in love or something. He started to reach for his phone and call him, but decided to wait and see what she would do. When she started walking his way, he snatched the phone up and paged his homeboy. He had strict orders and he wasn't about to break them.

****

"Whose pussy is this?" SL growled as he pounded the female bent over in front of him. He was imagining that it was the girl from that morning on the block who was on all fours, and the sex was amazing.

"It's yours, baby," the girl moaned. "It's all your pussy, baby." She was throwing it back for all she was worth. She was really working her vaginal muscles, trying to get the condom to slip off so she could trap SL with a baby. Every female in the hood wanted his baby because they knew that he would keep them and the child draped in the latest fashions and jewelry.

King Killa

SL was lost in his own world, imagining the girl he sold crack to, and didn't respond to the girl under him. He almost didn't respond when she told him that his pager was going off, but not even Vanessa Del Rio could make him forget about his money. He slowed his pace inside of her pussy, snatched his pager up, and looked at the number. When he saw the code from Jay Jay, he pulled out of her pussy and walked into the bathroom, where he flushed the condom he was wearing. He washed her scent off of him before he walked back into the room to find the girl still bent over on all fours, fingering herself as she waited for him to finish her off.

Dumb bitch, he thought as he got dressed.

"Where you going, baby?" she whined when she saw that he was leaving.

SL didn't bother to respond to her as he pulled out some money and tossed it at her. He left her apartment without a backwards glance. He had places to go and people to see.

****

Shinah pulled up on Angier Avenue and looked around, hoping to spot SL's car. When she didn't see him or his ride she parked and waited, praying that he showed up soon. She watched as the fiends were served and the line thinned out, leaving the block semi-deserted. She decided that she could no longer wait on SL because she was anxious to get high. She got out of her car and made her way towards the dealer. On the way she passed crackheads who were standing around begging, hoping to do something, anything, to earn a free high. She turned her nose up at them as she looked on in disgust. She vowed to never allow herself to become one of them. She finally made it to the man selling the drugs just as he was hanging up the phone.

****

Jay Jay hung up the phone after paging SL and watched her as she slowed to a stop in front of him.

Damn, she fine and thick, he thought as we looked at how the sweatpants she was wearing were hugging her hips and thighs like a second skin. *No wonder SL keeping her for himself,* he thought as he finished scoping her out. He knew that he was making her uncomfortable with his staring, but he didn't give a fuck because she was just a trick to him.

****

Shinah was uncomfortable with the way he was leering at her but she wanted, no, she needed to buy from him so she overlooked it. It just made her wish that she hadn't lost SL's number because even though she had only met him once, she could tell that he was more respectful than the man in front of her. She decided to just get the uncomfortable situation over with because she wanted to get high.

"Can I get a hundred dollars' worth please?" she asked politely.

Jay Jay snapped out of his reverie at the sound of her voice. He looked up at her beautiful face and smirked. "SL told us not to serve you. He's on his way to handle y'all's business himself," he told her, checking her reaction. "Unless you want to serve me. Then I'll serve you," he said, grabbing his crotch to make his meaning clear.

"You have me confused with one of these dirty crackheads standing around here begging," she snapped with an attitude. "I have money, so I don't have to degrade myself for nothing or nobody," she added, letting him know he had the wrong one. "And if I did do that, you would be the last one to touch me." She shot his pride because he disrespected her.

Jay Jay was about to open his month and tell her that she was on her way to becoming a full-fledged trick when he spotted SL's car bend the corner and blow the horn. "There go SL, bitch. I guess you like high-priced dick. Crack is crack, hoe." He sneered at her. "You will be begging me for a chance to suck this dick soon, real soon," he taunted.

Shinah felt tears well up in her eyes unexpectedly at his words but she blinked them back, refusing to cry in front of him and let him know that he hurt her. She turned abruptly and walking off, she spotted SL's car. She hurried to him as she tried to drown the dealer's laughter out of her mind. She opened up the passenger door to SL's car and slid into the seat, but refused to look at him. She knew that he would be able to tell that she was about to cry and she wasn't looking for his pity or sympathy; just his drugs.

"What's wrong, shorty?" SL asked after she was settled into his car. "Shorty, what's wrong?" he asked again when she didn't answer him the first time.

"My name is Shinah, not shorty, and nothing's wrong. I just want to handle business so I can go," she said stiffly, still not looking at him.

SL could tell that she was lying about her mood but decided not to press her. He looked over at Jay Jay, hoping he could clue him in to what happened but he was already back to making sales. He sighed and pulled off. After a few seconds of silence, he sparked the conversation. "Why didn't you call me, Shinah, like I asked you to do?" he asked, glancing over at her. He was glad she had told him her name again because after their first meeting, she had left him so flustered that he forgot everything but how she looked and her incredible body.

After a few more seconds of silence, she finally spoke. "I didn't call because I'm grown and can do what I want to," she said with attitude. She was still upset at what the dealer said to her earlier and she was taking it out on him.

SL didn't respond because he didn't do anything to deserve her anger, so he would just let it rest. She was just confirming to him that something was wrong with her. He hoped that due to her anger she didn't notice that he wasn't circling the block like the last time they were together. He wanted to spend more time with her than before.

When he didn't respond, she chanced a quick glance at him. She had to admit that he was handsome, but Roland still had her hating men. So she tamped those feelings down because she didn't want to get caught up. She also felt kind of bad for snapping on him when he did nothing to her. She tried to make amends. "And also I lost your number," she said quietly, hoping he heard the apology in her voice. She chuckled as he stopped at a red light because she knew that he would see right through her ploy to apologize without actually saying it.

SL turned to look at her and couldn't help laughing because she thought she was slick. "Oh, that's you way of telling me you're sorry for biting my head off earlier?" he asked with a smirk on his face.

Shinah could feel him staring at her and refused to give him the satisfaction of acknowledging it, but she smiled. She was glad that her assessment of him was on point. He was quick on his toes.

"So are you here to buy for your friend again?" he asked sarcastically. As soon as the question left his lips, he knew he had fucked up.

"Yes I am!" she snapped with anger. She turned in her seat to look at him with fire blazing in her eyes. "What is it with you drug dealers and all of these questions?" she continued before he could answer. "Do you get personal with everyone who buys from you?" she asked, giving him back his sarcasm hundred fold.

Before SL could respond and apologize for the question, someone behind them blew their horn. He looked up and noticed that the light was green, so he pulled off. He used that time to formulate a response that would ease the tension now hanging between them He actually thought he was making some progress with her until he opened his mouth, but now he felt like he was back to square one. He knew that trying to run game on her wouldn't work so he just came from the heart.

"Look, I apologize for that insensitive question. It was thoughtless of me and I'm sorry, Shinah. I just want to help you. I can't tell you why, but I do. I can tell that you are a good woman who got caught up with a low life-ass nigga. Don't let him drag you down that path of no return. If you let me help you, I promise to be there every step of the way. Just let me help you, please." He said this with every ounce of sincerity in his body. He couldn't even tell anyone why he was so invested in her because he didn't know himself, but he saw past the tough girl façade and realized that she was a woman he could give all of himself to.

Shinah heard the tenderness and sincerity in his voice and started crying. As horrified as she was about crying in front of him, she couldn't stop the tears from cascading down her cheeks. As bad as she wanted to reach out for his help, she wanted to get high even more. She angrily wiped her face and glared at him. "Are you gonna take my hundred dollars, or do I have to find somebody who will?" she asked angrily.

SL sighed and continued to drive with a heavy heart. He knew that he had fucked up bad and she might be lost to him forever. He thought about not selling to her at all, but he rejected that idea outright because he didn't want her scouring the city for drugs and getting taken advantage of. So at the next red light, he gave her the five rocks and took her money. The transaction was made in silence and he drove her back to her car the same way - in total silence. He wanted to say something that would put a smile on her face, but didn't know what to say. He pulled up behind her car and waited for her to get out so he could go take out his frustrations on some new pussy.

Shinah sat there, silenced by the tension inside of the car. She sighed and turned to face him. "Look, give me your number again so I can call you instead of coming out here to this block. Also, I'm sorry for snapping on you. I'm just stressed out. So excuse me and my rudeness."

SL wanted to smile because when she asked for his number again, he knew that he would see her again. For a minute he thought she might find another spot to cop from. He knew that if she ever did she would be taken advantage of or worse because of her naiveté, money, and beauty. He turned and handed her the piece of paper he had written his number on. "You want to talk about what's stressing you out?" He looked at her with hope etched onto his features. He wanted her to trust him badly. "We can go get something to eat and talk," he added hopefully.

Shinah saw the look on his face and smiled. She felt her barrier cracking more and more the longer she sat in his car. So she opened the door and prepared to leave. "Maybe some other time, but not now. I have things to do," she said, stepping out of the car. She turned and leaned back into the car before she closed the door. "And don't think I didn't notice that you took the scenic route today instead of circling the block. You not slick, Negro." She laughed then smirked at the look on his face before closing the door and heading towards her car.

SL smiled and watched her through the windshield as she walked towards her car. As much as he tried to deny it, she was getting to him. One way or another, he had to have her. He watched as she waved at him before pulling off. He waited until her car disappeared off the block before pulling off himself. He had to find a way to get her to open up and trust him because he wouldn't be able to accomplish his goals otherwise, which was to get her life back and off of drugs. Then she would become his.

Chapter 4

Over the next couple of months, Shinah was calling SL once or twice and sometimes three times a week to cop crack from him. She still hadn't admitted to him that she was buying the drugs for herself and he hadn't asked her to, so she left it alone. They were becoming close as a friendship blossomed between them. Every time she called him, he had her meet him in different locations like restaurants, movie theaters, and game arcades. Then he would tell her that she would have to eat with him, watch a movie, or play a few games before he sold her anything. She knew what he was doing and appreciated the effort he was going through to gain her trust and attention. She didn't mind spending time with him because he was a good-looking man and it had been a long time since she had the attention of a man. She never did anything to encourage him, but she never did anything to dissuade him either. When she started feeling uncomfortable she cut the rendezvous short. He kept trying to talk to her about her life, trying to find out stuff she didn't want him to know. Every time she responded angrily to something he asked her, he let it go immediately. She knew he wanted her but her mind and heart belonged to one man and one man only: her high.

She had just come from copping crack from SL and playing Putt Putt when she remembered to stop at the corner store before going home. She loaded up on junk food because that seemed to be all she ate these days unless SL had her meet him at some restaurant or some other place to eat. She was gaining weight, but she couldn't complain because it was all going to her breasts, thighs, and ass. She loved the way SL looked at her when they were together and how other women looked at her enviously. On the outside looking in, she had her life together, but on the inside, she was tormented. Her life was spiraling out of control. Her studies were slipping, not noticeably, but for a 4.0 GPA student, a 3.5 was slipping. She hadn't talked to her parents in months and the laced blunts weren't getting her as high anymore. She wanted to deny it, but she couldn't lie to herself. She wasn't feeling her secret lover like she used to. Her secret lover used to make her feel like a thousand hands were caressing her body at the same time, but not anymore. When she smoked, she didn't even reach cloud one, let alone cloud nine. She knew her body had become tolerant to the laced blunts and it was telling her it was time to take that next step, but that step scared her. She remembered Roland telling her that when the blunts stopped getting him high, he progressed to smoking crack straight out of a pipe. Was she ready to graduate to the glass dick?

Entering the store, she put the question out of her mind. She would answer that question at a later date. Right now she wanted to load up on junk food for the munchies she was sure to have after she got high. She stocked up on candy, chips, cakes and her favorite: Reese's peanut butter cups. When she got to the register to pay for her purchases, something caught her eye. Hanging up on the back wall behind the counter with the condoms and air fresheners were little plastic corn cobs she remembered Roland smoking crack out of the day she left him. She noticed that you could carry it around in your pocket or purse without anyone the wiser. She stood there staring at it, wondering whether or not to buy one, when the cashier cleared his throat, breaking her trance.

"Are you going to pay for your items, Miss?" he asked politely.

Embarrassed about getting caught, she asked him to add one of the corn cobs to her purchase, quickly paid him and left the store. She could've sworn that the cashier looked at her funny when she asked for it, or maybe it was her own imagination playing tricks on her. She got into her car and drove home with a lot on her mind. When she pulled up, she grabbed her bags and unlocked the front door. She noticed her two housemates were in the living room watching television and studying, but she didn't stop to speak. She just nodded her head and kept it moving to her room. She didn't have time to chat it up because she wanted to get high. Before she could get to the top of the stairs, she overheard one of them call her a stuck up bitch and it was loud enough to let her know that she was meant to hear it. She almost turned around to go and confront them, but figured there was no point.

Broke bitches, she thought angrily as she opened her bedroom door and set her groceries on her bed. She turned, slammed the door loud enough for them to hear it, and pushed the deadbolt home. She kicked off her shoes, pulled her hair into a ponytail, and wasted no time rolling up a laced blunt. After lighting up and taking her first pull, she knew instantly that she wouldn't receive the high she was looking for but she finished it anyway because she didn't want to waste her money. Wanting to feel her secret lover like she used to, she grabbed the little plastic corn cob and stared at it. She wondered if she would turn into one of those stinky, begging, disgraceful people she saw walking around looking lost all the time if she smoked the crack by itself.

Hell no, she thought fiercely, *I have more will power and self-control than those people*. She grabbed a bag of chips and ate them while she thought about what she wanted to do. She wanted - no, she needed - to feel her secret lover again and the laced blunts weren't doing it for her anymore. She figured she had more willpower than Roland and most definitely had more than enough money to do what she wanted, so she said fuck it and placed a crack rock on the open end of the corn cob. After securing the rock, she put the flame from her lighter to it and dived in head first. She took a long pull of the makeshift pipe and as soon as the smoke hit her lungs, she knew that she was in love. She felt like she was in an orgy. She felt like she was floating so high she thought she saw the pearly gates. She put the flame back to the rock and took another pull. When she got even higher, she was a goner. Before she knew it, she had smoked up all of the crack she had bought earlier and she was feeling the best she had ever felt in her life. She was feeling euphoric, like she didn't have a care in the world, and now that she was thinking about it, she really didn't have any problems she couldn't easily handle. As a matter of fact, she felt like Superwoman, like she could do anything. The way she was feeling had her in love. Goodbye to her secret lover. Hello to her new adventure.

Your loss, secret lover, she thought as she giggled uncontrollably. She was in a full-fledged affair with a new man and he had a glass dick.

Over the next couple of weeks, she completely lost herself. The only thing that mattered was her high. School fell to the wayside right along with everything else in her life. Her friends started distancing themselves from her because they said she was changing. Her attitude was changing, they said. She was becoming meaner, more sarcastic, and more cautious towards people where before she was such a sweetheart. She couldn't determine whether she cared or not. She just wanted to get high. Everything was changing, even her appearance. She had too much pride to let herself go, but all of the weight that she had gained from her junk food binges was steadily falling off of her because now she wasn't eating and she was staying up all night. The crack was keeping her active. She was falling and she knew it but she couldn't seem to slow her descent. The only thing that mattered was her high. The people in her life that loved her knew that she was doing something, but they would never guess that she was smoking crack. They probably thought she was snorting heroin like everybody else in Durham but no, she was in love with her glass dick.

Her housemates were starting to get on her nerves. They complained about everything and it had her thinking about getting her own spot to get away from them. She knew that she constantly talked about her when she was not around and on numerous occasions, she had caught them cutting their eyes at her when they thought she wasn't paying attention. She was also becoming paranoid. She was starting to think that everyone was out to get her. She felt like she could only trust her high. She felt like her high would never lie to her or let her down. She knew that she had hurt SL also because she had switched it up on him. They used to hang out and chill a little when she met him to cop, but now she bought what she was coming to buy and left. Whenever he tried to talk to her to find out what was wrong, she shut him down, partly because he wanted her to be something she wasn't, and that hurt her more than she was willing to admit. She didn't have time to listen to him talk to her about not using drugs and shit like that. She wanted to get high, nothing more, nothing less. The only conversation she wanted was from Mr. Glass Dick. Fuck what everybody else was talking about.

****

SL was going crazy. He knew that Shinah was falling and he needed to find a way to catch her on her downward spiral or she would die. He was in love with a woman he hadn't even kissed before and she smoked the same drug he made his money off of. Even though she was still denying it, he knew that she had officially graduated from the laced blunts to the pipe. She still wasn't even admitting to smoking at all, but he knew better. He had been hustling all of his life and he could recognize the signs of a smoker on their way to becoming a full-fledged crackhead. The last time she had copped from him it was bigger than her normal hundred dollar order, so he decided to test her to confirm his suspicions.

"What's up, shorty?" he asked when she settled into his passenger seat. He pulled off and awaited her answer.

"Same shit, different day. I'm trying to double my usual order today," she said as she looked out at traffic.

He looked at her strangely because he knew that she was escalating. All of a sudden she was changing up on him and in his line of work, change was great. But not today. She had stopped chilling with him when he tried to take her out to eat or to a movie. She stopped talking to him about anything. She had made their relationship impersonal to the point where it was one of strictly dealer and customer. Now here she was doubling the amount of crack she normally bought and she might've thought that he didn't notice her appearance, but he did. The changes weren't obvious to the casual observer, but to him, they were drastic. He could tell that she still took pride in how she looked, but the rapid weight loss had her face looking gaunt and the bags under her eyes were a clear sign of lack of sleep.

"Why you doubling up?" He asked seriously.

"Look, I don't understand you. Why do you continue to question what I do?" She turned from the window and looked at him with anger in her eyes. The bags under her eyes were so pronounced it looked like face paint. "You are probably the only drug dealer in the city who would question how much I'm spending with them. Are you going to sell it to me or not?" she asked seriously. She was ready to get high and didn't have time for games or small talk.

"Listen, I talk because I care," he said quietly. He didn't know if pouring his feelings out to her would work but he had to try. "I don't know what it is, but you are drawing me in. I wish I could kill the nigga who turned you dark. You are a smart, beautiful woman and have so much to offer, but you are traveling down a street that's usually one way. Not many make it back. So yes, I question your actions, but only because I care." He felt himself getting emotional, so he stopped talking.

Shinah didn't know how to respond to what he said. It touched her, but not enough to sway her. "Are you going to sell to me or not?" she asked coldly.

He heard the coldness in her voice and it was like a slap in the face.

"Nah, I can't see me selling you something I don't have," he replied just as coldly. Fuck it. If she wanted to keep it strictly business, then that's what he would do, he thought grimly.

"What!" she shouted with wide eyes as she tried to comprehend what he had just said. "What do you mean?" she asked urgently. She wanted to make sure that she heard him correctly.

"It's a drought, Shinah. Nobody in the city has any rocks," he said seriously, his heart slowly breaking as he watched the panicked look on her face turn to one of desperation.

"Nobody," she repeated softly. "Listen, SL, I need that two hundred or whatever you will sell me. If you're mad about me doubling up, I'll just keep it at a hundred, but sell me something." The desperation and hunger were coming through loud and clear.

SL sighed because he knew that she was lost. "Look, Shinah, you don't have to do this. Let me help y——" he tried to plead with her once again before she cut him off.

"SL, please, if you're not going to sell to me, then let me the fuck out of this car." She was trying to remain calm, but the prospect of not getting anything to smoke had her panicking.

SL pulled over to the curb and turned on his hazard lights. He felt her looking at him with a confused look on her face, but he ignored her as he pulled out a bag of rocks and counted out ten of them. He reached out to hand them to her without even glancing her way.

"Why did you lie to me, SL?" she asked calmly as she took the rocks. She tried to hand him the money, but he refused to take it. "Why you not taking my money?" She looked at him like he was crazy as she clutched the bills in her hand.

He pulled back into traffic before answering. "Keep your money, shorty, 'cause this will be the last time I sell you anything. The reason I lied to you is because I wanted you to see how these drugs are controlling you."

She opened her mouth to refute his claims, but he kept right on talking.

"You're a beautiful woman, intelligent, funny and perceptive, which I love, but you are gonna let this shit take you down. I can't front, at first I looked at you as major money, but now it's so much deeper than that. I know that some lowlife-ass nigga turned you out on laced blunts and left you to fend for yourself. When I first saw you in line with those dirty, fucked-up crackheads, I knew you didn't belong. You stood out like a light amidst the darkness. I knew you would eventually graduate to the pipe and you can keep denying it, but you're only lying to yourself. I know better. I thought I could help you, but I see now that you don't want it. Like I said, I looked at you as major money, but now I see a beautiful woman who's trapped chasing a high that's really an illusion. Shinah, I wanted you from the moment I set eyes on you, then I wanted to be more than you were willing to let me be. You would think a nigga had you out here buying work, scoping out the competition, and I was battling him for your affection, but you made me realize today that I was competing against that infamous high. So I quit trying to win a race rigged for me to lose. I refuse to be a part of taking you down any longer. So this will be the last time I give you drugs. How many rocks will it take before you're out here like a zombie? How many of these muthafuckas out here degrading themselves for a rock started out just like you? Thinking that they could control that high until it put them down? Always remember that I'm your friend, whether you believe it or not. I will help you if you ever need it." He pulled up behind her car and took a deep breath. He wasn't used to opening up like that, but he couldn't expect her to lay all of her cards on the table if he wasn't willing to do the same thing. He looked over at her and saw that she was crying. He grabbed a napkin out of his cup holder and jotted down his address. "Listen, nobody has this information. I don't have too many people I can trust, but I feel like you're one of them. I can't expect you to let me in if I don't do the same. If you ever need me for anything a place to feel safe, use it. Here, take it."

Shinah reached over and grabbed the napkin. She looked at it, then reached over and hugged him. Before he could react, she got out of the car and jogged to her own. She never once looked back at him as she drove away.

SL watched her pull off with a heavy heart and wondered if that would be the last time he ever saw her. He had to admit that he might've been a little too blunt with her, but it had to be done. He looked over, saw the two hundred dollars in his passenger seat, and shook his head ruefully. He pulled off, hoping she accepted his helping hand if she ever needed him.

Chapter 5

Shinah pulled up to her house mad at the world. She had just left the bank and found out that her parents had frozen her accounts. Every month like clockwork they deposited a couple of thousand dollars into her account so she could live comfortably while in school. They didn't want her to worry about paying bills and such, so when the teller had informed her that her accounts had been frozen, she was livid. She knew exactly what her parents were doing - or rather, what her mother was doing - because her father would never leave her out in the cold like this. But she wouldn't bite. She would show her mother that she didn't need them to make it in the world.

She got out of the car and made her way towards the house. She unlocked the front door and walked in to find her two housemates standing in the foyer with mean mugs on their faces and luggage at their feet.

I hope these bitches are moving, she thought as she stopped short of fully entering the house and assessed the situation. She looked down at the luggage by their feet and noticed that it was her luggage packed up. *Oh, these bitches done lost their minds*, she thought angrily as she walked fully into the house and slammed the door behind her. "What the hell were you two doing in my room, and who gave you permission to touch any of my shit?" she asked coldly. She was so angry that her body was shaking.

"We've discussed this, and we think it's best if you leave this house," Tiffany, one of her housemates, stated as she wrinkled up her nose like she was smelling something bad.

"Yes, you're a crackhead, and we don't want to be around that disgusting shit," Jasmine, her other housemate spat. She was ready for a fight. She had Vaseline on her face and her hair in a ponytail just in case Shinah tried to get violent.

"Girl, you are tripping. Me, a crackhead? Please! Shinah nervously tried to laugh off their accusations. "Y'all must be smoking too much weed," she added with a smirk.

"You must've forgotten that we come from the projects and we definitely know what crack smells like," Jasmine shot back with a smirk of her own.

"So we got together and searched your room because we didn't want to accuse you of anything without any proof," Tiffany said sympathetically. "We found this." She pulled the crack rocks and pipe out of her pocket, showing her the proof.

Shinah felt her heart drop when she laid eyes on her stash. She knew that she was busted, but tried to play it off. "I sell crack, bitch. Give me my shit." She angrily snatched her property out of her hand and placed it in her purse.

"Yeah, whatever. You're a drug dealer from the suburbs," Jasmine said sarcastically as she made air quotation marks with her fingers. "Whatever you claim to be doesn't make any difference because you're getting the fuck out of this house," she added seriously.

"Y'all can't kick me out. I pay rent just like you do. So I'm not going anywhere," Shinah said indignantly.

"Actually, we can, because your name is not on the lease. We were just looking out for you because we were friends. You using or selling crack is not something we fuck with," Tiffany said softly. She actually felt bad for her because she really liked Shinah.

"So you can and will get the fuck up out of here. Either on your own or with our help," Jasmine said as she balled her fists up so there wouldn't be any misunderstandings.

Shinah looked at them and knew that they had her dead to rights. She decided to leave peacefully because all she had left was her pride and dignity, and she refused to lose either by acting out of character.

"Can y'all at least help me load this stuff into my car?" she asked quietly.

"Yes, we'll help you," Tiffany said quickly, shooting a glance at Jasmine before she could open her mouth.

Jasmine blew out a frustrated breath, but she kept her mouth shut.

Together they loaded all of her luggage and possessions into her car in silence. What was there to say? When they were done, Tiffany tried to say something, but Shinah just hopped into her car and pulled off before they saw her tears. Her life was going downhill fast and she couldn't seem to slow it down.

****

"Was that really necessary, Charlene?" Bobby asked, exasperated after she had just informed him that she had frozen their daughter's bank account. "How will she survive if we don't help her? She is your only child!" he screamed. The worry for his daughter was evident on his face.

"We told her that she had to keep her grades up in school and she hasn't," Charlene said sternly as she looked at her husband crossly. "You are sitting there acting like your daughter isn't out in the streets running footloose, smoking drugs, and doing God knows what else and you expect me to continue to support her when it's obvious she's taking us for granted. I for one refuse to do so and I expect the same from you." She added seriously. As far as she was concerned, he had always coddled their daughter way too much and she felt like it hurt her more than it helped.

"First off, she's our daughter, not my daughter, and secondly, she's a child - our child," he said angrily. "She needs our help to overcome whatever it is she's going through. You won't even call or allow me to call to see if she's okay," he added, frustrated.

"She's not a child, but a grown woman who's showing us how much she needs us. As far as calling her, how many times has our child called us?" She crossed her arms over her breasts, glared at him, and awaited his answer. When none was forthcoming, she continued, "let me answer that for you: not one time. She's stubborn, but I will show her that it's time to grow up." Her anger was starting to rear its head also.

"Stubborn?" Bobby repeated incredulously. "I wonder who she got the particular trait from. Hmmm, let me answer that for you, sweetheart. You! She got it from you, Charlene. So stop acting like you haven't been young before, like you didn't experiment when you were her age. I will let you take the reins on this one, but I promise you that you will regret it if anything happens to our daughter." He stared at her for a few seconds to let her see the seriousness in his eyes, then he turned without another word and left the room.

Charlene watched him walk out of the room with that determined gait she was so used to him having whenever he was upset. She felt like she was right and would continue to be right until proven otherwise. He was right about one thing though. She did experiment when she was Shinah's age but she didn't have anyone to tell her what to do like she was doing for her daughter. So if Shinah wanted to experiment regardless of what she was told, then she would learn her lessons as she did: the hard way.

Chapter 6

Shinah had been sitting in the parking lot of Phoenix Square shopping center for hours crying her eyes out as she replayed the events of her life. She knew that she was out of control, but she couldn't seem to stop the spiraling affect her life had taken. She knew that she needed help, but she refused to give her mother the satisfaction of coming home with her head down and hand out. That's why she was sitting in an almost empty parking lot clutching the napkin SL had written his address on. She could go to a hotel for a little while, but the funds she had she needed to save because without her parents, she had no income coming in whatsoever. So she decided to show up at SL's house and see what happened. He had everything she needed at that moment: a place to regroup and get herself together. But more importantly, he had crack.

****

SL had finally reached the conclusion that he wouldn't see or hear from Shinah ever again and was about to go visit one of his old jump-offs. He grabbed his keys and opened his front door, receiving the shock of his life.

Shinah almost lost her nerve when she heard his front door opening up before she had a chance to knock, but she took a deep breath and steeled herself for his reaction in case it was negative. She hoped that he was a man of his word, because he was her last hope. She trudged on. "Hi," she said softly when they locked eyes.

SL looked at her with surprise etched onto his face. He was just thinking that he wouldn't see or hear from her ever again, and now here she was in the flesh standing on his front porch. "What's up? Are you okay?" he asked quietly despite the excitement he was feeling from seeing her again.

Shinah took another deep breath and exhaled slowly as she tried to figure out a way to tell him what it was she needed. The sight of him standing there looking handsome wasn't helping the situation either.

SL saw that she was trying to figure out a way to tell him something, so he decided to help her out. He had already peeped the packed bags in the backseat of her car anyway. "You need a place to stay for a while?" he asked gently.

She looked at him sharply, wondering if she really was that easy to read. "Why would you ask me that?" she asked in a voice she tried to make sound casual but failed miserably. She heard how it sounded and had the decency to look embarrassed.

SL chuckled at the look on her face and felt himself falling deeper into her. He pointed at the car and said, "The clothes in the backseat pretty much gave you away."

"Yeah, me and my roommates are not seeing eye to eye right now and I don't want to go to my parents' house for other reasons," she said honestly. She relaxed a little when she saw that he wasn't judging her.

"So you need to stay, right?" he asked again, wanting her to say it.

"Yes," she said and left it at that.

"Alright, but only on one condition," SL said as he tried to keep a straight face.

"What is it?" she asked as her anger grew.

"You have to tell me who you really are - and not some made up bullshit," he said, laughing at the look on her face.

"Oh," she said, embarrassed. She had thought that he wanted sex. If she sat down and really thought about it, he had never came off on her like it was just about sex. He let it be known that he was attracted to her, but never made her feel uncomfortable. "Okay, I can do that," she added with a smile.

And that's exactly what she did. He treated her so good and so comfortably she stayed up all night telling him about her life: the good, the bad and the ugly. She just kept it real and for the first time in a long time, she felt her burden ease a little.

"So you mean to tell me you walked into your crib and found this clown Roland smoking crack in the dark?" he asked with a frown on his face. He didn't even know the man, but he wanted to do something damaging to him.

"Yes. He took the money I gave him for the light bill and got high with it," she said with a look of disgust on her face from the memory.

"And he's the one who tricked you into smoking the laced blunts?" SL asked quietly.

Shinah just nodded her head yes because she was trying to fight back the tears that welled up in her eyes.

"If you want, I can make him disappear," he said seriously.

Shinah looked over at him to see if he was serious and shivered a little when she saw that he was. A long time ago she wouldn't have hesitated to take him up on his offer, but she wouldn't let him get into trouble over a lowlife like Roland. He would get his eventually. "No, but there is one thing you can do for me though," she said, looking him directly in his eyes.

"And what's that?" he asked when he noticed her nervousness.

"Make love to me," she said so quietly that he barely heard her.

"Are you sure this is what you want?" he asked because he didn't want to take advantage of her vulnerability. He couldn't believe that he was even asking the question in the first place, but he wanted to make sure that she didn't feel like she owed him anything.

Shinah nodded her heard yes, surprised by how badly she really wanted it to happen. If she was being honest with herself, she was attracted to him just as much as he was to her. She needed him to drown out her problems - at least for a little while.

SL grabbed her chin and tilted her face up until she was staring into his eyes." Are you sure?" he asked again.

She nodded yes again right before he touched his lips to hers. The sensations that shot through her body made her feel higher than any drug could. He picked her up and carried her into his bedroom. She clung to him, refusing to let his lips leave hers for more than a few breaths. He laid her down on his king-sized bed and stared at her for a second to see if she had changed her mind. When he saw fire burning inside her eyes, he wasted no time in undressing her before taking off his own clothes.

He looked down at her, lying naked on his bed, and realized that she was trusting him with more than just her body. She was exposing all of her vulnerabilities and secrets because she wanted him to see all of her. As he felt the connection she was making with him solidify, he felt a rage so intense course through his body because he wanted to kill Roland for trying to destroy something so beautiful.

Shinah reached up and cupped his face when she felt his energy change. "What's wrong?" she whispered, hoping he still wanted her.

SL didn't answer with words as he slid into her and became lost. He wanted her to feel the love growing inside of him for her. He thought about putting on a condom, but it was fleeting. He wanted to feel her - all of her. He looked down when he noticed her breathing change, and when her pussy started convulsing around him, he realized that she was climaxing. He knew right then from the way they fit, from the way she was responding to him, that they were meant to be. From the moment he penetrated her, she belonged to him, and vice versa. For the rest of the night, he made sure that no other man would ever be able to give her pleasure besides himself. He knew she was inexperienced, but eager to learn, and she responded well to his instruction. He put it all the way down so that when she screamed out that she loved him, he knew that she was his and wouldn't be going anywhere.

Chapter 7

SL slowly awoke from his satiated slumber with a smile on his face. He couldn't remember another morning he was happy to wake up in bed with a female. With his eyes still closed, he reached out for Shinah to go another round and felt her side of the bed empty. His eyes popped open quickly and he saw that she was indeed gone. Instincts kicking in, he quickly assessed the situation and hopped out of bed when realization finally dawned on him. He raced to his bathroom and snatched the lid off the back of the toilet. His heart stopped, threatening to burst out of his chest, when he saw that his dope was still where he hid it. He took off for the front door, but before he could open it, in walked Shinah. He breathed a sigh of relief when he saw her.

"What?" she questioned when she saw him standing there. "I just went to get some groceries to cook breakfast for you because there is absolutely nothing to eat in your kitchen," she said, laughing until she got a good look at his face. "You thought I had left with your shit and wouldn't come back, didn't you?" she asked seriously as she read the thoughts projected onto his face.

SL couldn't say anything in his defense because those were exactly his thoughts when he found her gone.

Shinah shook her head when he didn't respond. He didn't really need to say anything because his face clearly broadcasted his thoughts and feelings.

"Well, at least someone has faith in me," she said, nodding her head at his morning erection before taking the groceries into the kitchen to put them away.

SL looked down and realized that he was still naked, but put that out of his mind as he followed her into the kitchen. He walked up behind her and hugged her around the waist. "I can't deny that I thought you were gone, but can you blame me?" he asked regretfully.

Shinah shook her head no. She couldn't blame him for his thought because if the roles were reversed, she would've thought the same. But she also couldn't deny that those doubts coming from him hurt her more than she cared to admit. She wanted to talk to him, but she couldn't seem to put a coherent thought together with his dick pressed up against her backside. Last night was still very much on her mind and her feelings were confusing her.

She took a deep breath and spoke her mind. "Look, last night you made me feel…" She struggled to find the right words to describe it. "Wonderful, sexy, and brand new, but if we can't trust each other, then it's not worth it, SL." She started crying as soon as his name left her lips.

"Shhh, baby," he whispered in her ear as he turned her around to kiss her tears away. "I do trust you to a certain extent, Shinah, but we have to work to make the foundation strong so our feet will always be on solid ground."

Shinah didn't respond to what he was saying because the sound of his voice and the feel of his dick pressed against her stomach were turning her on. She lifted her face and captured his lips with her own. She squealed when he lifted her up and carried her back to the bedroom. Once there, she became the aggressor. She wiggled out of his arms and slid down his body to her knees. She took his dick in her hand and stroked it until the veins were bulging just beneath the surface, then she locked eyes with him as she wrapped her lips around him. After bringing him to the verge of climax twice, she released him and stood up.

"Stop teasing me, Shinah," SL groaned as he watched her through slitted eyes.

Shinah just smiled wickedly at him as she slowly undressed. She could tell that he was fighting the urge to take her, but he held back, and that power she had over him was intoxicating. When she was completely naked, she pushed him onto the bed and straddled him. She leaned forward a little so he could enter her, then she took the reins. She rode him like a champion jockey at the Kentucky Derby. When they both reached the peak of pleasure, she collapsed onto his chest and sighed happily.

"I love you," she mumbled right before drifting off to sleep.

SL stroked her hair and followed her into dreamland with his dick still inside of her.

Later on that day he was awakened by the ringing of his phone. He snatched it up before it could wake Shinah and answered, "Talk to me." He listened as Jay Jay told him about a situation that he needed to handle personally. "Alright, give me twenty minutes and I'll be there."

He hung up and slid out of bed. He stretched as he watched Shinah still snuggled under the covers and wanted to get back in bed, but he was missing money. He looked at the clock on his dresser and noticed it was already one o' clock in the afternoon. He hadn't made one move to leave the house and he was missing bread that he was usually getting before the sun came up. He shook his head and looked down at the woman he was in love with. She had a hold on him he wouldn't have thought could happen so quickly. He had a few reservations about the test he set up for her because he didn't know if it was too soon, but he needed to know if he could trust her. In his line of work, one mistake could cost you your life, and he couldn't afford to take that chance unless he knew he could trust her.

With that thought in mind, he went and hopped into the shower. Twenty minutes later, he was dressed and ready to go. He wrote a quick note letting her know he would be back as soon as possible. He kissed her on the cheek and left the house.

About an hour later, Shinah was awakened by the growling of her stomach. She opened her eyes and saw that it was a little after two o'clock in the afternoon. She looked around for SL and noticed the note he left for her. She got up and grabbed it. A smile blossomed on her face as she read the message he left for her. She hopped into the shower and got dressed before cooking herself something to eat. After finishing her meal, she grew bored with herself and decided to clean up the house to give herself an excuse to explore. She needed a hit badly, but she had kept it under control around SL because she didn't want him to think that she was having sex with him for crack. She hoped she found a rock or two to calm her demons as she tried to quit smoking altogether.

She looked around at the messiness of the house and shook her head.

Typical man, she thought as she got started with her task. By the time she reached the bathroom, she was dead tired and irritable. She had searched the whole house and couldn't find anything to smoke - not even a crumb. More than once she had the urge to leave and go find something to smoke, but she had successfully fought those urges with everything inside of her and she was proud of herself because the little devil on her shoulder could be very convincing at times. She put the dilemma out of her mind and got back to work. She lifted the lid off the back of the toilet and felt her heart skip a beat. Sitting in front of her wrapped in plastic baggies and submerged in water was what her heart had been yearning for the last couple of days: crack. She lifted the lid all the way off and carefully pulled the drugs out of the water. She checked to make sure no water had seeped inside of the baggies before setting the drugs onto the sink counter. She replaced the lid, sat down on the toilet seat, and stared at the crack with her heart thudding inside of her chest. Sweat beads started popping up on her brow as she thought about SL and the consequences of taking his dope. Last night combined with that morning was the best she had ever felt with a man and she had actually told him that she loved him, but was she really in love or just vulnerable?

Take your secret lover and let him show you what real love is, the devil on her left shoulder whispered in her ear.

Don't do it. Let SL help you fight your demons, the angel on her right shoulder whispered into her other ear.

Shinah thought about her options and knew that she really didn't have any. She wasn't strong enough to resist her greatest lover. SL sold the drug she craved. So she couldn't possibly be with him and defeat her demons, could she?

Rationalizing in a way that made sense to her, she grabbed the dope and left the bathroom to repack her bags. She put all of her stuff into her car, even all of the groceries she had bought that morning. Before she left, she realized that she was low on funds, so she ran back into the house to where she saw the bundles of money SL had hidden in his closet. She grabbed the money and stuffed it in her purse. Feeling bad about stealing his stuff and leaving, she wrote him a letter and placed it in the middle of his bed so he wouldn't miss it. She didn't know what time he would return, so she ran back to her car and pulled off. Before she reached the end of the block, she had tears cascading down her face because she had just left behind the best thing to ever happen to her.

A couple of hours later when SL pulled up to his house, he knew in his heart that he wouldn't find Shinah inside. He grabbed the bag of Chinese he had bought and the videos he had rented and hoped that his intuition was wrong. He hoped that he was jumping to conclusions again like he did that morning but his gut told him that he was right. Besides, her car was gone. He opened his front door and headed straight towards his bathroom. Lifting the back off of the toilet, his eyes confirmed what his heart already knew. He put the lid back heartbroken and walked into his room, spotting the letter almost immediately. He rushed over, picked it up and started reading. When he got to the end, his heart dropped. He reread it to make sure his eyes weren't playing tricks on him.

Dear SL,

Why did you leave that dope in the back of the toilet? I know you left it there on purpose because you are too intelligent to just forget about it! If you were testing me, then I'm sorry to say that I failed miserably. It was too early for tests when you knew that I wasn't strong enough yet. One night and morning wouldn't be enough to clean me up. I'm also sorry about your money, but I needed it. I promise to pay you back. I told you about my parents. We will probably never see each other again because I am weak and don't like the path that I'm on. I really want to thank you for making me feel so special while I was with you, even if it was only for a day. I will never forget you. Maybe we'll see each other in the next life or maybe not. Don't hate me please!

Love,

Shinah

He dropped the letter and bolted out of the house. He had to find her because she had taken over two ounces of work from him, and that was enough to kill anyone if they didn't know what they were doing. He felt horrible because he should've known better. He figured she would get nosy and start searching the house but he was hoping - no, praying - that she could defeat temptation when she eventually found the drugs. He should've followed his instinct not to do it, but he didn't, and now he regretted it. He had wanted to know if he could trust her, but he knew that it was too soon. A person who hadn't smoked in years would've been tempted by two ounces of crack and a couple of thousand dollars just lying around. Hindsight was 20-20 though and now he had to find her.

He hopped into his car and broke every speed limit in the city as he raced to Shinah's parents' house. He had called everybody he knew in the city, especially his team along the way and had them on the lookout for her and her car. He had to find her before she killed herself. Last night she confided in him all about her life, especially the problems she had with her mother. He already didn't like her because she was cutting her daughter off when it was obvious that she needed help. Shinah didn't know it, but when he had first met her, he was so intrigued with her that he had followed her to the neighborhood said to contain her parents' home. That's why he was on his way to their house now, despite the problems Shinah said she had with them. He would think they had a way to contact her in case of emergencies, and this definitely was an emergency.

When he arrived at the gated community, he had to wait for someone to leave or enter before he could get inside. When he was finally inside, he had no problem locating her parents' home because the family name was posted on their mailbox. He parked his car and sat there for a few seconds, thinking that they probably wouldn't tell him where she was even if they knew. Deciding that he would be content just to know that she was okay, he got out of the car and knocked on the front door. A few seconds later, it was answered by a woman who was undoubtedly Shinah's mother. They looked like they could be twins. SL knew that he was staring, but the resemblance was uncanny.

"Yes, how may I help you?" Charlene asked as she looked him up and down with a frown on her face. Her expression showed him exactly what she thought of him.

"Um, I'm looking for your daughter Shinah," SL said, getting back to the business at hand.

"Why are you looking for my daughter?" she asked as her frown deepened, diminishing her beauty a little.

SL looked at her and shook his head. He was starting to understand what Shinah was talking about. This woman just had a snobbish air about her. He also noticed that she didn't seem too concerned when it came to Shinah. He was gonna be nice and spare feelings, but decided to give it to her raw and uncut.

"Your *daughter*," he emphasized the word, "got ahold of a lot of drugs and went missing. I'm trying to find her before she hurts herself." He waited on her response.

"Did you sell her the drugs?" Charlene asked with an amused glint in her eyes.

SL looked at her like she had two heads after she asked him that. "No, I didn't sell her the drugs, but why is that important?" He was starting to lose his cool with her nonchalant attitude, but she didn't want to see that side of him so he stayed respectful. "We need to find her before it's too late," he added seriously.

"We?" Charlene asked incredulously as she looked at him like he had lost his mind. "We don't need to do anything Mister whatever your name is. Shinah is grown and can look after herself. She will have to live with the consequences of her choices," she said while looking him directly in the eyes.

"Why are you acting like you don't care about your daughter?" SL asked, disgusted at her attitude.

"Like I said, Shinah is grown and can take care of herself. Now will you please remove yourself from my property before the proper authorities are called?"

SL looked at her for a few seconds before turning around and walking back to his car. He got in and pulled off. He quickly dismissed the woman from his mind. He had to find Shinah.

****

If Shinah wants to associate herself with trash like that, she is no longer my daughter, Charlene thought as she watched him drive off.

"Who was that, sweetheart?" Bobby asked, walking up behind her and peeking over her shoulder.

"Oh, nobody important. Just some young kid trying to sell us newspapers," she said as she made a mental note to get the guard at the gate house fired tomorrow. She grabbed her husband's hand and pulled him back into the house, closing the door behind them.

****

SL checked every hotel and dope spot he knew of in the city, but he couldn't find a trace of Shinah anywhere. No one he had on the lookout for her or her car had spotted her either. He knew that the chances of her still being in the city were slim to none, but if she went out of town, he wouldn't even know where to begin looking. He wouldn't give up on looking for her, but he wouldn't hold his breath either on ever seeing her again. He just hoped she was okay. He finally gave up his search and went home praying for the best, but preparing for the worst.

Chapter 8

Eight months later

SL was the man to see in the streets of Durham now. He had graduated from a team owner to the commissioner of the city. His rise to the top wasn't without its usual hiccups: police kicking in his spots, niggas hating, other crews testing his strength and bitches doing whatever they could to get to his dick and his pockets. He handled every situation with his usual aplomb. For the police, he bought the ones who had a price and ducked the ones who didn't. The haters, he evaluated them, weeded out the threats, and eliminated them. For the ones who tested the strength of his foundation, he let his murder game do the talking, and it spoke loud and clear. They listened and played their positions. As far as the women, he kept them at arm's length and stuck to his number one rule, M.O.B.: money over bitches.

For the last eight months, there was only one woman who occupied his thoughts, and that was Shinah. No matter how many other females he dealt with, he couldn't get her off of his mind. He hadn't given up on finding her. He still had people on the lookout for her. He still watched for her white Acura every time he was out and about because despite everything, he still loved her. His heart didn't want to accept the logical answer his brain was telling it: that if Shinah wasn't dead, then she was either turning tricks in someone's stable or was roaming the streets as a full-blown crackhead doing all kinds of degrading shit for a hit. He shook his head to clear it of the depressing images that flooded his brain. He didn't give a damn what she was doing. He vowed to find and help her, and that's what he would do. It was the least he could do, seeing that he was the reason she was in the predicament she was in. Not to mention that he still wanted her.

****

Shinah had finally hit rock bottom. After she had stolen from SL, she drove until she ended up at a twenty dollar a week motel called the Red Carpet Inn in Creedmoor, a little country town about thirty minutes down the highway from Durham. Once there, she paid for the room for a couple of months, paid another resident to unload her car, locked her room door after they were done, and pulled the dope out. She sat there for a few minutes staring at it, amazed by how much crack she actually had in her possession. She was a little scared to get started because she had a feeling she wouldn't be able to stop. She didn't know anything about cutting crack down to rocks, so she just broke a big piece off and put it in her rooms air conditioner unit to hide it just in case. She broke off a much smaller piece and placed it in her stem. Once she put the flame to it and took her first pull, her worries vanished. Her secret lover was back and he made her feel so good that she didn't have a care in the world. She smoked rock after rock until she felt like she could touch the sun. The only time she took a break was to eat and use the bathroom. The more she smoked, the more she started noticing little subtle changes in herself. She stopped caring about her hair and nails being done like she used to. She didn't care if she skipped a shower or two. She wasn't too concerned about anything except getting high.

It wasn't until a couple weeks into her binge that she would finally meet the man who would turn her into the person she dreaded becoming the most: a crackhead.

****

Mike Billy was a predator in every sense of the word. There was no other way to describe the things he did. He was 5'10", 160 pounds, with stringy, greasy brown hair, pale white skin, and numerous tattoos, he wasn't much to look at physically. He wasn't attractive at all, especially to the opposite sex, but he was very aware of this and it didn't stop him from doing what he wanted to do because he had connections. The Red Carpet Inn was home to junkies, crackheads, whores, pimps, and drug dealers and as the manager, but more importantly the owner's son, he had a pool of weak-minded women to take advantage of. He used every tactic he could think of to get what he wanted: the threat of eviction, calling the police, to free rent or whatever else he could think of to bribe the tenants he wanted something from. Everybody who stayed at the Red Carpet knew him so they knew what it was when they saw him coming. The Red Carpet was his life and that was where he felt like a king. He worked there seven days a week and did whatever he wanted to do whenever he wanted to do it. His parents basically let him as long as he kept away from them. On the rare days he did take off, he had one of his friends watch the office until he came back.

When he did return from one of his rare days off, his friend told him about the new woman that had checked in while he was gone. He said she had paid for a couple of months in advance, so it looked like she would be around for a while. His friend went on and on about how gorgeous she was and how he had never seen anything like her at the Red Carpet. He was talking about her so much that Mike Billy finally got fed up and sent his friend home, but he couldn't deny that his interest was piqued. That's why for the past couple of weeks, he had been watching the room waiting to see her, but she hadn't stepped foot outside of her room once since he had been back. He finally made the decision to go knock on her door and introduce himself as the manager and owner, which he sometimes lied about because people seemed a lot more gullible to what he was saying when they thought he owned the motel. He looked in the mirror and made sure his hair was slicked back before he made his way across the parking lot towards her room.

As he walked, he was greeted by different tenants like he was the president or something. He smirked because he knew that they really didn't like him, but they tolerated him because they knew that he ran his domain with an iron fist. He made it to her door and took a deep breath before knocking. For some unknown reason he was nervous, because he usually knew some dirt about the tenant he could use before he decided to make his move, but he knew nothing about this one, something he planned on rectifying soon - real soon. He took another deep breath before knocking again.

****

Shinah was sitting Indian style on the bed getting high when she heard the knock at the door. The sound startled her because she had been left alone since she had been there. Other than the food delivery people, nobody had bothered her. And she preferred that. Now it seemed as if someone had gotten curious and wanted to be nosy. She hopped up and hid the drugs and paraphernalia in the bathroom. On her way to answer the door she looked down and saw that she was only wearing her panties and baby tee. She decided not to get dressed because she didn't plan on letting anyone into her room.

"Yes, may I help you?" she asked politely when she opened the door halfway and saw a white man standing on her threshold twitching like he was nervous or something. She stood behind the door so he couldn't see that she wasn't dressed.

"Um, I'm the manager and owner of this motel and I need to do a room inspection, Miss," Mike Billy said, trying to muster up his best authoritarian voice but he was flustered by her beauty. She was everything his friend said she was and more. He noticed that she looked tired what with the dark circles under her eyes, but it did nothing to detract from her beauty. He also noticed that she was hiding behind her door and tried to peek around at her in case she was naked.

Shinah's eyes opened wide with fear when he mentioned a room inspection. She needed to hide her drugs better first before she let him into the room. "Hold on, let me get dressed first," she said as she started closing the door.

Mike Billy noticed the fear in her eyes and put his foot out to stop her from closing the door. He knew that look of fear all too well and didn't expect to see it on her face, but he decided to see if his intuition was correct. He leaned forward a little and sniffed the air.

"Is that crack I'm smelling in the air?" he asked with an incredulous look on his face. He would recognize that smell anywhere. It was a wonder he didn't smell it before as strong as it was coming out of her room.

"You are crazy, Mister." Shinah was trying to sound indignant as she tried to close the door. Her heart was hammering inside of her chest. Images of jail, handcuffs, and police were flashing through her mind and she was scared.

Mike Billy smiled as he saw right through her act. He knew that he had her right where he wanted her. He forced his way into the room and silenced her before she could speak. "Do you want me to call the police to come search the room, or would you rather we handled this ourselves?" he asked as he stared at her body lasciviously.

Shinah couldn't deny his claims because he had her between a rock and a hard place. She just stood there speechless as he lusted after her body.

Mike Billy smirked because he had her. "That's what I thought. Now come over to the bed and discuss your options," he demanded.

Shinah did as she was told and waited meekly to see what he would do.

"Go get the crack from your little hiding spot. Or do you want me to do it?" He looked at her to let her know that she didn't want him to waste the time to look for it.

She silently went into the bathroom to get the drugs.

Mike Billy watched her ass in her little panties as she walked away and felt himself become erect.

Shinah grabbed the drugs and broke some off just in case he tried to take it from her. She re-hid that before she went back into the room and handed him the rest of the product.

Mike quickly calculated that she had about seventeen, eighteen grams. His mouth started to water at the sight of so much crack. "Okay here's what's going to happen we're going to smoke and fuck," he said seriously. He was praying that she took the bait.

"What!" Shinah screamed as her fear disappeared and was replaced by anger. She couldn't believe that he had come at her like a prostitute.

"Or I can call the police and you deal with them. You have about twenty-five years' worth of crack here," he said, smirking at her.

Shinah looked at him with disgust in her eyes as she tried to decide whether or not to believe him or not. She quickly came to the conclusion that she couldn't afford not to believe him. The possibility of spending the rest of her life behind bars terrified her.

"Okay, but we're only having sex one time and I need to take a hit first," she said, taking what she thought was her best option.

"Okay, that's cool," Mike Billy said, smiling because he knew better. He was staring at a gold mine and he planned on milking it for everything it was worth. "Come on and get your hit so we can handle business," he ordered, ready to fuck.

Shinah prepared her stem with a big rock because she didn't want to remember any of this experience. She wished she could disappear, but she would have to settle for going on a trip to outer space. She put the flame to the stem and took a big pull. Instantly she was in her zone. Her secret lover would take care of her. She was feeling so good that she didn't even protest when she felt him pull down her panties.

Mike Billy looked at the most perfect ass he had ever seen and almost climaxed on himself from pure excitement. He bent her over the bed and started fingering her pussy.

"You need to put on a condom," she said, trying to keep some control of the situation. She didn't want to end up pregnant by this nasty-looking white boy.

"Shut up and smoke your crack," he said, using his tongue to lick her pussy. He didn't plan on putting a condom on but he didn't plan on cumming inside of her either. A whore baby was exactly what he didn't need. He could picture his parents' reaction if he got hit with a paternity suit. But he wanted to feel the inside of her without any barriers. He pulled out his dick and rammed it in her hot, wet pussy.

King Killa

Shinah knew without a doubt that she wouldn't have been able to get through the ordeal of having sex with him without her secret lover. She also knew without a doubt that she had made a mistake by dealing with him and in the end, she would pay dearly for it.

****

"You have to get rid of that baby in your stomach, bitch, when it slides out of your worn pussy," Mike Billy said, sneering at Shinah as he paced her room. He was trying to remember if he had ever cum inside of her, but the drugs had his brain addled. Ever since he found out about the pregnancy months ago, he had been trying to figure out the percentages of the whore's baby being his, but he couldn't come up with a number, even though he knew it was high, and he was scared. He was terrified that she would sue him for child support because she believe he owned the motel, but he didn't own anything; his parents did. And if this hit the fan, they would finally disown him. That's why he was trying to talk her into giving the baby up for adoption when it was born.

Shinah didn't even respond to his suggestion that she get rid of her baby. They had been having this same discussion every day since he found out that she was pregnant six months ago. When she had missed her period twice, she instantly knew that she was pregnant, but she went and bought a pregnancy test anyway just to be sure. When it came back positive, she found a free clinic where she could get a checkup. When the doctor informed her that she was two months pregnant, she knew exactly who the father was. She tried to hide it from Mike Billy at first because she didn't want him to know, but when she tried to cut back on smoking with him, he became suspicious and started beating on her until she was forced to tell him that she was pregnant. She feared he would beat her into a miscarriage and by no means would she lose this baby, not after Roland tricked her into an abortion the last time she was pregnant. Regardless of what happened to her, she would protect her baby at all costs.

So from that point on, she stopped smoking cold turkey. It was one of the hardest things she ever had to do in her life, but her baby gave her the strength she needed to pull through. Now she had to figure out a way to get from under Mike Billy's thumb. He had a hold on her because of the threat to call the police on her, but she was starting to prefer the thought of jail rather than be with him any longer. He still tried to make her smoke in hopes she would lose the baby, but she refused, and when he threatened to beat her, she kept him at bay by telling him that he wouldn't want to catch a charge for killing their baby. That was enough to get him to never raise a hand to her again. But he continued to have sex with her and then he started prostituting her out to other new men and sometimes women for money. You would think that people wouldn't want sex with a pregnant woman, but he never had a shortage of takers. He made her sell all of her possessions, including her car, to drug dealers to buy crack that he kept control of. He rationed money out to her like she was a cadet in his army, but she started putting a little away every time because she had to get away from him before the baby was born. He had her totally dependent on him for everything - or at least he thought he did.

The closer she got to her due date, the more adamant he became about her giving her baby up, and that wasn't an option for her. At eight months pregnant, she was running out of time to make a move. She thought about calling her parents, but she figured that they would disown her if they saw her now. Even though she maintained her weight, you could tell that she had abused drugs for a while and she didn't want to get into it with her mother. She also thought about calling SL, but figured that he would kill her for robbing him, so she felt lost. She got herself into her predicament and she would get herself out of it. She had a plan that she would execute soon.

Mike Billy stopped pacing and looked at Shinah with an evil look on his face. He hated when she acted like she didn't hear him, which she did a lot lately. He felt like she was mocking him with her silence, like he wasn't important. He would show her. He had to figure out a way to get rid of the baby, and her too, if necessary.

He had a plan, and he would execute it as soon as she dropped her load, but in the meantime, he would continue to enjoy the best piece of ass he ever had. He unzipped his pants, pulled out his dick, and sneered at her.

"Since you don't want to talk, put your lips to good use and suck me off," he demanded as he grabbed her by her hair.

Real soon, Shinah thought bitterly as she did as she was told.

Vincent "Vito" Holloway

Chapter 9

"It's been almost a year, Charlene, and I haven't seen or heard from my daughter," Bobby said to his wife.

"She's grown and she knows how to pick up a phone to call us," she said, not giving an inch on the subject.

"I don't care about what she'd doing or has done. She's stubborn - a trait she inherited from you, I might add - and that's why she hasn't called. She wants to show you that she can make it without our help. She's gullible, Charlene, because we sheltered her too much and she can be taken advantage of," he said seriously.

"If she wants to use drugs and act like common trash, then she's no daughter of mine," Charlene said, just as serious.

"You are a conniving, trifling, and hypocritical woman. Sometimes I wonder what possessed me to marry you. The greatest thing to come out of this marriage is our daughter. It's funny how you're condemning her for abusing drugs when you used to do the same thing. You have money now, but I've always had it." He smirked at her before continuing. "You married up; not me. So don't forget how I found you twenty-five years ago," he said with a look of disgust on his face.

"Don't act like you are all high and mighty when you are selling the same drugs your daughter is abusing," Charlene said as she returned his look of disgust. "You're no better than I am because you make your transactions in boardrooms instead of dope houses and street corners. Blood money is blood money. Hypocritical, trifling, and conniving I might be, but look in the mirror, Bobby dear, and recognize what you see in me," she added, chuckling.

"Believe me when I say that you will lose if you fight me on this," he said furiously. "I'm going out of town later tonight to handle business, but take heed, and I'm not asking. I'm telling you to find my daughter or I will make you regret living, Charlene." Bobby gave her one last look before turning on his heel and leaving the room.

Charlene waited until she heard him slam the door to his bed-room before she picked up the phone and dialed a number she had acquired months ago when she started putting her plan together. She didn't plan on finding her daughter because as far as she was concerned, Shinah was one less piece she would have to remove from the board as she positioned her pieces to attack. She had looked into the eyes of a burgeoning king almost a year ago and she would need to replace the one who would soon be checkmat-ed. Bobby would soon learn not to underestimate her: a true Queen!

****

After having sex with Mike Billy for what she hoped was the last time, Shinah slipped out of bed and started getting dressed. Her stomach was poking out so much now that she had a tendency to become clumsy. The normal time it took her to put on clothes was doubled, but she managed to get everything on without falling over or making too much noise. Earlier that night she had crushed up some extra strength sleeping pills and slipped them into Mike Billy's drink before they had sex. She had gotten them from another pregnant woman who also stayed at the Red Carpet and sympathized with her situation. She was praying that they would kick in before he was able to stick his dick inside of her, but that prayer went unanswered as she faked her way through another uninspiring performance. She shook his shoulder one last time to make sure that he was really out before she went into his pants pocket and grabbed all of his money and the keys to the manager's office. She left all of the drugs because she wanted nothing to do with them anymore. Everything she took with her was what she could fit in her purse or pockets. If she couldn't carry it, she left it in the room for somebody else to have. She was already toting around another person, and that was enough. As she left the room she left the door opened, a clear indication that everything left inside was up for grabs. She made her way towards the manager's office and was greeted by everyone who was out that night. Her plan was only a secret from Mike Billy. Everybody else knew because she had to enlist the help of some of the other residents to succeed. The hatred for Mike Billy amongst the residents was a universal thing, so she wasn't lacking any volunteers. She had gotten to know quite a few people staying at the Red Carpet and under different circumstances, she would even consider some of them friends. But she was on a mission that night to save her child. When she arrived at the office, she used the key she took from Mike Billy's pocket to unlock the door. Once inside, she headed directly for the safe and opened it up. Mike Billy was so sure he had the residents in fear of him that he left the safe open - a move he would regret in the morning.

Stupid motherfucker, she thought as she cleaned it out. She didn't bother relocking the door after she left the office because she wanted the people to clean Mike Billy out. She felt a lot of eyes on her, but she didn't care. She wanted Mike Billy to know that she was the one who set him up. She was sure that his informants would be ready to sell her out when the opportunity presented itself. She finally made it to the corner of the building and breathed a sigh of relief when she saw her ride waiting for her in the agreed upon spot. She hopped in and buckled up because she was anxious to get away from Mike Billy. She started breathing a little easier when they were on the highway, but she didn't relax until she saw the "Welcome to Durham, The City of Medicine" sign. She was home, and she would face whatever consequences awaited her return.

****

Jay Jay was sitting in his brand new money green Saab watching one of the dope houses SL had put under his control. They had the city jumping, but they needed a new connect. The Dominican they were dealing with, named Pep, was holding them back from reaching their potential. He supplied them with work when he had it, but he wasn't consistent enough. He never could meet their demand, and if he did, he gave them product that had been stepped on so much that they couldn't bring anything back. SL felt that Pep was conning them on some country bammer type of shit, thinking that he could get over on them because they were from the south. Jay Jay knew that he would be able to give Pep the dirt nap he deserved, but only after they found a new connect.

He was about to leave when he spotted a car he didn't recognize pull up and drop off a female. He shook his head when he noticed that she was a pregnant woman. To keep his conscience somewhat clear, he didn't allow pregnant women into his spots, so he was about to get out and stop her from entering his spot when she walked directly under a street light and looked his way. He laughed and snatched up his phone when he recognized her. *SL is gonna love this*, he thought as he dialed his number.

****

Shinah got out of the car and wondered just what the hell she was doing at a dope house. Upon entering the city, she had wanted to go to a hotel and rest up, but then she suddenly was overcome with the urge to find SL. She tried to ignore the urge because the thought of confronting SL scared her to death, but she couldn't shake the feeling that she needed to face him. When she committed herself to finding him, she racked her brain trying to remember his address, but couldn't. So she had her ride drop her off at the spot where they first met. When she got out of the car, she felt like someone was staring at her, but didn't notice anyone in particular watching her. She was sure a pregnant woman at a dope spot drew a lot of eyes so she put it out of her mind and wobbled up to the house, wondering exactly what she would say when she finally saw him again or if he would even be in the mood to talk.

****

SL hung up his phone, wondering if he could believe everything he had just heard. He had been looking for a new connect for a couple of months now, so he found it odd that one would just drop into his lap if he was willing to handle business, which he had no problem doing, but his benefactor was a mystery. He couldn't even tell the gender of his caller because they were using some type of voice disguiser, which made the situation even stranger, and he wouldn't know who it was unless he agreed to a percentage of his profits going their way. They promised that the money would be more than enough to share the pie. He was glad they gave him time to think about it because he didn't make rash decisions. He was about to call Jay Jay when his phone rang.

"Talk to me," he answered. "What!" he exclaimed, making sure he heard him right. He started making plans. Too much was happening in one night and he didn't believe in coincidences. "Make sure she doesn't leave and wait for me," he added before hanging up his phone and starting his car. For the second time that night, he had received a surprising phone call. Shinah was back on the scene, and to top it off, she was pregnant.

Ten minutes later he pulled up behind Jay Jay's car. He got out and walked up to the driver's side window.

Jay Jay rolled his window down and smiled up at SL. "She still in there, dog, and I called the workers to make sure nobody sold her anything."

"Good, good," SL said more to himself than him. "Set up a buy with Pep and cop everything he's got. Don't pay him shit." He paused and looked Jay Jay in his eyes. "Give him the dirt nap he's been begging for," he finished as he made a few decisions he hoped were the right ones.

Jay Jay smiled at the order because it was one he had been waiting for. He figured that they had secured a new connect or else SL wouldn't be giving the order to dead Pep. "You good here?" he asked, ready to handle business.

"Yeah, I'm good. Just get at me when you are good and I'll fill you in on everything," he said before crossing the street towards the dope house.

Jay Jay watched SL cross the street and wondered what it was about this girl that had his boss locked in like he was. That was a question he wouldn't be able to answer that night, so he pulled off after watching SL enter the spot. He was eager to chop another snake's head off.

****

Shinah sat on a dingy couch inside the dope house beside a woman who was begging somebody to let her suck their dick for a hit, wondering how long she would sit there waiting on SL. She figured that he had people on the lookout for her that would let him know the moment she was spotted. She was also fighting the urge to buy some crack. Even though she had been clean for months, it was still hard to be around it and now want to smoke. She kept rubbing her stomach to remind herself that it wasn't just about her anymore.

She was about to finally leave when she heard her name being called by the voice she remembered so well. She looked towards the door and saw the person she wanted to find her. The look on his face let her know how he was feeling, and it wasn't happiness, but she vowed to face whatever wrath he had in store for her.

****

SL walked into the house and let his eyes adjust to the smoke and gloom permeating the room. Almost immediately, he spotted Shinah fidgeting on the couch looking nervous. When he noticed her stomach protruding from her body with her obvious pregnancy, his anger reached a new level and he couldn't stop himself from the obvious thoughts that raced through his brain.

This bitch might be pregnant with my baby and she sitting in a dope house probably high or worse, trying to trick off, he thought angrily.

"Shinah!" he yelled, not giving a damn about all of the eyes that were now staring at him. He didn't give a fuck who didn't like it. He was SL.

Shinah sat there stuck as SL made his way towards her. She saw by the way people were staring at him and whispering that he was still the man to see. She watched how he walked with a commanding presence like a general ready to lead his troops into battle. She had to admit that he was still as handsome as she remembered. When he stopped in front of her, she looked up at him, ready to apologize, but he spoke before she could open her mouth.

"Let's go," he ordered harshly.

She was about to curse him out for his tone, but figured that she deserved it, no matter how much she didn't like it. She kept her mouth shut as she got up to follow him outside. She was about to protest again when he grabbed her by the arm, but she saw how everybody was looking at them and decided to wait until they were alone before she gave him a piece of her mind. Once they were outside, she tried to yank her arm out of his grasp but he gave her a look, squeezed tighter, and led her to his car. When she was safely inside, she folded her arms across her chest and stared out of the window.

SL got into the car, started it, and pulled off. He really didn't know what to say to her so he concentrated on controlling his anger. After a few minutes of letting the tension build, he broke his silence. "Why did you run?" he asked quietly. He kept his eyes on the road because he couldn't stand to look at her. He really wanted to ask her whose baby she was carrying around in her stomach, but he was scared of what her response would be.

"Why did I run?" she repeated incredulously. She turned to look at him. She couldn't believe that he asked her that question when they both knew what he did. "I ran because you knew I finally surrendered to you and you left me out to dry by leaving drugs and money where I would find it easily. You knew I was still weak and would run. One night of some good sex wouldn't change that. Don't flatter yourself. So save the bullshit questions," she spat angrily. She wore an expression that would scare most people, but it didn't faze SL.

"Yes, I left it there because I needed to know if I could trust you before I let you all the way in. Don't try to flip this shit on me because you were afraid to admit you had a problem. I was the one willing to help you. I was the one who took you in. I was the one who told you I would be there through it all. I was the one you told you loved. I was the one you stole from." He was so mad that he was seeing red. "Now look at you, pregnant with a trick baby because you were out there fucking and sucking every dick you could find for a hit. Wouldn't surprise me if you let a nigga pimp you," he added as he tried to hurt her.

Shinah wanted to cry because he didn't know how true his words were, but she wouldn't waste tears on a man who obviously didn't care anymore.

"Nigga, fuck you. You don't know what I've had to overcome the last eight, nine months. So fuck you, nigga." She lashed out to hurt him like he hurt her. "Drop me off anywhere please," she said suddenly as exhaustion overcame her. She needed to sleep.

"Nah, shorty, you owe me," SL told her as he maneuvered through traffic. He had plans to drop her off, but not where she was expecting.

"Oh, you want to fuck a pregnant trick?" she asked sarcastically as she rolled her eyes at him.

SL just smirked in response and kept quiet.

Shinah sucked her teeth and faced the passenger side window again. She figured that he wasn't going to let her off the hook that easily, that he was gonna get his money back somehow. So she sat back and waited to see how the events unfolded. After a few minutes though, the unknown was killing her and she started asking questions. "Where are we going? Where are you taking me?" She used a polite tone, even though she was still pissed at him, but she figured that being nice would get her an answer and she was correct. It was just not the answer she was looking for.

"The hospital," he told her and watched her eyes grow wide with fear. He pulled into Durham Regional Hospital's parking lot.

Shinah looked up and saw that they were indeed at the hospital. "Why are you taking me here?" she asked nervously as she placed her hands protectively on her stomach.

King Killa

SL saw the look of fear on her face and felt his heart soften. He could only imagine the horrors she had endured if she thought he was going to do something to her unborn child. He decided to put her mind at ease. "When was the last time you had a checkup by a doctor?" he asked as he looked at her in the eyes.

Shinah was ashamed to tell him that Mike Billy never let her go to the doctor after he found out that she was pregnant for fear that she would disappear on him. She broke eye contact with him and put her head down.

"Look, I'm checking you in and you will stay here until you have your baby. After you deliver, you can do what you want, but I'm not gonna let you kill this baby before he or she has a chance to live. You will not run because somebody will be watching your room day and night, even if I have to do it myself. This is not you, and I'm offering you my help one last time." He smirked at her when surprise lit her features up with happiness. "But shit on me again, and it's over. No more do-overs," he said seriously. He couldn't let her continue on the path she was on when he knew that it wasn't her fault for being on the path in the first place.

Shinah couldn't believe her ears as she sat there quiet. She closed her eyes and remembered her father's favorite saying. "God answers all prayers but only in his time; not yours." She wanted to thank SL for all his help, but was too overcome with emotion to speak. Also, she didn't want to come off as fake so she let SL check her in.

To her surprise, he stayed with her while the doctors performed their tests. From the very beginning she told her doctor that she didn't want to know the sex or any other information about the baby, only that they it was healthy. She really wanted to be surprised when she delivered because her baby really was a gift from God, a new beginning for the both of them. Another thing she was grateful to SL for was the fact that he didn't hesitate to foot the bill for her hospital stay because she no longer had insurance. He paid for everything out of pocket.

She looked at him now watching the doctors and nurses performing their tests and vowed to never hurt him again. She also promised herself to pay him back for everything he had done for her by getting clean and becoming the woman he claimed to see in her. For the first time in a long time, she smiled and believed that she would be all right.

Chapter 10

For the next week, SL kept constant watch over Shinah, catering to her needs and making sure that she was doing alright. If it wasn't for Jay Jay keeping him appraised of what was going on in the streets, he would've never called his mysterious benefactor back to agree to terms. The only reason he was leaving Shinah's side was because they wanted to meet with him and go over the details to the job he would have to complete in order to get his new connect.

"How long are you going to be?" she asked, pouting a little bit. Over the last week, SL had made her fall in love with him all over again because of the way he was treating her, despite the fact that she had done him wrong.

"It shouldn't be long, but don't worry because my homeboy is going to watch your room until I get back. If you need anything, he will get it for you," he said, ready to go handle business so he could get back to her.

"I'm not gonna run again, SL," she said, trying to make a joke of it by rubbing her bulging stomach, but she knew that the only thing that would heal that wound was time. She would do whatever she had to do so that he would trust her again.

"I believe you, Shinah, but humor me until I get back." He kissed her on the forehead before leaving. As bad as he wanted to stay, he had money on his mind and it was always M.O.E.: money over everything.

As soon as he left, Shinah felt a cramp in her stomach and closed her eyes until it subsided. She was so ready to have this baby and move on with her life, hopefully with SL.

Thirty minutes later, SL pulled into an abandoned parking garage and waited like he was instructed to do. After about ten minutes of sitting there and nothing happening he was about to pull off when a black Mercedes Benz pulled up behind him and flashed the high beams twice, the prearranged signal he was told to wait for. He got out of his car and walked towards the passenger side, trying to see who was driving. He couldn't really see any features that would jog his memory, but he could tell that it was a female, and that was a shock in of itself because he didn't expect a woman to be meeting him. Discreetly, he pulled his pistol from his waist and hid it behind his leg as he cautiously opened the passenger side door and looked inside. Who he saw staring back at him with a smirk gracing her pouty lips only confused him even more. His instincts were telling him to walk away and never look back, but his team expected him to secure this connect. If she could give him what he needed, then nothing else mattered to him.

"What are you doing here?" he asked aggressively.

"What do you think, Mr. SL?" Charlene replied sarcastically. "Now put your gun up and get in please. Tine is of the essence," she added, looking at him with an eyebrow arched.

SL tried to quickly figure out why Shinah's mother was sitting in this car, at this meeting, at this time. The voice on the phone had been distorted, but he would've never thought that his mysterious benefactor was a woman. Was it a coincidence that Shinah popped back up on the scene all of a sudden? He didn't believe in coincidences, so he would play his cards close to his vest and let it unfold in due time. If she could deliver on her promises, then who her daughter was didn't matter. He tucked his gun and slid into the car, closing the door behind him. Something she said when he first met her months ago was bothering him, so he threw a question in the air just to hear her answer. Her response would let him know how to carry her.

"How's Shinah doing?" He turned to look her in the eye so he could see her reaction. He had to check himself because her beauty and aura still threw him a little bit.

"Oh, she's overseas recuperating and getting her life back together. Don't worry about her," she said smoothly, not missing a beat. She didn't have to let him know that she hadn't seen her daughter in almost a year, not yet at least.

Well, at least I know that she's a lying bitch, SL thought as she looked at him. His face never revealed his feelings. "So tell me about this job - and let me warn you that I have little patience for lies and games," he said seriously, never once breaking eye contact.

"Honey, trust that I don't have any reason to lie or play games with you. We both have the same aspirations: to be as rich as possible. So you play your part and I'll play mine." Charlene wasn't intimidated and let him know it by maintaining the eye contact. To her, he was just a piece on her board.

Yeah, right, he thought as he smirked at her. He had to admit that he liked her attitude, but she was a snake and had to be watched. "Alright, tell me about this job," he said, deciding to speed things up.

"Here's a picture of the man you are to get rid of," she said as she handed him an 8 x 10 photo.

"Who is this supposed to be?" he asked after studying the photo for a few seconds.

"Let's just say that he's the man currently occupying your position," Charlene said coyly.

"So how do you want this done and when?" SL asked anxiously. He was ready to do what he had to do to secure the connect. He was wary of her, but he would lay her to sleep right beside of her mark if she played him for a fool.

"I want him to disappear. No body, no case. Completely gone, and I need it done now. Here's your plane ticket and all of the information you need. Your plane leaves in exactly three hours," she said, handing him the paperwork. "Oh, you notice that watch that he's wearing?" she asked pointedly. "Bring it back to me for verification. It has a special engraving on the underside of it." She wished that she could be there to see him take his last breath, but the plan didn't allow her that luxury.

"I'll get it done. You just have your end in order because when I get back, it's on," SL said before getting out of the car.

Charlene watched as he got back into his car and pull off. "Oh, my end will definitely be in order, believe that," she mumbled to herself as she watched his taillights disappear into the night.

Check, King. Protect yourself or you die, she thought wickedly as she pulled off. She had other pieces to put into play. Superior position always beat superior pieces.

****

After another round of tests, Shinah was tired of getting poked and prodded. She had told her doctor about her drug use because she wanted to give her baby all the help she could. The doctor kept trying to tell her details about the baby, but she really wanted to be surprised when she delivered. As long as he or she was healthy, that's all that mattered to her. Her doctor was an older African American lady by the name of Geraldine Hammonds, and she was taking very good care of her. It seemed as if she had taken special interest in her. She made Shinah feel like she could tell her anything. She wanted to tell Doctor Hammonds about the life she had led up to that point, but she didn't know if she could take it if she was judged, so she kept it to herself. She also missed SL. He had been gone for almost a week and she hadn't called him because she was waiting for him to call and check on her. As irrational as that sounded, she was the one pregnant and shouldn't have to call him. He had left Jay Jay there to watch her, but other than telling her his name and getting what she asked for, he ignored her attempts at conversation. She remembered him looking at her like a piece of meat about a year ago when she attempted to buy some crack from him, so she didn't really like him anyway, but she wanted to find out about SL. Every time she brought his name up, she received a look like it was her fault that he was there watching over her.

Fuck him, she thought after Jay Jay ignored her questions again. She pressed the button to lift her bed up. As she was rising, a sharp pain in her stomach stopped her halfway up. She waited for the pain to subside, but another one hit her twice as hard, making her scream. She saw Jay Jay poke his head into her room and ask what was wrong, but she couldn't answer because she felt another pain wrack her body. Then she felt the telltale wetness between her legs, letting her know that her water had broken and that her baby was on the way, whether she was ready or not.

****

Jay Jay was mad SL had him watching his little crackhead trick when he had better shit to do. For the last six months or so, SL had been showing him weaknesses that he hadn't spotted before and now he was playing guard dog to one of his biggest weaknesses. He didn't understand the logic behind taking care of a bitch who robbed you and ran. He didn't plan to dwell on it too much because he would soon be his own boss with his own team. He had met a woman who he felt would change his life if he put her on his team. She was grown sexy and screamed money with her looks, attitude, and attire. She was so unlike the usual hoodrats he dealt with that he didn't know how to handle her, but he was confident that once he put the dick on her, she would fall in line just like all the rest. He picked up his phone to call her, but he heard Shinah scream. He poked his head into the room to ask what was wrong, only to find her holding her stomach with a grimace on her face.

"What's wrong?" he asked, even though he could see that she was in pain. "Crackhead-ass bitch," he mumbled to himself when she ignored him. He went to alert the nurses anyway because she looked like she was ready to pop.

Shinah was in so much pain it left her speechless. She hoped Jay Jay went to alert the nurses because she couldn't reach the button to do it herself. She looked up when she heard footsteps running and saw her doctor with a few nurses rush into her room pushing carts of equipment.

"Are you ready to deliver these babies?" Doctor Hammonds asked with a smile as she checked her vitals to see how far her contractions were apart.

"Yes, please get this baby out of me!" Shinah screamed as another contraction hit her. *Babies? Did she say babies, as in more than one?* she asked herself, wondering if her doctor was stable enough to perform the delivery.

Doctor Hammond just smiled as they rolled her into the delivery room.

Jay Jay watched them roll Shinah by and hoped that the whole ordeal would soon be over. He dialed the number to who he hoped was his future Queen.

Ten hours later, Shinah was finally done feeling like she was dying. She couldn't believe that she had been carrying around four babies instead of one. They stretched her vagina so much that the doctor had to stitch her back up after delivery. She wished SL had been there to hold her hand throughout the whole ordeal, but he still hadn't called. She also thought about her parents and figured that it was time to let bygones be bygones so that they could be a part of their grandchildrens' lives. She promised herself to call them later after she got some rest. She was so exhausted that she drifted to sleep immediately.

****

"I don't care how you get it done, just get it done!" Charlene screamed as she slammed the phone down. She was mildly upset because her opponent had pushed a pawn to her side of the board and there was now another Queen back in play. But she wasn't worried because she had pieces everywhere. Remember, superior position always beats superior pieces.

****

A couple of hours later, Shinah awoke with a strong desire to see her babies. She hit the button to alert the nurse that she needed assistance. When she appeared at her door, she let her know that she wanted to go see her children. Even though she was still a little groggy and sore, she managed to get dressed in the gown and robe provided for her, then she was helped into a wheelchair and rolled down to the nursery. When she finally laid eyes on her children, her breath caught from the blessing God gave her.

Damn, they look just like their daddy, she thought to herself, smiling. She vowed right then and there to get her life back in order. She would start off by going back to her room and calling her parents to make things right. A few minutes later when she was tucked back into bed, she picked up the hospital phone, took a deep breath, and dialed the number she had vowed at one time to never call again.

****

Charlene snatched her ringing phone up, thinking that it was one of her many pawns reporting in, but she received the surprise of her life.

"Hello?" she said sweetly.

"Hey Mommy," Shinah answered tentatively.

"And to what do I owe the pleasure?" Charlene asked as she immediately recognized the voice.

"I just gave birth and I want you and Daddy to meet them. I also want to talk to you both so I can apologize," she rushed out before she lost her nerve.

"Your father is out of town once again, but I would love to see your baby and I want to apologize to you also. So I will be there in the morning," Charlene promised as a plan came together in her mind.

"Okay Mommy, see you in the morning," Shinah said, relieved that everything was going right.

"Okay baby, see you then," Charlene said before hanging up with a smile on her face. She loved when plans came together. It made her job so much easier.

Shinah hung up the phone with a smile on her face. She felt like God was finally blessing her. All she needed now was SL to show back up and everything would be perfect. She decided to close her eyes and get some more sleep. She had a feeling that she would need her energy for tomorrow.

Vincent "Vito" Holloway

King Killa

Chapter 11

Jay Jay had been up all night trying to figure out how to solve a problem that had suddenly popped up on his radar. He figured that he could get it done and get away with it, but he needed the opportunity to present itself. An idea came to him on how he would go about accomplishing his goal. He started smiling because he had figured out a way to solve his dilemma, and it would be easy. He stood up to stretch the kinks out of his body and felt someone walk into his personal space. He spun around and felt his heart skip a beat when he saw who it was.

"When did you get here?"

****

For the second time, Shinah awoke with a strong desire to see her kids. She was getting ready to alert the nurse to come help her when she decided that she would get ready on her own then go see her babies. After she finished getting dressed, she thought about asking Jay Jay if he would like to go with her. She wondered what he would say when he saw them. She smiled at the thought. She was about to go ask him when she heard him arguing with someone. She was about to walk out of the room to go see her kids anyway when she heard something that took her breath away.

"Shinah has to die."

"I told you I'ma handle it so chill the fuck out," Jay Jay whispered nervously. He looked around to make sure that no one was paying them any attention.

"Her father is already dead. You need to handle business before I find someone who will."

"I'ma kill that crackhead-ass bitch, but I can't rush this shit!" Jay Jay spat angrily.

Shinah was terrified at what she was hearing. *My father is dead,* she thought as she tried not to cry. She needed to know who Jay Jay was talking to because she would avenge her father. She crept to the door and pulled it open just an inch. What she saw bewildered her as well as made her angry beyond reason. She closed the door back, maybe too hard. She ran back to the bed as fast as her fatigued body could carry her and slid back under the covers. She was afraid Jay Jay or his guest had heard the door close and would speed up their plan to murder her. The only thing on her mind was survival and how she would exact her revenge.

"Let me go check and see if she's still sleeping. I could've sworn that I just heard the door close." he said before checking on Shinah. He opened her door wide enough to poke his head in and breathed a sigh of relief when he saw that she was still resting. He watched her for a few seconds to make sure that she was really sleeping before backing out of the room.

"Why don't you slip in there and suffocate the bitch with her pillow?"

Jay Jay looked back at the smiling face peering over his shoulder and shook his head.

This motherfucker is crazy and reckless, he thought. But they were giving him a chance to be the boss he knew he could be, so he put up with it for now. He actually looked around to see if he could slip into her room and handle business without notice, but he saw a nurse walking their way and knew without a doubt that they were headed to check on Shinah. He looked back into the room one more time to make sure she was still sleeping before closing the door.

****

Shinah's heart felt like it was going to burst out of her chest because it was beating so hard. She tried to keep as still as possible as she listened to them talk about ending her life so casually, but she was scared. She knew that if Jay Jay took his guest's advice and tried to smother her with her pillow, she wouldn't be able to fight him off because her body was still weak from delivery. Her mind was scrambling, trying to figure out a way to get out of her predicament. She also wanted to mourn her father, but her survival prevented her from doing so. As much as she loved her father, she didn't want to join him wherever he was resting. She peered out of slitted eyes to find Jay Jay looking around like he was contemplating doing what his visitor suggested he do: suffocate her. She snaked her hand under her blankets, searching for the call button to alert the nurse. She was getting the impression Jay Jay was in a hurry to get rid of her. When she found the button, she pressed it and hoped that the nurse got to her room quickly. She was finally able to breathe a sigh of relief when he finally closed her room door. She laid there waiting to see if he would come back. When her door opened again, she almost screamed until she spotted the nurse she had paged.

"Are you all right, Shinah?" she asked tenderly when she laid eyes on her patient. A lot of the nurses on the maternity ward had grown fond of her since she had been there, and even more so since she had her babies.

"I'm fine, Mrs. Jones. I just wanted to know if I could go down to the nursery by myself and look at my babies?" she asked as a plan came together in her mind.

"Of course, baby, but are you sure you're up to going by yourself. Do you want me to push you in the wheelchair?" Mrs. Jones asked as she looked at Shinah like a mother would her daughter.

"I can do it, Mrs. Jones. I just want to spend some time alone with them," Shinah said sincerely.

"Well, okay, but try to make it back soon because Doctor Hammonds will be here to check up on you." Mrs. Jones said as she prepared to leave.

"Okay. Did you see my brother out there anywhere?" Shinah asked nonchalantly as she used the lie SL came up with before leaving to explain Jay Jay's presence at the hospital.

"I saw him get on the elevator right before I came in," Mrs. Jones said with a frown on her face. There was something about her brother that rubbed her the wrong way, but she kept it to herself. "He might've been going to the cafeteria." She added with a smile for Shinah's benefit.

"Okay, well I'll see you later," Shinah said as she followed the nurse out of her room. She had noticed the frown on Mrs. Jones's face when she mentioned Jay Jay's name and knew that she didn't like him much. None of the nurses did. She filed that information away in the back of her mind as she shuffled toward the nursery.

When she arrived, she peered through the window to where her babies were resting and became overcome with emotion. She felt her heart swell at the sight of her children lying in their incubators and tears started falling down her face because looking at them reaffirmed what she had to do. She had to get out of the hospital unseen and knew that would be next to impossible if she tried to take her kids with her. So she turned and walked away without looking back. She hoped that she would be able to come back for them, but the cards had been dealt and she would have to let it play out.

****

Charlene walked up to the front desk on the maternity ward and asked to see her daughter.

"And may I ask who you are?" the nurse asked as she studied the expensively-dressed woman standing in front of her.

"I'm her mother, Charlene Lloyd," she replied with a frown.

"Oh, well let me call the head nurse Mrs. Jones. She's with the doctor now," the nurse said as she picked up the phone to page Mrs. Jones.

"Is there a problem?" Charlene asked when she noticed the nurse's nervousness.

"I will let Mrs. Jones and Doctor Hammonds inform you of what's going on," the nurse said as she nodded her head towards where Mrs. Jones and Doctor Hammonds were hurrying up the hallway.

Charlene looked over her shoulder and knew that something was wrong. The look of panic on their faces spoke volumes.

"What is it, Ms. Greer?" Nurse Jones asked, not even bothering to spare Charlene a glance. "I hope it has something to do with the situation," she added sternly. She was silently chastising herself because she felt like it was her fault.

"This lady says that she's Shinah's mother," Nurse Greer said, pointing at Charlene.

Nurse Jones immediately directed her attention to Charlene. "Have we met before?" she asked as she stared at her. She was feeling an uncanny sense of déjà vu.

"No, I don't think we have. But can someone tell me what's going on with my daughter?" Charlene looked between the nurses and the doctor standing in front of her with looks of panic and concern on their faces.

"I'm sorry to inform you that from all indications it seems as if your daughter is missing," Doctor Hammonds said, taking the reins from Nurse Jones, who was standing beside her with a frown on her face.

"Missing! What do you mean she's missing?" Charlene asked as she looked at the doctor with a quizzical look on her face. "Didn't she just give birth?" she added.

"Yes, she did just give birth, and we think that she walked out of the hospital. What we've been able to gather from camera footage shows her leaving the grounds alone, but we don't know the reason yet," Doctor Hammonds said, shaking her head sadly. She tried to figure out what would make Shinah just leave her babies when she seemed so happy about them.

"We are trying to locate her brother who was here with her. He seems to have disappeared at the same time she did," Nurse Jones said as she narrowed her eyes suspiciously. *This woman is entirely too calm to have just been told that her daughter is missing*, she thought.

"Her brother had been staying here, but he's seemed to have disappeared along with her," Doctor Hammonds said, silently asking God for help.

"Brother?" Charlene asked, confused. "Shinah doesn't have a brother. She's an only child, Doctor whatever your name is," she added with a frown.

Nurse Jones and Doctor Hammonds both exchanged worried glances with each other. They both knew that something was tragically wrong with this picture.

"Well, your daughter was claiming him as such." Nurse Jones said, trying to make sense of it.

"Well, I'm telling you as her mother that I only had one child during birth," Charlene said incredulously. "I can't believe how incompetent this hospital is. My lawyers will be contacting the administration here about a lawsuit. So I would start looking for new jobs, ladies. Also, my grandchildren need to be removed from this despicable place. Please make the necessary arrangements." Charlene was acting livid, but inside she was overjoyed with the turn of events.

"Mrs. Lloyd, I wouldn't advise——" Doctor Hammond started to say before she was rudely cut off.

"I don't care about what you advise," Charlene said sarcastically. "I've seemed to have lost a daughter under your care and I refuse to lose my grandchildren. They are leaving with me. So I would advise you pack them up now," she added sternly.

Pack them up, like she's talking about clothes or shoes, Nurse Jones thought as she looked at the woman with disgust evident on her face.

"As you wish, Mrs. Lloyd," Doctor Hammonds acquiesced. She wanted to argue further, but realized that it was futile. They were standing on a legal precipice already, and all it would take to blow them all over the edge was a formal complaint. "Come help me get them ready, Mrs. Jones, please," she added before walking away.

Nurse Jones shot one last frown at Mrs. Lloyd before turning and following the doctor.

Charlene caught the look and smirked. She just loved when a plan came together.

King Killa

Chapter 12

SL had just arrived back in the city a little after midnight and went straight to the hospital. He figured that Shinah would be angry, so he had a teddy bear for her. He also had a lot on his mind and most of it didn't make sense - at least not at the moment. The job had taken longer than expected, but he had gotten it done.

He got onto the elevator and pressed the button for the maternity ward. When the doors opened, he automatically noticed the extra security walking around and posted up in different areas of the ward. Wary of their presence, he made his way to Shinah's room. He looked around for Jay Jay and wasn't at all surprised not to find him. His second in command was allergic to the police just as much as he was. When he got to her room door, he gently pushed it open in case she was resting. He peeped his head in and was shocked to see another woman lying in the bed.

"Can I help you?" she asked with a smile.

"No, I think I have the wrong room," SL said, backing out quickly and closing the door behind him. Figuring that they had moved Shinah to another room, he walked to the front desk to find out where.

"Yes, may I help you?" the nurse asked with a tired smile.

"Can you tell me what room Shinah Lloyd is in?" he asked politely.

"And may I ask who you are?" the nurse asked suspiciously.

"I'm her fiancé," SL stated when he noticed the change in her demeanor. He held up the teddy bear to help ease the tension in the air.

The nurse relaxed a little at his answer. "Well, sir, it seems as if your fiancée walked out of the hospital earlier today," she informed him regrettably.

"Walked out?" SL said with a sick feeling in his stomach. "But she was pregnant, almost nine months," he added, hoping she was mistaken.

"She gave birth a few days ago," she told him sympathetically.

"Where is the baby?" he asked as he held his breath.

"The children are gone also," she said shaking her head.

SL abruptly walked off in a daze. He knew that something like this might happen, and that's why he had left Jay Jay there to watch her. To know that Shinah was out there with a baby doing God knows what left him sick to his stomach. Before he left she has happy, ready to give birth and get herself together so she could be a good mother to her child, but now she was gone, and with a baby in tow.

As he headed towards the elevators, he pulled out his cell phone to call Jay Jay. When the doors opened up, he hurriedly got on, ready to go. Before the doors could close, he tossed the teddy bear into the trash can. Something wasn't right, and he would find out what it was.

****

Shinah was all cried out. She had cried for her mother and father because they were both dead to her - her mother figuratively and her father literally. She cried for her children because she knew that she would have to leave them behind. Revenge was the only thing on her mind, and revenge she would get.

****

SL pulled up in front of a house he hadn't been to in almost a year since Shinah ran away the first time, but he was back and this time he was invited. He had talked to Jay Jay on his way over and received his version of what happened at the hospital, but for some reason, he felt like Jay Jay was either holding something back or lying to him. He couldn't give a good reason as to why he felt like that but he did, and he never went against his intuition. He put that on the back burner as he got out of his car to go handle a more pressing matter. Shinah had decided to burn her bridges with him, so he would put her out of his mind.

He walked up to the front door but before he could knock or ring the doorbell, it swung open and there stood Charlene, wearing a form-fitting dress like she was ready to celebrate.

"Do you have the watch?" she asked without formality.

SL looked at her for a few seconds before reaching into his pocket and pulling out the watch she was inquiring about. It was a hundred thousand dollar Audemers Peugeot watch. He handed it to her and watched as she flipped it over to read the inscription the underside. "To my King, the one and only".

"Come in, Mr. SL, because we have a lot to discuss," Charlene said as she stepped to the side with a brilliant smile on her face.

SL stepped into the house with the knowledge that he was selling his soul to the devil, but money was the root to all of his evil and he would get as much of it as possible before he had to pay the piper.

Shinah couldn't believe her eyes. Her heart broke into a million pieces as she watched SL walk into her parents' home with her mother smiling at him like she had just hit the lotto. The fact that SL had disappeared the week her father ended up dead and was now meeting with her mother didn't sit well with her. She didn't believe in coincidences and she didn't believe this one. She knew they had killed her father, and the watch she saw SL give her mother only confirmed that fact. It was the same one her father wore every time he left the house. The same one her mother gave him for their 20th anniversary. Her desires forgotten, she only wanted revenge. SL would find out soon enough the power of a woman scorned. She would make sure of that.

****

"Oh my God, Sister Mary!" Sister Gloria screamed out hysterically. She looked down at the bundles somebody had left on their doorstep.

"What is it, Sister Gloria?" Sister Mary asked when she finally reached her. She was breathing kind of hard because she had been at the back of the orphanage when she was called.

Sister Gloria just pointed down at the bundles.

Sister Mary looked down and felt her heart skip a beat. "Did you see who left them?" she asked as she looked up and down the street they were situated on. No one was in sight.

"No, Sister. I came out to get the mail and they were right here," Sister Gloria said.

"Well, help me get them out of this weather because there's no telling how long they've been out here," Sister Mary said as she started moving the babies inside. She sent up a quick prayer for whoever left these precious gifts in their care. She didn't know what would possess someone to give up their children, but she would make sure that they found a loving home. She and God both knew that this life was only the beginning - the beginning to the end.

Chapter 13

Majestic stood in front of the Islands Way restaurant with trepidation, wondering how his family would receive him, especially with him being the bearer of bad news. It had taken him longer than he expected to get off of the island because after his father passed, the hunt for him had intensified. But he had made it to America with the help of some friends still loyal to his father. He looked around at all of the bustling traffic entering and exiting the restaurant and figured that business was good for his mother and sisters. He looked through the big plate glass windows and saw that most of the workers were from the islands or descendants of people from the islands, but he didn't see anyone who resembled his sisters or mother. He noticed people walking by cutting their eyes at him because he was just standing there staring at the restaurant like he was staking it out for a robbery, but he didn't care about the strangers around him. He only cared for his remaining family. He finally spotted one of his sisters serving some customers and breathed a sigh of relief. He wanted to rush in and hug her, but decided to come back at closing because he knew that the tears would flow at the news he was bringing. He melted into the traffic moving up and down the sidewalks. He had to find a way to occupy his time.

****

"King, Sergeant Harris wants to see you in her office," Officer Sanchez said as she stood there at his room door.

King ignored her as he went about his business of packing up his property - or at least the stuff he was taking home with him. Tomorrow he was a free man. Out of his peripheral vision, he saw her still standing there watching him, but he didn't acknowledge her until she sucked her teeth. He finally turned to look at her, but he didn't say anything. He just looked.

"Why do you always do this shit?" she asked with an attitude as she folded her arms across her chest.

"Do what?" King asked, knowing exactly what she was referring to. He didn't give her what every other convict on the yard gave her, which was attention.

"Ignore me and play hard to get." She couldn't understand why he did what he did and it pissed her off, but it also turned her on.

King stared at her for a few seconds before he decided to indulge her a little bit. He was going to put her on the team, but she didn't need to know that yet. "I ignore you because you are an attention seeker. And I don't play hard to get, ma. I am hard to get. What you want is not free. Whether or not I put you on my team is entirely up to you. I get money. I don't play games. I will fuck you, but money is first and foremost on my mind," he said, switching to his first language.

"What do I need to do?" she asked seriously. This is what she had been waiting on, and she would do whatever he wanted.

"Give me your number and wait on me to call," King said.

"Okay," she said, then recited her number.

"I got you," King said, committing her number to memory. "Come here." He crooked his finger at her.

Officer Sanchez pulled the door up a little bit so that nobody walking by would be able to look directly in the room. She walked over and stood in front of him. Her panties were getting wet just from being so close to him.

King smirked at her and leaned in like he was about to kiss her, but put his mouth close enough to her ear where his lips were touching her earrings. "Loyalty is not everything; it's the only thing. Remember that," he whispered before kissing her on the neck and leaving the room, once again giving her his back to watch as he left her.

****

"So what are you going to do, St. Pierre?" Ms. Annie asked after failing to talk Czar into resting up for a few more weeks.

"I'ma kill that snake Jimmy Slim and then I'ma reclaim my city," Czar said as he strapped on the new bulletproof vest she had acquired for him while he was recuperating. His thirst for revenge only grew the more he heard about Jimmy Slim balling out of control in his city. At first he couldn't believe what Ms. Annie told him was going down, but the streets never lied, and the streets were crowning Jimmy King - a position he would make sure that he didn't hold for long.

"You think Jimmy Slim don't know you gonna try him if Martinez doesn't succeed in putting you down first?" she asked, raising an eloquently arched eyebrow as she looked at him like he was crazy. "He knows you were the brains and muscle behind the operation. He knows that he stole your legacy. He knows he's a rat, and he knows you know too. So he has a team of killers around him at all times, and word on the streets is that they are blazing a trail of terror to make sure you are labeled as a rat and forgotten."

"I know the odds against me, Ms. Annie, but Jimmy Slim could never do anything better than me, especially when it came to thinking. So I'ma use arrogance - his arrogance - against him and trap him off. Regardless of the fact, that's been the case forever with him. He always wants to shine and be seen. I will use that against him and put him where he belongs: six feet under. Despite the rumors out about me, I know its people out there who are not believing the hype, and I will reach out to those people to help me." Czar made sure that both of his bulldogs were loaded before stuffing then into his hoody.

Ms. Annie sighed because she knew that he had his mind made up. He had that look in his eye that she had seen so many times before, the look that said, "watch out, the beast is coming." She would keep her promise to his mother and try to keep him alive, but the job was getting harder by the day.

****

Pharaoh stared at his mother in disbelief. The information she had just told him blew his mind. He looked down at her lying there, saw that steely determination she was so famous for in her eyes, and knew that she was telling the truth.

"So you're telling me that my father was a perpetrator, a fraud masquerading as a legitimate businessman when in fact he was a drug dealer. Then on top of that you're telling me that I'm adopted. I've been lied to my whole life," he said angrily. He could tell that he was making his mother upset and that wasn't good considering her present condition, but he really didn't care at that moment. He wasn't as upset about being adopted as he let on because he had figured that out on his own a few years ago. He looked nothing like either of his parents and his mannerisms were nothing like theirs either. So the adoption didn't surprise him. But the part about his father being a drug dealer really upset him.

Olivia watched her son as he processed the information she had just given him. She could tell that he was upset about his father being a dope dealer, but sensed that he wasn't as upset about the adoption. Pharaoh was very perceptive and she got the feeling years ago that he had figured it out, or at least guessed the truth, but vowed she would only tell him the truth if he asked or in dire circumstances, like now.

"Baby, listen, your father wasn't a perpetrator. He just wanted better for you. He did what he had to do and I'm not making any excuses for him, but he had his reasons as far as the adoption. I couldn't conceive and your father wanted a son. We raised you as our own and couldn't have loved you more. You are a Carter and you have to carry the flag. Your father must be avenged."

"And what is it that you want me to do, Mother?" he asked incredulously. "You want me to take his place as the top drug dealer and find his killer? You want me to assume my rightful place in the hierarchy? Tell me what it is you expect me to do." He stared at her, waiting on an answer.

"Yes, that is exactly what I expect you to do," Olivia said as she returned his stare. "The pharmaceutical company is for you. Your father never intended for you to be involved in the illegal aspect of his life, but death has a way of changing priorities. He was in the process of transitioning from illegal dealings to a hundred percent legitimate, but he was murdered, gunned down right in front of us like a rabid dog by his enemies. I'm asking you, not demanding you, to take your father's place in both the legal and illegal worlds and finish what he started. He wanted to get out, but somebody stopped him from doing so and they did this to me," she added seriously as she waved at her lifeless legs.

Pharaoh looked down at his mother and felt his rage spike to another level. She was paralyzed from the waist down and he couldn't help but remember the man who stared him down and decided that he was too insignificant to kill. It was a face he would remember until he was able to put a hole in it.

Olivia watched her son warring with his emotions and decided to press the issue. "I'm not gonna be here much longer, Pharaoh. Avenge me and your father and then you can do what you want to, but you are a Carter and you are expected to do great things."

"I will do what you ask, Mother, but I cannot guarantee I will be the same when it's all said and done," he said seriously. He already felt different. The day he saw his father murdered and mother paralyzed changed him forever.

"Promise me you will do as I ask," she told him.

"Mother——" he started to say.

"Promise me," she said cutting him off.

"I promise, Mother but only if you promise I will have a hundred percent control of everything," he said, staring at her.

"You are the man now, son," she said, smiling sadly.

"Get some rest, Mother, because I'm going to need you," Pharaoh said as he kissed her cheek.

"Okay, baby," Olivia said, fighting off the tears that threatened to fall.

Pharaoh smiled at his mother one last time before walking out of the room in their house that they had converted into a private hospital room specifically for his mother's care.

When the door closed behind Pharaoh, another one opened up and in walked the family lawyer, Mr. Riley.

"You heard everything, right?" Olivia asked him.

"Yes. Are you sure that this is how you want to do things?" Mr. Riley asked, pleading with her with his eyes.

Olivia didn't even bother to respond. Her mind was already made up.

Mr. Riley sighed because he knew that it was impossible to change her mind once it was made up. He could inform Pharaoh of her decision, but one learned early not to disobey Olivia. "May God keep you," he said before kissing her on her cheek and exiting out the same door he just entered.

When the door closed, Olivia reached under her covers and pulled out the .38 revolver she had hidden there. She let one tear fall from her eye before she put it in her mouth and pulled the trigger.

Chapter 14

Mega had just seen the last customer out and was about to lock up the doors when they were pulled open.

"Hey. We're closed, mon," he said, trying to block the man's entrance into the restaurant. He did a quick inventory of the man from his rude locs to his Timberland boots and instantly thought "robber".

Majestic paid no heed to the man as he brushed past him, knocking him out of his way with his shoulder. He had only one thing on his mind and that was his family.

Mega instantly grew angry at the blatant disrespect and tried to grab Majestic.

Big mistake!

Majestic whipped out his pistol and hit him on the bridge of his nose with the butt of the gun, breaking it instantly. "Don't ye ever put yer 'ands on mem again or mem gwan kill ye, pussy bwoy," he growled as he pointed his gun at Mega's head.

"Please, sir, don't kill mem," Mega pleaded loudly to attract the attention of the people in the back.

"Who de fuck are ye in mem damn business?" a female voice asked calmly but deadly.

Majestic looked up and smiled for the first time in a long time. Even though a gun was pointed at him, he couldn't help but to laugh.

"What's de problem, sista?" another female who resembled the first asked as she walked from the back with a gun also in her hand.

"Dis mon crazy," the first female said, never taking her eyes off of Majestic.

Still laughing, Majestic looked up and flipped his dreads out of his face. "Don't recognize ye own brudda, Star, Sky?" he asked with a devilish smirk on his face. The way he suddenly stopped laughing was disconcerting.

Star gasped. "Majestic!" she screamed, lowering her gun.

"Mudda!" Sky yelled towards the back. "Get ye gun off Mega's 'ead, brudda," she added as she rolled her eyes.

"Dis ye brudda." Mega asked after getting up off the floor. He was still trying to stop the blood from leaking out of his nose with his shirt.

"Yes, and ye can go 'ome. We will lock up," Sky said sternly.

Mega knew not to say anything when she used that tone of voice. He grabbed his bag and watched Majestic warily until he was out the door.

Sky locked the door behind him and turned to look at Majestic with questions in her eyes.

"Why ye still 'ave ye guns out?" he asked with amusement in his eyes.

"Why ye still 'ave ye gun out?" Star countered, smirking at him.

Majestic looked at his gun and reluctantly slid it back into his pants.

Star and Sky both put their guns up and looked at each other before they both rushed their brother.

Majestic tensed, not knowing what their true intentions were or how to react, but he relaxed when they both hugged him and started crying.

"We've missed ye so much, brudda," Star said, overwhelmed at the sight and feel of her younger brother.

"It's been too long, bwoy," Sky whispered, happy and sad at the same time. She knew that his presence meant bad news.

Majestic didn't know how to react to this display of his sisters' emotions. His father told him to never show them, so he didn't know what to do about the tears welling up in his eyes.

"Majestic."

He looked up when he heard the melodic voice and let the tears fall as he laid eyes on his mother for the first time in over ten years. His sisters released him as their mother walked over and took him into her arms. He lifted his head and started to speak, but she stopped him.

"Shhh." His mother wiped his tears as her fingers traced his face like she was trying to become familiar with the man he had become in her absence. She took a step back out of his arms and gently picked up the Lion's head medallion lying on his chest. She lovingly caressed it as she thought about the implications of him wearing his father's, her husband's necklace.

"Mudda, me——" Majestic started to speak, but was cut off again.

"Shhh, bwoy," she said, placing her fingers on his lips. "Mem knew de moment ye fadda took de last air. Mem felt it in 'ere." She pointed to her heart. "Mem sure 'e gave ye instructions to follow, so let's go talk. Ye fadda wouldn't want us to mourn 'im, but to reclaim what is rightfully ours and avenge his death. Ye are de man in de family, son. Mem glad ye are 'ere, bwoy, but time is of de essence. Ye and yer sisters are de future of de Livingstons. What are ye gwan do?"

****

Today was the day King became a free man and he couldn't wait. He was standing at the account window, waiting for the officer to process the funds out of his trust fund account.

"Damn, King, what you gonna do with all this money?"

He looked up and recognized Officer Green. She worked the yards sometimes, but mostly she worked in administration. She was brown-skinned with a short pixie cut and freckles. Her hazel eyes were by far her best feature along with her thick hips and big ass.

"I'ma use it to make more money," he told her as he maintained eye contact.

"Well, I wish I could get some money like this," she said, laughing as she handed him his check.

King could tell that he was making her nervous and that was his objective. He could also tell that she was serious about the money despite her joking manner. He saw an opportunity and he never passed one up if it was beneficial to him.

"You can get it if you want it," he said seriously.

"What do you mean?" she asked curiously. She looked around to make sure that nobody was close enough to eavesdrop on their conversation.

"I don't have time to really get into details right now, but give me your number and I'll hit you this week or next week," he said, ready to go.

"For you, I'll do it." She blushed as she whispered her number to him.

"I got you, mami," he said, committing her number to memory.

"You not gonna remember my number," she said poking her bottom lip out playfully.

"Like I said, I got you," he said over his shoulders as we walked out into free air.

People didn't understand that the air inside of the penitentiary was different from the air in the free world. He closed his eyes, took a deep breath, and savored his first few minutes as a free man.

"Can I get a hug, King?"

He looked up and saw his lawyer leaning up against a brand new, pearl white Mercedes Benz SL 500 with Chanel shades covering her eyes, wearing a huge smile on her face and a pair of jeans so tight that they looked painted on. He had to admit that he was looking at the only person he could trust in this world. The betrayal Marco and Sophia extended his way still had him bitter, but he put that out of his mind and put a smile on his face as he walked over to her.

"Isn't it against the rules for a client to hug his lawyer while she's looking like this?" he teased as he looked her up and down.

Latoya put her head down so he wouldn't see her blush. He was looking too good to her, and the moisture pooling inside her thighs was evidence of that. She looked back up at him and saw her future. She just wondered how long it would take him to realize it. "Come here, boy, and hug me. I don't care about the rules right now," she said grabbing him into her arms. Whew he slid his strong arms around her waist, she sighed. They fit so perfectly together. She wanted to stay there forever.

"We gonna stand here all day, or are we going back to the city?" he asked playfully. He couldn't front though; she felt good in his arms. But he faced something more sinister than house and home, so he forced that out of his mind because pussy was the last thing on his mind. M.O.E.: money over everything!

"Come on. Let's go," she said, reluctantly releasing him. They got into the car and slowly pulled off.

"I'm proud of you, mami. You're one of the best criminal defense lawyers in the tri-state area now," King said, silently applauding himself for recognizing her potential first. "I'm really proud of you." He wanted her to know that he really appreciated her.

Latoya beamed and blushed at his sincere praise. "You remember how we met?" she asked, involuntarily frowning at the memory.

King noticed her look and laughed. "How could I not?"

"Whatever, nigga," she said, rolling her eyes even though she couldn't help but laugh also.

King would forever remember that day because it was the day that changed his life.

"I got that information you asked me to get, Marco and Sophia's address," she said, watching him out of the corner of her eye.

King felt his body go rigid and his jaw tense. No matter how calm he tried to act, their betrayal affected him deeply and would until they got what they deserved: dirt naps. "Wake me up when we get back to the city," he said, not responding to her statement as he closed his eyes and leaned his chair back.

Latoya knew that he didn't want to talk about them snakes. Hell, she didn't either, but she was glad that he finally woke up and saw what she had been trying to tell him was happening since he had been locked up and probably even before that. She smiled to herself as she sped down the highway. If King didn't already know, he would soon enough that his wish was her command.

****

Czar sat low in his hoopty as he watched the apartment of Gauge, one of his little homies he had on the team before all the shit with him and Jimmy Slim went down. He knew this nigga should still be loyal to him, but he wasn't taking anything for granted, especially when Jimmy Slim had money on his head. Out of his whole team, Gauge should be the one who didn't believe the hype going around about him because he had taken the little nigga off of the streets, cleaned him up, and made sure that he and his moms were taken care of. So he had the most faith in Gauge to still be loyal. He sat up a little in his seat when he spotted Gauge's black on black Dodge Charger circle the block a few times like he taught him to do. He smiled because that move only solidified Gauge's trustworthiness in his eyes. He watched him park, get out, and check his surroundings out. Gauge looked directly at his hoopty and narrowed his eyes. Czar wasn't worried about being seen because of the dark tint, but he gripped the handle of one of his Bulldogs just in case shit got hectic. He breathed a sigh of relief when Gauge turned and disappeared into his apartment building. He waited about ten minutes before getting out of the hoopty and running across the street. He went right up to the door and knocked like he was the police.

"Who is it?" Gauge asked angrily.

"It's the police, sir," Czar said disguising his voice. He wondered if he still followed all of his lessons he taught him about hustling.

"What's u——" Gauge started to say until he saw who was standing at his door. "Oh shit, Czar, what's up, nigga?" He grabbed his mentor into a bear hug. "Shit been crazy the last couple of weeks around the wards." He stepped back so they could enter the apartment and close the door.

"Yeah, that bitch Jimmy Slim flipped on me and got the city fooled to what's really going on," Czar said, happy his little homie didn't believe the stories about him.

"Jimmy Slim saying all types of bullshit about you and niggas turning 'cause he was your man, then he popping up with better prices talking about he the plug now," Gauge said, putting him on point.

"What about you?" Czar asked seriously as he looked at him intently.

"Homie, I play any position to live and eat. I wouldn't trust Jimmy Slim to piss on me if I was on fire," Gauge said seriously.

Czar looked at him for a few seconds then decided that he was telling the truth. Either that or he was a damn good actor. "That's what up," he finally said.

"So tell me the real scoop on what happened. It's niggas out here who still fucks with you, but Jimmy Slim is the only voice being heard right now," Gauge said, wanting to know what really happened.

Czar settled in and dived into the story. He could finally make plans to reclaim his throne.

****

"How in the hell did my mother get a gun when she's paralyzed from the waist down?" Pharaoh screamed at the men assembled in one of his father's warehouses. His voice was full of anguish and he wanted to cry over his mother's suicide, but he couldn't show weakness because these were the men who controlled every aspect of his father's underworld empire and they were ruthless.

"Mr. Carter, please, let's start the meeting first," Mr. Riley begged because he knew that these men were animalistic when it came to business and respect, and Pharaoh was on the verge of crossing the lines of both.

"No, I want to know how my mother got a gun," Pharaoh said firmly as he looked the lawyer in his eyes.

"Who the fuck are these young cabrons you brought to this meeting of the family?" Juan asked, not bothering to hide his contempt for Pharaoh's leadership. After Bear was killed, he became the head of security and street dealings. He didn't understand why they were now taking orders from a virtual kid to the streets. He, for one, wasn't going for it and would let it be known.

Pharaoh stared at Juan silently. He could tell that he was opposed to his leadership and would become a problem if left unchecked. He looked around at the other men and saw that they felt the same way. He made a promise to his mother to avenge his father's death, and he would do so with or without them. He smiled cruelly at Juan before he addressed the "young cabrons" he was referring to. "Lion, you and the fellas introduce yourselves," he ordered.

Lion smiled as he signaled his team to spread out and surround Juan and his men.

Juan tensed as they were surrounded. He wanted to reach for his gun, but he wouldn't let Pharaoh see any weakness from him and his men. Besides, Pharaoh wouldn't dare try anything stupid. "Is this little show for a reason?" he asked as he laughed in Pharaoh's face.

At 6'4" and 250 pounds with locs that looked like a mane, Lion was intimidating. He walked up to Juan and without warning punched him in the face, sitting him on his ass. Juan's men started to react, but the sound of pistols cocking stopped them in their tracks.

"You are a dead man, fucking bitch-ass pussy!" Juan screamed at Lion as he held his busted lips and nose. He had plans to kill Pharaoh for the disrespect, but he kept that thought to himself.

"My father is dead and I've been forced to take his place. I can tell you men don't like this turn of events because of my lack of knowledge regarding the street life, but this is the way it is. This meeting was called to let you know that I am in charge. Quite frankly, I don't have time to bring you guys around to my way of thinking. So I'm just gonna remove the old ways." He looked at Lion and nodded his head.

Juan watched in horror as each one of his men were shot down. He turned and looked at Pharaoh with a question in his eyes.

"Yes, you too will die." Pardoning him wasn't even a thought in Pharaoh's mind.

Lion looked down at Juan and smiled. "By the way, my name is Lion," he said before he grabbed his head and twisted it violently, breaking his neck.

Mr. Riley stood there horrified as he watched the carnage happening around him. He couldn't believe the transformation of Pharaoh. He flinched when Pharaoh turned and looked him in the eye. Gone was the childlike innocence he used to possess and in its place was a murderous rage.

"Now you can start the meeting."

Vincent "Vito" Holloway

Chapter 15

Majestic looked at the boyfriends of his sisters and kept his thoughts to himself. After telling his mother what his father said and instructed him to do, she gave her blessing and a warning before leaving him and his sisters be.

"Mem don't like de pigs. So stay clear." Now he was meeting his sisters' "big ballers".

"Sky and Star told us you trying to get money," Bang said, sizing Majestic up.

"We can front you the work or we can put you on the team," Petey said, not really feeling the idea, but doing it as a favor for Star.

Sky and Star looked at each other before looking at their brother, wondering what he was thinking.

Majestic noticed their looks and wondered what they saw in these clowns. They were fronting for him like they were bosses when they were nobody important. His father told him to recognize the strengths and weaknesses in each man, and with these two, the cons outweighed the pros. Bang was a show-off and a follower, but he knew how to hustle. Petey fashioned himself a leader, but was also a follower. He played the background while Bang put his face out there to be seen. He was more of a snake and took advantage of the first sign of weakness. Both of them were pussy - or at least to him they were. He knew they were sizing him up. They thought that he was fresh off the banana boat and was gullible to their game, but he had a trick for them.

"So what you wanna do?" Petey asked, looking at Majestic.

"Yeah, fuck with us and we'll put you on your feet," Bang said excitedly.

Majestic looked at Bang and Petey and shook his head. He was saddened that his sisters were associating with these clowns, but he would rectify that with his next move. "Ye two pussy bwoys got de game fucked up. Mem don't need ya charity, fuck bwoy. Now get de fuck out of 'ere," he said before pulling his pistol out and pointing it at them. Their shocked expressions made him want to laugh, but he kept his face stern.

"Man, what the fuck is wrong with you?" Bang asked, shocked at the turn of events. "Look, you can have everything in my pockets, man." He looked over at Sky like "get your brother.'

Sky looked at him and rolled her eyes. She was disgusted. Bye-bye were the only two words she had for his pussy ass.

"Nigga, shut up," Petey said to Bang as he eyed Majestic. "This nigga not gonna do shit, are you? Are you?" he asked, taunting Majestic as he stood up. "Because if you don't kill me, I'ma put you in the dirt."

"Ye want to play, pussy bwoy, and get fucked?" Majestic asked, pulling the trigger.

Blocka! Blocka! Blocka!

"No problem, mon," he said before finally letting his smile touch his lips. He didn't even look at the body lying at his feet.

"Man, please don't kill me. Listen, I'll give you whatever, man, just let me go. I promise I won't say nothing. Hell, I didn't even like that nigga Petey," Bang said as he begged for his life.

"Sky!" Majestic called out, never taking his eyes off Bang.

"Say no more, brudda," she said before pulling out her own pistol and ending the coward's life.

"If dis city full of de pussy bwoys like dese two dead men, I will 'ave easier time den mem thought," he said, eyeing his two sisters.

"Ye crazy, blood clot," Star said, trying not to laugh. "Ye lucky mudda not 'ere or she would pop ye," she added before finally letting out the laugh she had been trying to hold in.

Majestic shrugged his shoulders nonchalantly like he didn't just murder a man in his mother's restaurant.

"Mem can't believe dey were pussy bwoys like dat," Sky said, still disgusted.

"We been knew, but ye can't deny dat de dick was good," Star said, smiling.

"Show ye right." Sky said, laughing as she slapped hands with her sister.

Majestic just shook his head at them. It was like he was meeting them for the very first time. In Jamaica they didn't act like this, at least not that he could remember.

"'elp us get dese bodies ta de incinerator," Sky said, getting up to grab rubber gloves, trash bags, and bleach to clean up with.

"And in de morning, we'll take ye to meet some real rude bwoys," Star said with a wicked gleam in her eyes.

Majestic didn't respond as he went about the business of bagging the bodies of Band and Petey. He just hoped that they were as real as she said they were, or he would have a lot more bodies lying around Miami.

****

"King? King, we're home," Latoya said as she shook his shoulder to wake him.

King slowly opened his eyes and took in his surroundings. It took a few seconds for him to remember that he wasn't in prison anymore. He noticed that it was nightfall and that they were parked in a very nice neighborhood full of renovated brownstones. "Where exactly is home?" he finally asked.

Latoya took a few minutes to answer because she was too busy admiring him.

King turned to find her locked in on his face. He saw the desire in her eyes, but decided to ignore it. "What's up with you, T?" he asked quietly. He knew that she wanted him to be more than just her client, but he didn't know if he wanted that yet. The betrayal of Sophia was still too fresh and raw.

"You," she said quietly. That one word held all the love and passion she had for him.

"I'm no good for you," King said seriously.

"Says who?" she asked with an arched eyebrow.

"Me," he said firmly. "We on two different paths. You are a great lawyer but me? I'm a great hustler. Find you someone who is willing to leave the streets alone, because I'm not ready," he added, looking into her eyes, hoping to convey his seriousness.

"I'm a big girl, and I can live with the consequences for my actions and decisions," she said heatedly as she fought the tears that were threatening to fall.

"I'm no good for you." He looked away from her because she was making him weak.

Latoya looked at his profile, his firm jaw, and how hard he was being with her and grew frustrated. She grabbed her purse and got out of the car, slamming the door behind her. She rushed into the house before he could see her tears.

King watched her run into the house and regretted the position he was in. He wanted to go after her but decided not to. He slid over into the driver's seat and started the car up. He looked at the brownstone one last time before pulling off. He had shit to do.

Latoya heard the car pull off and sank down to the floor with her back against her door as her tears started cascading down her face. Her heart was breaking into a million pieces as she thought about the man she loved more than life itself not loving her.

****

Jimmy Slim was feeling himself. He had the connect, he had the team, he had the money and bitches but most importantly, he had the respect he'd long coveted. With Czar on the run and not showing his face to refute his claims of him being a snitch, his transition to the top had been smooth so far. He planned on making sure that Czar never got a chance to tell his side of the story, that's why he had a brick and five stacks on his head.

"Nobody found where Czar hiding at yet?" he asked his second in command Tilly.

"Naw, dog. That rat motherfucka hiding real good," Tilly said before sparking up the blunt he had just rolled.

"Raise that five stacks to ten. Let's see how long he can stay in hiding with the whole city after his rat ass," he added before cutting the radio up to listen to the announcement the disc jockey was making.

King Killa

"Already! Big D. Friday night the executive club is where you need to be. The baddest strippers in the Dallas area reside in this hotspot. Fellas, bring the bankrolls out, and for all my ladies who get down like that, bring yours too. Ha! Ha! Ha! Friday night, make your way to the executive club. Doors open at nine and shut down at five the next morning. This is Fat Mack from 97.9 The Beat1"

"We up in there, homie," Tilly said, blowing smoke rings.

Jimmy Slim had already planned to slide through there anyway. There was one stripper in particular he wanted to notice him, and Friday he would get noticed. Money made the pussy go whoo, whoo! You ain't know?

****

Dior Eva and Bianca Calle were two of the baddest women in the Dallas metropolitan area. Dior, originally from New Orleans, stood 5'6" with 36D-27-40 measurements that came directly from her mama. Her tattoos and blond hair stood out, but her butterscotch skin and hazel eyes were the two features that captivated the masses. Bianca was born and raised in Dallas and she repped her city to the fullest. The small Dallas Cowboys star under her left eye could attest to that. She had five piercings: her tongue, her clit, her eyebrow, her nose, and a Monroe. The way her 36D-28-40 measurements stretched over her 5'8" frame stopped traffic. She had dark brown eyes and fire red hair. Her light skin made her a certified redbone. Alone, they were both fifty cent pieces, but together like they always were, they were a whole dollar that niggas desperately wanted to spend.

"Dior and Bianca, tell me where that rat Czar at so I can go collect that money Jimmy Slim got on his head," a dude named Don Don yelled across the parking lot, making his homeboys laugh along with a few other people.

It was Saturday morning and everybody who was somebody was at Sparkles Wash and Wax detail shop getting their whips done.

"Miss me with that, Don Don, you pussy-ass nigga!" Dior spat, mad that these lames were fronting on Czar. "When he was out here, yo' bitch ass was a yes man. So stop stuntin' for your little friends," she added, starting to regret the decision to come out that morning.

"Bitch..." Don Don started to go in before his man grabbed his arm.

"Yeah, think it's a game, soft-ass nigga," Bianca said, pulling her 9mm Beretta out of her purse.

"Chill, B, ain't no need for all that," a man named Chris said. He turned to Don Don and said, "Chill."

"Yeah, whatever," Don Don mumbled, snatching his arm out of his grasp. Then he sat in his car.

"What's up with Czar though, Dior?" Chris asked seriously. He didn't really believe the hype, but with Czar missing in action and Jimmy Slim beating down the block with his prices, he was rocking with the money. Nothing personal, just business. "If what's being said is not true, then why is he not showing his face if he's still alive?"

"First off, I'm not going to discuss Czar with you or nobody else, but I will say this ... whoever believing that snake Jimmy Slim is a snake too. Let's go, Bianca," Dior said as she hopped into the driver's seat of her 2014 black Dodge Charger sitting on 22 inch Giovanis. Bianca got in the car and they pulled off.

"That bitch knows where that nigga at," Don Don said after they were gone.

Chris had that same thought running through his mind, but he kept it to himself. He had a lot of things to think about as he pulled out his cell phone to call Jimmy Slim because if it didn't make money, it didn't make sense.

Chapter 16

"Mem only gwan ask ye one more time," Terror said as he placed the hot fire place poker close to Jacques's body. "Where in de States in Majestic and 'is family?"

"Dey in Miami, sir," Jacques whimpered.

For the last couple of weeks, Terror had been putting him through different kinds of torture, trying to find out the location of the remaining Livingstons, especially Majestic. At first Jacques held out because he felt disgraced for betraying Buju, then when that no longer sufficed he held out because of his hatred for Terror. But he was relentless and he couldn't take it anymore. He was ready to die.

Terror smiled, frightening Jacques even more before Terror pushed the hot poker through his chest and into his heart.

With his last breath, Jacques spoke words he hoped one day would come true. "Master Majestic will kill ye painfully." With that said, he took his final breath and died.

Terror turned and looked at his most trusted comrade, Chaka. Without a word being exchanged, Chaka turned and left the room to go prepare a team for the trip to Miami.

Terror sat down and sparked up a fat blunt of ganja and thought about the Livingstons, who were still beloved in Jamaica. Buju was a leader loved for his fairness and love for his people. His family was considered royalty on the island because of that, but with Buju gone and the remaining Livingstons in hiding, he ruled with fear and pressure. He didn't care about love; only fear and respect. He knew the people didn't like him and for that reason alone he feared Majestic, not as a man but as a ray of hope for the people he now ruled with an iron fist. He feared Majestic could lead a rebellion against him and for that alone he had to die, along with the rest of his family.

****

"Whose pussy is this?" Marco grunted as he pumped his dick in and out of Sophia's warm, wet pussy. He had her bent over the couch in their apartment in Brooklyn.

"It's yours, papi. It's yours, Marco!" Sophia screamed as she threw her ass back. She reached back and spread one of her ass cheeks so he could go deeper. "Fuck me, baby. Fuck me."

"My dick better than King's, right?" he asked as he tried to touch her uterus on his down stroke.

Sophia rolled her eyes. *Not even close, papi but it's good*, she thought as she fed his ego. "You got the best dick, papi. King couldn't fuck me like you can. Cum with me. I'm cumming!" she screamed as her orgasm turned her body into jelly.

"Oh shit!" he yelled as he shot his kids deep inside of her. He wanted to get her pregnant.

Sophia was glad that she was on birth control pills. She knew Marco was trying to get her pregnant, but she wasn't having it. The last couple of years since King had been locked up, it was like Marco wanted to be him. She couldn't front; she missed King daily. But twenty-five years was just too much time to ride with. She felt bad for abandoning him, but Marco wanted proof that she was down for him, so he had her tell King it was over when he called that day. She had been with King since they were thirteen and he was her first everything. Her first kiss, her first piece of dick, the first to eat her out. He taught her everything she knew. But she couldn't do a prison bid with him.

At first she ignored Marco when he tried to get with her out of respect for King, but then he started spending money on her and since King had been gone, he had a lot of money to spend. She didn't love Marco. That was still reserved for King. But she loved the things that he could do for her. She knew that King would never forgive her betrayal, so she was with Marco as long as he had the money.

"Boy, get up off of me so I can go clean up," she said, giggling.

"Go ahead, 'cause I'ma want some of this good pussy again in a few hours," Marco said, smacking her on the ass as she walked towards the bathroom.

He is a nympho, she thought as she hurried to the bathroom to push his cum out of her because she didn't trust birth control a hundred percent. Before closing the bathroom door, she heard a knock at the front door, but she paid it no mind as she focused on cleaning up.

Ten minutes later, she walked back into the living room to find Marco conducting business with Lil Trey.

"No more money needs to be missing, son. If it is, I'm holding you responsible for it. I can't afford to take any losses fucking with you little niggas," Marco said sternly. He looked at Lil Trey for a few seconds to make sure he understood how serious he was.

Lil Trey stared back at him unflinchingly, but he played his position for the time being. "You got it, Marco." He got up to leave. "What's up, Sophia?" he asked as he mean mugged her a little bit.

Is this little nigga grilling me? she questioned herself. The look disappeared so quickly she thought she might've imagined it, but had a feeling that she didn't. "What's good, Trey?" she replied with a smile.

"Money is the only thing good my way," he said with a smirk. "I'll get at y'all later." He walked out without waiting for a response.

"Why do you deal with him when you know he's loyal to King?" she asked skeptically.

"He not loyal to nothing but the money," Marco said confidently.

"How are you so confident?" she asked as she watched him count money.

"Because I'm not King," he said, never taking his eyes off the money.

"No, you're Marco," she said, gassing him up. Deep down she felt that something bad was about to happen, but she didn't know what. She just hoped she didn't get caught up.

****

Czar was starting to get that feeling he knew so well. He never knew what his mother used to talk about when she said she used to get that feeling, but now he knew. Something wasn't right. He had trusted Gauge to make a few runs for him, but he had been gone longer than expected and that feeling was growing stronger. He had been at the window for the last twenty minutes waiting to see Gauge's car bend the corner. He had started to leave a few times but he wanted - no, he needed - to trust somebody so he stayed put. He peeked out the blinds one more time and knew his instincts were right. Pulling up to the curb was a black on black Yukon Denali with police tint that he knew hid shooters to take him out. He looked at the door and thought about making a run for it, but the building had only one entrance. He knew that by the time he got to the door, they would be on him. He went back to the window and saw three men get out of the truck dressed in all black. With the sun setting and night fast approaching it was hard to identify who they were, or if he knew them at all. He pulled his Bulldogs and waited. If he was gonna die, he wasn't going alone.

He didn't have to wait long before he heard their footsteps outside of the door. Their next move surprised him. They knocked on the door like this was a social visit. He looked at the door for a few seconds before deciding to play along.

"Who is it?" he called out as he tightened his grip on his bulldogs.

"Gauge sent us to holla at you," one of the shooters said calmly.

I know that bitch nigga did, Czar thought bitterly as he snuck up to the door and looked out of the peephole. "Amateurs," he whispered to himself when he saw all three men standing directly in front of the door. He backed up a few steps and let his dogs bark.

Boom! Boom! Boom!

Their screams were like music to his ears as he pressed his attack. Through the holes made in the door, he saw two of the men on the floor holding wounds to their chests and stomachs. The other one he heard taking off back down the stairs in a fast retreat. He put two in the heads of the wounded and took off after the third. By the time he made it to the ground floor, the Denali was pulling off. He put the remaining slugs into the windshield and hood trying to stop the truck, but it kept going.

"Fuck," he cursed as he watched the truck bend the corner. He heard the sirens getting closer, so he pulled his hoody up over his head and jogged to his hoopty. Jimmy Slim was upping the ante, and it was his turn to bet or fold his hand.

****

"So tell me what you have for me, Riley?" Pharaoh said as he sat down with the lawyer to discuss his father's will.

Mr. Riley sat there looking at the person he had watched grow from a baby in diapers to a man whose ruthlessness surpassed that of even his father. He was still amazed at the transformation Pharaoh had undergone. He couldn't deny that the man seated across from him scared him.

"Riley," Pharaoh called again to get his attention. "You all right?"

"Yes, yes, I'm fine." Mr. Riley said, shuffling some paperwork to cover the awkward moment. "It's just hard to believe that Michael and Olivia are both gone," he added sadly.

"I know," Pharaoh said quietly. His face grew taut at the thought of his mother's suicide. He was still searching for the man who gave her a gun. "When I find the man who gave her the gun, he will follow her into the afterlife," he added seriously.

Mr. Riley saw the look in his eyes and knew that he was telling the truth. He cleared his throat to give himself a moment. "Well, let's get down to business." He pulled the file for Michael Carter's legitimate businesses. "Your father's main source of income comes from Tri-med Pharmaceutical. It's worth an estimated seven hundred million. His Carter Ford car dealerships brings in another hundred million a year off of sales. His stocks and bonds are worth a hundred and fifty million. He owns coffee fields in Columbia, oil fields in Africa, and tobacco fields here in the states. Legally, you're worth around two and a half billion, give or take a million or two. Now your father's illegal activities are just as extensive." Mr. Riley looked at Pharaoh over his eye glasses.

"Continue," Pharaoh said sitting there, expression stoic. The old Pharaoh would've been shocked at his newfound wealth, but the new Pharaoh didn't deal with emotions.

"Ecstasy and other prescription pills bring in an estimated fifty million a year. Heroin brings in close to two hundred million a year. Cocaine another hundred million and marijuana brings in another twenty million," Mr. Riley said, once again amazed at the many dealings of the Carter Conglomerate.

"Finish out the year with the illegal business, then shut it down. Take the profits and diversify my portfolio. I don't want anything to do with drugs, period," Pharaoh said seriously.

"As you wish. There's one last thing before we end," Mr. Riley said reaching into his briefcase and pulling out a set of photographs.

"Who is this?" Pharaoh asked as he flipped through the pictures.

"The man suspected of having your father murdered," Mr. Riley said seriously.

"What's his name and what was his problem with my father?" Pharaoh asked as he studied the features of the man he was going to personally kill.

"He is called Sincere, and he was your father's biggest rival in the drug market." Mr. Riley said.

"Okay, thank you, Mr. Riley. I'll get back to you soon," Pharaoh said, dismissing him. He set the pictures on the table face down.

After Mr. Riley packed up his papers and left the room he picked the pictures back up and continued to study the man responsible for altering his world. He couldn't help but feel like he knew the man from somewhere. The longer he stared at the pictures, the stronger the feeling got.

"You are a dead man." he whispered to the picture as the tears started to fall.

Vincent "Vito" Holloway

Chapter 17

"So ye are de famous Majestic de pretty star been talking 'bout," Mantay said over Star's shoulder as he hugged her. He was studying Majestic to see what all the hype was about. Let Star and Sky tell it, he was the end all be all, but he wasn't impressed. Majestic didn't respond to the comment. He just gave the man his dead stare.

Sky noticed the silence from her brother and spoke up. "Yes, dis 'im, Mantay."

"'E can't speak?" Mantay asked, eyeing Majestic.

"Mem can when de mon mem speaking to speaking 'bout sumting," Majestic said seriously.

Mantay chucked as he nodded his head to Big Tree, the biggest dread in little Haiti. He started walking towards Majestic.

Star started to say something because she knew what Mantay was doing, but Majestic stopped her with a look as he pulled out his pistol.

The sound of guns being cocked was heard as every dread on the block pulled a pistol hidden somewhere on their bodies.

"No guns, mon. End to end. Lion ta lion," Mantay said seriously.

Majestic felt his rage rise at the mention of lion to lion. He was the lion, but he didn't trust Mantay and was reluctant to put down his gun. Fighting wasn't a problem, but trusting them to fight fair was.

"No jumping, mon," Mantay said reading his mind. "Mem word," he added, touching two fingers to his heart.

Majestic gave his gun to Sky and turned to face Big Tree. He was big 6'8" and at least 250 pounds compared to his 6'1" 200 pounds, but he wasn't worried because his father taught him how to fight, especially against bigger opponents. He grabbed the lion's head lying on his chest and felt his father coursing through him. He tucked the necklace into his shirt and tied his locs back. "Let's go, pussy bwoy," he said seriously. He heard his sisters gasp and it almost made him laugh. He could tell that they were scared for him, but he would show them that their brother was the real lion.

Big Tree charged him, just like he thought he would. He waited until Big Tree was a few feet away before he went low. "Soft spots, mon," he whispered before making Big Tree squeal like a struck pig. He executed a perfect uppercut into his genitals. The momentum from Big Tree's charge took them both to the ground, but Big Tree was in no mood to fight as he cradled his family jewels and moaned on the concrete. "Soft spots," he whispered once again as he got on top of the big man and started pounding his eyes, nose, lips, and throat.

"Enough!" Mantay shouted. He was amazed at the outcome. Big Tree had never lost a fight.

Majestic got up off of Big Tree and stood staring at Mantay, breathing hard.

"Mem give ye respect, mon," Mantay said sincerely.

Majestic looked at him for a few seconds to gauge his sincerity, then nodded.

"Okay den, mon. Let's go and discuss what ye came ta discuss." Mantay turned and walked into a house on the corner.

Majestic and his sisters followed him to talk about what would become one of the most dangerous island gangs Miami had ever seen.

****

King walked into the brownstone to find Latoya cooking breakfast in the first floor kitchen. She looked back, saw that it was him, and went back to cooking without saying a word to him. He knew that she was mad at him for staying out all night and coming home that morning without checking in at all. He stood there watching her cook and couldn't stop his dick from getting hard. She had on a wife beater with no bra and some shorts that barely contained her ass. Throwing caution to the wind, he walked up behind her and pressed himself against her, letting her feel what

King Killa

she was doing to him. "Do you think you can handle being my number one?" he asked, kissing her on the neck.

Latoya was shocked to feel him hard and pressed up against her backside. She couldn't hold in her moan when he kissed her neck. She was mad at him, but her anger was slowly fading away the longer he grinded himself into her. Plus, she always grew extra wet every time he talked to her in Spanish. "You already know I can. Why are you playing with me?"

"You already know I don't play, but the life I live is serious and dangerous," King said as he reached a hand inside of her shorts to slide a finger in her soaking wet pussy.

Latoya felt her knees buckle when he entered her, so she reached over and cut the stove off. Her concentration was solely on him. "I'm with you a hundred percent, but sooner or later, choices will come up and decisions will be made," she moaned. She wasn't going to be with him just to be with him. She wanted him to think about the future.

"You got that," he said, pulling her shorts down before releasing his rock hard dick from his pants.

"Well, it's about time you came to your senses," she said right before he entered her, taking her breath away.

****

Pharaoh stood in the pouring rain in front of his parents' headstones, talking to them, asking for advice.

"What am I supposed to do, Father?" he said, looking at the picture engraved into the stone. "I don't want to get caught up in this life, but I know I am not the same person I was before you died and I feel that I will never be that person again. Why did you deal drugs? Why did you feel the need when there wasn't any reason to? Sometimes I want to join you and Mother, but you left me too much to do. This man Sincere will be in hell soon. I promise you that. I love you, Father. Mother I'm going to find the person who gave you that gun and I'm going to kill them, even though I'm sure it was your decision to take your life. You shouldn't have left me, Mother, because I needed you. Still do. I'm taking our family out of the drug market. I won't have a part in killing communities. It's time for me to go, but I'll be back next week. Love you both."

He laid the flowers he was holding on the gravestones and walked away. Anybody looking would've seen a young man with the weight of the world on his shoulders.

****

"Fellas, put your drinks down and get your paper up. Coming to the stage is the lovely beautiful and gorgeous Dior. Throw ya money and get a show already!" the deejay screamed into his microphone as he dropped that "Wet" by Chris Brown and Ludacris.

Dior came out crawling on her hands and knees. Her cat eye contacts had her looking like a sexy tigress. The way she was bouncing her ass cheeks to the beat had the crowd going crazy. She went from her knees into her signature move, a handstand where she popped her ass and made each cheek move independently to the beat. She came down into a split and popped her pussy before crawling to the edge of the stage to let the men and women put money into her garter belts. Something was drawing her attention to the shadows of the club. She did a double take because the silhouette of the man standing in the corner looked real familiar. A nigga trying to cop a quick feel drew her attention back to what she was doing. After finishing her set, she looked back over to the corner but found the spot empty. She gathered up her money and quickly left the stage. She had to find Bianca.

****

"Did you know King was out?" Sophia asked hysterically as she rushed into the apartment she shared with Marco.

"What!" Marco shouted when what she was saying registered in his mind. "Who told you that?" he asked as he looked at her skeptically.

"Apparently he was seen in Castle Hill yesterday, pushing a brand new Benz," she said with a worried look on her face.

"What he do, beat his appeal?" Marco asked as he wondered how King was going to react.

"Probably so. He had that lawyer bitch working on his case nonstop," Sophia said bitterly. She couldn't hide her jealousy for Latoya Watkins.

"So what? Fuck him and that bitch," Marco said, trying to figure out what he was going to do. He knew King wouldn't take his betrayal lightly. He had to do the only thing he knew to do: put money on his head. "You sound like you still have feelings for him or something," he added, looking at her sharply.

"No, fuck that puto, but you need to do something about him," she said unconvincingly. She knew Marco couldn't hold a candle to King and her betrayal was weighing heavy on her mind.

Marco looked at her like she was crazy. He stood up and roughly grabbed her by her neck. "Who the fuck you think you're giving orders to?" he growled as he squeezed her neck, cutting off her air.

Sophia gasped as she tried to breathe. She tried to pry his hand loose, but he was too strong

"Always remember your place. I will kill you and that bitch-ass nigga if I catch you sniffing around him. You belong to me now. You hear me? You hear me!" He screamed in her face.

When Sophia nodded her assent, he let her go. She fell to the floor, gasping for air. Marco looked at her and wanted to apologize because putting his hands on a woman wasn't his thing, but the news about King was unsettling to say the least. He grabbed his hoody and fitted cap before leaving the apartment.

The tears started flowing as soon as the door slammed shut behind him. Sophia massaged her neck and knew without a doubt that she had fucked up. Now it was about to hit the fan.

****

King opened his eyes when he heard his phone ringing. He reached over to grab it, but Latoya stopped him.

"Uh-uh," she moaned in disagreement as she cracked open her eyes to look at him. "Let me get today, baby, please?" she asked as she pressed her body into his.

He had put it down all day long, and she couldn't get enough. They had christened every room in her brownstone and ended up in the bedroom. She wanted - no, she needed - this day with him before he dived head first back into the streets.

King chuckled as he kissed her on her neck. "You got that, but let me cut my phone off," he said, reaching over her and doing just that. "I wasn't finished with you yet anyway," he added before he slid his hand down to her warm pussy.

Latoya gasped when his fingers entered her "And I'm most definitely not done with this guy," she said, grabbing his dick.

****

The private jet that landed at Miami Dade International Airport didn't draw much attention amongst the other million dollar planes, but the men who disembarked did. They were clearly rich, attired in expensive suit and shoes. The briefcases they were carrying made them seem businesslike, but they gave off an aura of danger that was almost palpable. Maybe it was the looks they all wore or the scowls they gave to anyone brave enough to hold eye contact long enough. They meant business. That much was clear. One probably could describe them as sophisticated rudeness.

Chapter 18

Majestic and Mantay had Miami terrified. They had come together to form an organization called The Rude Boys. Dade County hadn't seen a group like this since the John Does ran Liberty City, Vonda's gang in Overtown and the Thomas Family in Carol City. Miami is a multicultural city and the island population is usually considered to be at the bottom of the totem pole, but Majestic and Mantay were setting out to change that narrative. They were getting money any way they could, but their main hustle was hitting cargo ships. They had a few connections amongst the longshoremen at the Port of Miami that let them know when certain ships would dock. Their weapons of choice were assault rifles when they wanted to make a point, and the machete for when they wanted to kill silently. The city at Miami was on fire and The Rude Boys were holding the torch.

****

The Executive Club was jumping. It was Friday night and all of the ballers were out to see the baddest strippers in the state of Texas.

"Girl, cheer up. It's money all around here and you're sitting here moping over something you think you saw," Bianca said to Dior as they sat at the bar.

She had on purple fishnet stockings with garters, a purple thong, lip-shaped pasties covering her nipples and glitter covering her body. Dior was dressed in the exact same except her color scheme was pink. They both had on wigs the color of their outfits.

"You don't even know if it was him. You think he would show up and not get at you?" she asked seriously as she looked around at all the money she was missing because her girl was seeing ghosts.

"I know, B, but something about that nigga standing in the shadows made me look that way," Dior said, remembering how her attention kept being drawn to him how she felt like he was looking at her and only her. "Plus I'm tired of these bitch-ass niggas fronting since he been M.I.A. Niggas dick riding Jimmy Slim like he's the shit when he was nothing more than a do-boy when Czar was on deck," she added bitterly. She was also upset that Czar hadn't contacted her. He was making it easy for people to believe what Jimmy Slim was saying about him.

"Speaking of the devil. Look," Bianca said, nodding her head towards the entrance.

Dior looked that way and spotted Jimmy Slim leading his entourage into the club. She frowned because niggas were acting like the presidents had just walked into the club, but she couldn't front. Jimmy and his team reeked of money. A smile blossomed on her face as she turned back to Bianca. "You have some of those pills with you?" she asked devilishly.

"You know I do," Bianca replied, looking at her friend with an arched eyebrow raised. "What you trying to do?" she asked curiously.

"Follow me and watch your girl work," Dior said before sliding off of the barstool and making her way through the crowd towards Jimmy Slim.

****

Jimmy Slim was feeling himself. He was the man to see, and it wasn't just his inflated ego talking. It was the reception he got when he walked into The Executive Club. Niggas was dick riding, but he knew that as soon as he lost the plug, they would be onto the next nigga. So he kept them at a distance and let them build his legend. The women were flocking around trying to get his attention, hoping he chose and took one of them home. The strippers were flaunting, hoping he made it rain. He was the man and everybody knew it.

"Jimmy, look who's walking this way," Tilly said, tapping him on the arm and pointing.

Jimmy Slim looked where he was pointing and felt his dick jump to attention.

Dior and Bianca were walking through the crowd like they owned it. They were the two baddest women in the club that night, and every other woman knew it. The crowd surrounding Jimmy Slim parted like the red sea as they stopped in front of him. "What's up, playa?" Dior asked seductively. She placed a hand on her hip and put all of her weight on one leg so that her best asset was on display. She was sexy personified and she knew it.

I knew this bitch wanted me with her fronting ass, Jimmy Slim thought gleefully as he licked his lips. "What's up with you, Dior?" he asked excitedly as his eyes roamed her body.

Dior had to fight not to roll her eyes at this thirsty lame nigga. "Me and B trying to get you and one of your homeboys into the private rooms," she said licking her glossy lips. "You already know you're gonna get your money's worth," she added slyly. She knew he would give her whatever she wanted for a night with her.

"Say no more. Me and Tilly down," Jimmy Slim said, throwing his arm around her shoulder, staking his claim. "Tell the bartender I'm buying the bar and tell him to send two bottles each of Rosé and Ace of Spades to the private rooms," he told one of his entourage before moving towards the back where the private rooms were located.

Dior caught Bianca's eyes and winked. Her plans were coming together easier than she expected. Jimmy Slim was a sucker and she was gonna see how many licks it took for her to get to the bottom of his pockets.

****

Sasha Livingston was a simple woman. She worked hard to make sure her family was happy and secure. When Majestic, her only son, showed up at the restaurant, her heart broke because his presence assured her of her husband's, her one-time love's, death. She had kept it together at the time because she knew that her children needed her. When Buju sent her and the girls to America over ten years ago, it was with a purpose. He knew that the cancer would eventually kill him and he wanted to train their son to be a man without any interference from a woman, plus he wanted the women safe.

She remembered the words Buju told her that night he put them on a boat headed for Florida. "Don't ye ever forget mem love fa ye, Sasha. Mem lucky ta 'ave ye as mem wife. Ye understand what must be done. De next time ye see our son, mem will be dead. Ye must raise our daughters to be strong, because Majestic will need 'elp. Mem love ye. Always 'old dat in ye 'eart."

She remembered the last kiss he gave her before he turned and walked away so he wouldn't have to see her tears. That kiss was something she cherished and would continue to cherish until she joined him. Every time she thought about Buju, she grew sad and tears flooded her eyes, like now, but she never allowed them to fall because she knew how much Buju hated her crying.

She heard the doorbell ring and went to see who was at the door. She shook her head to clear her memories of her beloved before peering out of the peephole and seeing a beautiful Jamaican woman standing on the stoop. Most people couldn't tell the difference between a Haitian, a Jamaican, a West Indian, or a Trinidadian, but she could. She would always be able to tell if someone was from her homeland, but the fact that she was from Jamaica and on her doorstep gave her pause. Majestic had told her that Terror was the one who took over after Buju passed and she knew that he would try and hunt down the remaining Livingstons. Despite knowing all of that, she opened her door.

"May mem 'elp ye?" she asked politely.

"Are ye Sasha Livingston?"

Hearing her name come out of this woman's mouth alarmed Sasha and she knew that she would die. Surprisingly, that thought didn't bother her as much as she thought it would. Maybe subconsciously, she was ready to join Buju. "Who are ye?" she asked warily.

The woman reached out faster than a cobra and grabbed her neck, cutting off her air supply. "Dey call mem death back 'ome,"

Chaka smiled and replied as she backed Sasha up into the house and kicked the door shut behind her.

Terror had come to call, and Terror would be answered.

****

"How much is it going to cost me for the pussy, Dior?" Jimmy Slim asked as she danced in front of him. He was feeling good as he watched her through half slitted eyes.

They had smoked three blunts together, but he was the only one drinking. He was mixing codeine cough syrup and Sprite together to sip on. The Rosé and Ace of Spades were consumed as soon as they arrived. Bianca and Tilly had taken a bottle of each with them to their private room. He had been alone with Dior for a couple of hours now and he was ready to fuck. He pulled his dick out and started stroking it.

I can't front, this nigga got a big dick, she thought as she danced and watched him stroke himself. Despite herself she was getting horny. Her pussy was getting wet and that was a clear sign that she was ready to fuck. "How much you got in your pocket?" she asked to buy time.

Jimmy Slim paused what he was doing and started pulling out knots of money. "Is this enough?" he asked, throwing it at her feet.

This nigga want the pussy bad, she thought as she looked down at the money lying at her feet. "How much is that?" she asked nonchalantly as she continued to dance.

"I don't know, but it's probably ten stacks or more," he said growing agitated with her attitude. "What's up with that pussy?" he asked seriously.

Damn, when is these pills gonna kick in? she thought as she looked in his eyes. She could tell that he was serious and might be trouble if she didn't give him some pussy. Besides, she wasn't even thinking about giving the money back. "Chill, boy, I got you," she said, walking over to him and grabbing his dick. She started slow stroking him, making him moan.

"Yeah, that what I'm talking about," Jimmy Slim groaned as he reached over and slid her thong to the side before sticking two fingers inside her wet pussy. "Damn, you wet as hell and you got a fat pussy," he moaned, using his thumb to play with her clit as he finger fucked her.

"Can I ride your face?" Dior asked as she bit her bottom lip to hold her moans in. She couldn't front, he was working her pussy. It had been so long since she had some dick and if she didn't do something to hold him off until the pills kicked in, she was going to give him some pussy.

"Hell yeah, you can ride my face," Jimmy Slim slurred excitedly as he laid back on the velvet couch in the private room.

Dior pulled her thong off and climbed onto his face. She started rocking back and forth as Jimmy Slim used his tongue like a little dick and sucked on her clit. He grabbed her ass cheeks and started bouncing her up and down. "Oh my God," she moaned as she felt her orgasm building. She turned around on his face until she was face to face with his dick she grabbed it and starting jacking him off. She hoped that if he came with her, he wouldn't want to fuck because he was eating her pussy so good she would give it to him and that would be the ultimate betrayal to Czar. She was already doing him dirty, but she couldn't turn down ten stacks just to let a nigga eat her pussy.

"I'm cumming," she moaned as her body started convulsing. Her orgasm was so intense because Jimmy Slim was sucking the juices right out of her as he sucked on her clit. It only took a couple of more strokes before he was shooting his cum all over her hands. She climbed up off of his face.

Jimmy Slim slurred something unintelligible and started snoring.

Dior smiled and then she started laughing. Her plan had worked to perfection. She looked at Jimmy Slim laying there with his dick out and her cum drying on his face and wished she had a camera. She knew he would be mad if he woke up and remembered what happened, but she wasn't worried about him doing shit. She put her thong back on and ran his pockets. After relieving him of all of his money, she left the room to go find Bianca, hoping that Czar never found out about this night.

****

Majestic, Star, and Sky were racing towards their mother's home. Majestic had been planning another raid with Mantay and the team when he got the feeling that something wasn't right. He grabbed his father's lion head medallion and closed his eyes. His father was telling him that danger was lurking around their family and since he was with his sisters, that left one person his father would warn him about: his favorite girl, his mother. He opened his eyes to find everybody staring at him, but he paid them no heed as his eyes locked onto his sisters.

"Let's go!" he barked, getting up and rapidly leaving the room without giving an explanation.

Star and Sky were as confused as everybody else, if not more, but they got up and followed their brother without question. "What tis de problem, brudda?" Sky asked once they caught up to him.

"Fadda let mem know dat Mudda is in trouble," he said before sliding into the backseat of their car.

"Sky, mem believe Majestic," Star said worriedly.

"'urry, 'urry," Majestic said frantically from the car. "Mem get de feeling we might be too late," he added quietly.

With those words, Sky hopped into the driver's seat and burnt rubber, taking off out of the parking lot. She broke every traffic law in an effort to stop whatever Majestic was foreseeing. When she pulled onto their mother's street and parked in front of her house, Majestic was out of the car before it had come to a complete stop with his guns in his hands. He slowed down when he noticed that the front door was cracked open and knew that his father had been right. He kicked the door the rest of the way open, raised his guns up, ready to dead anything outside of his mother, and felt his heart freeze inside of his chest. He felt his sanity disappear as he absorbed the sight in front of him. He dropped his guns and let out an anguished scream that registered with his sisters who started crying when they reached him. Hanging from the ceiling fan was their mother's decapitated head staring at them as it slowly rotated but that wasn't what had Majestic's attention. It was the words written on the wall in what he knew to be blood. Terror has come. Terror has Reign!

****

"Girl, we got off on them sucker ass niggas," Bianca said as she finished counting the money they had gotten off of Jimmy Slim and Tilly. "We got twenty-three stacks, Dior," she added as she put the rubber banded stacks into her purse.

"I told you we would get off," Dior said as she pulled into their driveway.

"Bitch, you didn't tell me shit," Bianca said with a smirk. "I had to figure it out as we went along," she added, laughing.

"Great minds think alike," Dior said, laughing along with her. "That's why we sisters," she added.

"Already!" Bianca agreed.

"But girl, let me tell you, that nigga Jimmy Slim can eat some pussy," Dior said as they got out of the car. She was getting wet just thinking about it, but she knew that she could never experience his tongue again, no matter how good it was.

"That nigga Tilly was a freak," Bianca said, fanning herself. "He ate my ass and pussy from the back, front, and sides," she added as they made it to their front door.

Before Dior could respond, they were rudely interrupted.

"If either of you two bitches act crazy, I'ma lay you down," Don Don growled seriously as he held his gun on them.

"Just be easy, ladies, and shit will go as smooth as your pussies," Chris added, laughing a little.

Dior and Bianca both turned around slowly. "Oh, y'all some big men robbing two women, huh?" Dior asked sarcastically. She was actually terrified, but she wouldn't let on in front of them when she knew they were bitch made.

"Pussy-ass niggas is what they are," Bianca said seriously. She was also scared but didn't show it.

"Bitch, I'm tired of your mouth," Don Don snarled as he smacked her across the face with his pistol.

Bianca screamed and fell to the ground holding her busted lip. She glared at him because she would make him pay for that.

"Please, please," Dior begged, finally letting her fear show.

"Oh, you not so tough now are you?" Chris asked, smirking at the fear in her eyes.

"Just take the money and leave," Dior said, trying to get this over with.

"Get me the info we looking for and we will leave," Chris said seriously.

"What info?" she asked confused.

"Bitch, stop playing dumb," Don Don said raising his gun to her head. "We know you know where that nigga Czar at."

"I promise you that I haven't heard from him since everything went down," Dior said seriously, but she knew that they wouldn't believe her because she been going hard for Czar from the beginning.

"Bitch, give me that," Don Don said, snatching Bianca's purse when he noticed her reaching inside. "Well look at what we found." He showed Chris the stacks of money.

"Get Bianca up and open the door. We came to find out where Czar is and we not leaving until we find him," Chris said. "Jimmy upped the price on his head and we need that. Nothing personal, just business." He added smiling.

Dior glared at him as she helped Bianca up. She wondered what they would do to them when they found out they really didn't know where Czar was. She used her key to open the front door and led them inside. She started to reach over and cut the lights on but decided to leave it dark. She grabbed Bianca's hand and led them further into the house.

"Cut the fucking lights on in this bitch," Don Don said as they closed the door behind them.

"You're the closest to the switch," Dior aid.

Don Don reached out, groping for the switch, and felt something more solid. "What the fuck?" he said, confused.

"I heard you bitch niggas looking for me."

The voice shocked everyone in the room, but before anyone could react, the room was filled with thunder.

Boom! Boom! Boom!

Dior and Bianca both screamed and fell to the ground when the gunfire started.

Czar cut the lights on and turned to face them. They were both looking at him like he was a ghost.

"What took you so long?" Dior asked seriously. She was happy to see him, but she was also mad as hell at him for not contacting her sooner.

"I should kill both of you bitches," he said seriously. He didn't know who he could trust anymore.

"What the fuck for, nigga?" Bianca asked with attitude, even though she was scared he might actually shoot them.

"For fucking with them snake-ass niggas," he said, grilling them. He saw them go into the private rooms with them snakes.

Dior knew that she had been right. He had been at the club and probably saw them go into the private rooms with Jimmy Slim and Tilly. "Nigga, miss me with that bullshit. If you believed that, then we wouldn't be standing here talking," she said confidently. "We would be laid out on the floor with them bitch-ass niggas." She knew how he gave it up so she didn't doubt her last statement at all.

"She's been holding you down hard since everything hit the fan," Bianca said truthfully. "She loves your dirty drawers," she added playfully.

Czar never took his eyes off of Dior. In fact, he never gave an indication that he even heard what Bianca said. "You love me?" he questioned Dior.

She looked at him like the answer should've been obvious, but answered anyway. "Of course."

"Are you in love with me?" he asked quietly.

164

Dior paused before answering as she looked at him because she had never heard him talk like this before and honestly, it was scaring her. Bianca even looked perplexed by his questioning. "You know that I'm in love with you," she answered seriously, trying but failing to meet his intensity.

"Then why did you let a nigga that wants me dead by any means touch what's supposed to belong to me?" he asked coldly.

Dior was shocked by his question. The guilt she was already feeling over her tryst with Jimmy Slim intensified because she had hurt Czar with her actions, and that was something she never wanted to do. She was so embarrassed and ashamed that she couldn't answer his question.

Bianca saw that her girl was at a loss for words, so she tried to help her. "That was all my——" she stopped talking when Czar looked at her because his eyes were so cold, the words froze in her throat. She threw Dior a sympathetic look and kept silent.

"There's nothing I can say that will make this situation better, so I'll just tell you that my love for you has no boundaries and I know that I've damaged your trust in me, but I'm prepared to do whatever I have to do to repair your faith in me." Her words were so sincere that tears were falling from her eyes as she looked at him.

"Loyalty is not everything. It's the only thing," Czar said quietly. He knew how tenuous trust could be so he didn't take it for granted. He needed to know that he could trust her without question before he let her in because death was lurking and he refused to be caught slipping. "Clean these niggas up and be ready to go when I get back," he instructed before leaving the house.

Dior and Bianca looked at each other, confused about the turn of events, but they kept their thought to themselves as they went about the business of wrapping and cleaning up two bodies.

Vincent "Vito" Holloway

Chapter 19

Latoya was on the phone talking to a client when her secretary poked her head into her office. "Yes, Mrs. Williams?" she asked after covering the mouthpiece of the phone with her hand.

"Sorry to interrupt you, Ms. Watkins, but there's a Sophia Gomez waiting in the reception area waiting to see you. She says it's urgent," Mrs. Williams said, frowning her face up because she knew how her boss hated unscheduled visits from people. But the girl was very insistent.

What the hell does this hoe want with me? Latoya asked herself silently. *I hope she needs legal representation so I can turn her trifling ass down.* "Send her on in, Mrs. Williams, and hold any calls until she leaves please." She smiled at her older receptionist to let her know it was all right.

"As you wish, Ms. Watkins," Mrs. Williams said, breathing a sigh of relief as she backed out of the office to go do her bidding.

"Sorry about that, Mr. Gregory, but look, just come in tomorrow and we'll finish up the details for your trial. Okay, bye."

She hung up just as Sophia walked into her office wearing her usual scowl. She sat down across from her and remained silent.

Latoya was content to let the silence build as she looked over Sophia just as she was being studied. They both had similar thoughts running through their minds about each other.

This bitch ain't nothing special, Latoya thought sardonically as visions of King loving her filled her head.

I don't know what King sees in this bitch, Sophia thought angrily as images of King making love to her invaded her mind.

"What is it that you want?" Latoya asked. As much as she loved having the upper hand, she hated the childish games.

"Is King really out of prison?" Sophia asked urgently. She hated how desperate she sounded, but she needed to know if the rumors were true.

Oh, she must've heard King was out and wants to beg for his forgiveness, Latoya thought, wanting to laugh in her face. "Yes, he's out," she answered, loving the look of fear that crossed her face. "He hasn't contacted you or Marco yet?" she asked with a smirk on her lips.

Sophia knew that Latoya was mocking her and wanted to curse her out but she held her tongue. "Tell him I really need to talk to him and that Marco put money on his head," she said seriously as she unconsciously rubbed her neck where Marco had choked her.

Latoya noticed the bruises and almost felt sorry for the girl - almost. "Did Marco do that to you?" she asked, indicating the bruises on her neck.

"Look, this is my new number," Sophia said, placing a piece of paper on the desk and ignoring her question. "Tell him to get at me soon. It's important," she added before turning and walking out of the office, leaving Latoya with a lot to think about, especially about Marco putting money on King's head.

She picked up her phone to call and warn him to be careful. After getting his voicemail, she asked him to call her back ASAP and then hung up just as her receptionist was showing in her next appointment. She looked up at the beautiful expensively-dressed woman walking into her office and smiled. She stood up to shake her extended hand.

"Mrs. Lloyd, how can I help you?"

****

Pharaoh had been in the ring sparring for hours until the sweat was pouring off of his skin. He took out his anger on whoever got in the ring and still it wasn't abated. Every time he looked at his opponent, he saw the face of the man who had killed his parents. His hatred for the man was so strong he dreamed about killing him. His father always told him to never move off of emotions because they would get you killed, but this would be one instance where he let his emotions drive him. He wouldn't be able to rest until those responsible for his pain were dead.

"PC...PC..."

King Killa

Pharaoh heard his nickname and snapped out of his anger induced haze. He looked over to see his longtime girlfriend Laura standing there waiting to be acknowledged. He sighed because he really didn't feel like dealing with her at that moment, but he knew how persistent she could be so it was best to see what she wanted.

"Yes, Laura." He tried to keep the irritation out of his voice, but didn't quite accomplish that.

"Are you going to fight all day, or are we going out like you promised?" she asked, either ignoring his tone of voice or completely oblivious to it.

Pharaoh looked down at the woman who was chosen by his mother to be his wife when they were teenagers and came to the conclusion that he really didn't like her. "We will after I finish sparring," he said before turning back to Herb, his opponent.

"But you promised, PC," she said, poking her bottom lip out in a fake pout, a move that got her whatever she wanted.

"Listen, Laura," he said, turning to glare at her as he let his irritation show in full. "I told you that we will go after I finish. And my name is not P.C. It's Pharaoh. Now go and wait on me or you can leave. Your choice."

Laura stood there with her mouth hanging open, stunned at the way he had just talked to her. Since they'd been together he'd been nothing but respectful and courteous, but the man she was looking at was not the same man. She looked at him in a new light and had to admit that even though he was acting a little brash and abrupt with her, she was a little turned on. She wouldn't let him know that she kind of liked the new him. She turned on her heels and stomped out of the gym.

Pharaoh watched her stomp off and knew what was running through her mind, but he wouldn't apologize because he wasn't the same man he used to be and never would be again.

****

"What de fuck ye mean it be not yer concern dat mem mudda twas murdered?" Majestic asked as he grilled Mantay, who was sitting behind his desk like he was the president.

"It be exactly like mem said, mon," Mantay said, returning Majestic's glare. "Mem not worried 'bout yer mudda, mon. Mem sorry it 'ad ta 'appen, but mem mind tis on money. Death is a part of life. Deal with it," he added coldly.

Star and Sky couldn't believe Mantay was acting so cold and callous towards their mother's death, especially when she had fed him plenty of nights and let him hide from the police in the basement of her restaurant numerous times. They wanted to curse his soul out of his body, but Majestic told them not to open their mouths and they would not. He made it clear that he was now the head of family and they accepted this. They would follow his lead.

The whole room was quiet as the two leaders of The Rude Boys stared at each other with hate in their eyes. The room was also divided because half of them felt Majestic's pain. The believed family came before anything and they weren't feeling Mantay's nonchalant attitude towards the death of one of their leader's mother, but they kept silent to scc how things unfolded.

"So ye will not 'elp mem avenge mem mudda?" Majestic asked quietly as he looked into Mantay's eyes. He almost smiled when he saw fear lurking there.

"Mem said once man and mem will twice," Mantay said sitting there like a king. He felt like Majestic hadn't fully respected his position within Rude Boys but after today, he would one way or another. "Mem don't care about ye mudda's death."

Majestic wasted no time as he pulled his two pistols and riddled Mantay's body with bullet holes. Before Mantay's body slumped over his desk, he put three holes in Big Tree's face. He didn't have to look behind him to know that his sisters had pistols out, trained on the rest of the room.

"Whoever doesn't believe in family can leave de same way Mantay left dis earth," Majestic said as he looked around the room.

King Killa

On some faces he saw fear, on some he saw respect, and on the rest he saw awe, but it was the fear he saw that he relished the most because it had a way of paralyzing the person who experienced it. His father always taught him to recognize the strengths and weaknesses in people and with this group it was easy. "As a whole, we will prosper. Money will be spread evenly and families will be brought up; loyalty is a must, and ye already ave de example of de punishment for betrayal. If ye are wit mem, ye are wit mem but turn snake on mem and mem will kill ye whole bloodlines. Rude Boys! Rude Boys! Rude Boys! Rude Boys!" he started chanting until the whole room was screaming the name at a fevered pitch.

He looked over at his sisters who were also looking at him with a respectful awe on their faces and smiled at them. The Lion would soon rise again, and terror would most definitely reign.

****

After wrapping Chris and Don Don up in plastic, Dior and Bianca helped Czar carry them to his hoopty and put them in the trunk. After they finished sanitizing the house, they packed up a couple of bags worth of clothes and other essentials then followed Czar to Glendale Park, where he parked the hoopty under a tree and wiped it down before hopping into the Charger with the girls. They stopped and ordered a couple of pizzas before getting a room at the Mi'Amor Motel on Scyene Avenue After taking showers, they sat down on the beds to eat and hear the whole story from Czar.

"Before I tell y'all anything, tell me what been going on in the streets," Czar said as he reached for another slice of pizza.

"At first it was all rumors that was going on around town. Niggas was telling their own stories, like you set up the connect. Jimmy Slim popped up as the man to see, and I couldn't believe niggas was eating up his stories about you. We thought niggas were just hating like usual until Jimmy Slim tried to get at me one day and let it be known you were a rat and he was putting money on your head. We spoke up to anybody who said something crazy in our presence, but we played our positions until we heard from you," Dior said, running down everything she knew.

"When Jimmy Slim popped up with the connect and beating your old prices, niggas took what he said as gospel. I think a lot of niggas didn't go for the bullshit, but Jimmy had the connect so they kept silent," Bianca said, adding her two cents. "Plus with you missing in action, it was easy for people to believe that bitch-ass nigga. You already know you had haters from here to Florida who were praying for your downfall."

"I thought you didn't tell Jimmy who your connect was?" Dior asked curiously. She could remember him always saying he trusted Jimmy Slim with everything but the connect.

"I didn't tell that snake who the connect was. It's hard for me to believe that the connect would fuck with him unless he was sponsored, and that bitch nigga didn't know anybody like that," Czar said angrily. He was trying to fit the pieces to the puzzle, but some of them didn't fit.

"You know all of this is your fault, right?" Bianca said seriously. "We've been telling you for years that nigga wasn't kosher."

Czar couldn't even defend himself because she was right. Over the years a lot of people had told him Jimmy Slim was a snake, but he defended who he once considered his brother against all backbiting and slander.

"What happened to your arm?" Dior asked when she noticed the bandages.

"I was down in the Quarter shopping…"

"You probably had that bitch Chrissy with you," Dior said sarcastically as she felt her jealousy spike.

Czar kept talking like he didn't even hear her. "I noticed two dudes following me and Chrissy. Somehow they got the drop on me and tried to kill me. I killed them both, but I got hit in the process."

"What happened to Chrissy?" Dior asked, figuring that he was leaving something out.

"She died," Czar said quietly as he looked at her.

"That's what the bitch get for fucking with you after I whooped her ass and told her to leave you alone," she said, dismissing his look.

"You crazy, Dior," Bianca said, laughing at them.

"Naw, she not crazy, she tripping," Czar said seriously.

"Naw, you tripping for fucking around on me. I'm glad the bitch dead," Dior said, letting emotions get the best of her.

"Before we even took it to that level, you knew about Chrissy. She was loyal and you chose to play the side chick when I told you it was about her. I wasn't going to cut her off until she gave me reason to do so. I gave you a taste of my dick and you went crazy. Miss me with that silly shit, because you not off the bench yet." He grimaced because his ribs still hurt. He regretted the fact that Chrissy died because of him, but that was the life he lived and he never sugar coated that fact with anybody on his team.

"Nigga, you know I'm the realist bitch. You like to play games. I keep it real with you on all levels. What other bitch you got on your team that can shoot a gun? Weigh, cut, and bag dope? Make her own money? Is loyal? And look like this?" she asked, pointing at her face.

"You say you keep it real with me on all levels and you're loyal, right?" He maintained eye contact with her.

"Damn right," she answered emphatically.

"But you let Jimmy Slim put his hands and mouth on my pussy," he said sarcastically.

Dior looked at Bianca but she looked away, not wanting to get caught up in their relationship. She tried to help earlier and it almost got her shot, so she minded her business. Dior couldn't say shit because she was dipping with his enemy, but it was all about the money with her and she wouldn't apologize for that. She didn't need a man to take care of her. Czar knew that, but she kept silent out of respect for him and the situation.

"You even let yourself get caught slipping because you were too busy running your trap about how good Jimmy Slim eats pussy," he said when she kept silent. "So stop with all the insincere shit because in the past couple of weeks I've deaded four niggas and I'm far from finished. All I need now is loyalty and heart. If you can't give that, there go the door." He laid back on the bed and closed his eyes, effectively ending all conversation.

Dior looked over at Bianca and rolled her eyes when she saw her friend trying not to laugh at her. She looked at Czar lying there and sucked her teeth because he was so brash and arrogant, but that was what had drawn her to him and she fell in love with it. Whatever faults he had, she was glad he was back because now they would get a chance to see how real niggas were.

Chapter 20

Raul was laying on his bunk in his cell at the federal detention center in downtown Dallas pondering his situation. Something wasn't right. He didn't believe that Czar snitched him out, but his father wasn't trying to hear anything to the contrary, and it was very unlike his father not to take his counsel when it came to the street branch of their organization. It was like he was getting information from somewhere else. But when he broached this subject, all he received in response was silence. Also there was the fact his father was now supplying Jimmy Slim, a man he neither liked or trusted and on many occasions counseled Czar to distance himself from him. He had told Czar to build distance between his personal and business relationships, but Czar had always assured him that he kept Jimmy Slim in the dark when it came to him and his father, but if that was the case, that would mean that Czar, always a trustworthy man, had snitched him out, and he just couldn't make himself believe that without proof.

His father was trying to find Czar and kill him. He had also heard that Jimmy Slim had money on his head. So he had to work fast. It seemed to him that somebody badly wanted Czar out of the way. Something wasn't right and he had a few of his people checking into some things. The alphabet boys were protecting their rat well but he knew from personal experience that money made circles out of squares. So he would soon know for a fact whether Czar was a charlatan or not.

****

Marco pulled up on East Tremont Avenue in South Bronx and found Lil Trey on the block with a couple of his homeboys making money. He rolled down his passenger side window and called out for him to come holla at him for a minute.

"Marco, what up?" Lil Trey asked when he got to the car. He noticed that Marco was sweating and, from the look of the car's ashtray, chain smoking Newports. He wondered if he was getting high off of something other than weed.

"Have you seen King?" Marco asked as he stared intently into Lil Trey's eyes.

"King?" Lil Trey said with a confused look on his face. "I thought King was locked up?"

"No, he out. But look, I got five thousand for whoever kills that clown," Marco said, lighting up another cigarette.

"Word?" Lil Trey asked excitedly.

"Word," Marco said smirking at his excitement.

"I thought King was your brother?" Lil Trey asked as his face grew serious.

"Yeah, shit happens. But spread the word about the money," Marco said somberly as he looked out the windshield. If he would've been paying attention, he would've seen Lil Trey's expression, but he was too busy thinking about Karma.

"I got you," Lil Trey said stepping back away from the car.

Without another word, Marco pulled off. Lil Trey waited until the car disappeared off the block before pulling out his cell phone. Shit was starting to get hot and niggas was gonna feel the fire.

****

"Riley."

He turned his head to regard the woman lying beside him and still couldn't believe that she would give him the time of day. Their relationship was a discreet one and had been going on for years, but he wasn't under any illusion about love or even sexual satisfaction. He knew that she was using him, but he found that he couldn't resist her even when he knew she was forbidden. She had been Michael Carter's mistress for years before he died, even though they were both married. She was greedy, conniving, and a bitch, but he knew that he would do whatever she wanted, even if he didn't like it.

"Yes?" he answered. He felt another erection forming as he looked at her erect nipples. Even though she was an older woman, her appetite for sex was insatiable, and she was like Viagra for his old body.

"Are you proceeding with our plans?" she asked as she grabbed his rising penis and started stroking him slowly.

"It's not as easy as we once planned." He moaned as she rubbed her thumb over the head of his penis. "He is not the same naïve little boy he once was. His parents' deaths took his innocence away from him," he added, trying to keep his wits about him. She had a way of making him forget himself.

"With his parents out of the way, it should be a cake walk, darling," she said, gripping his penis tightly. "I'm glad you were able to talk that bitch Olivia into killing herself. I just wish I could've been there to witness it," she added as she felt herself getting even wetter at the thought of her suicide.

Riley closed his eyes partly out of desire but mostly out of regret. Olivia had been a strong, vain woman and he had convinced her to join her husband because a woman of her caliber shouldn't be confined to a wheelchair for the rest of her life. He had been surprised at how easy it was to talk her into killing herself, but it was and she did it. He didn't tell her how at the end he had tried to talk her out of it. He also didn't tell her of Pharaoh's vow to kill whoever gave her the gun. He shuddered as he remembered the look in Pharaoh's eyes as he made that vow. "Pharaoh is a ruthless man now and he's becoming more and more involved in the daily operations of his businesses," he said as she moved her mouth close to the head of his penis.

"Set up more dummy corporations to siphon more money from him," she said, using her tongue to circle the head of his penis. "Then kill him. You can do that, right, Riley?" she asked seriously as she continued her tongue bath on his penis.

Riley's breathing was coming out in gasps as she made him feel like he's never felt before in his life. "Yes, I can do it." He moaned as she stuck her tongue in the tip of his penis. He knew what she was asking of him wouldn't be easy but he would agree to just about anything as long as she continued to pleasure him like she did.

"That's a good boy," she said before her mouth enveloped him.

****

"Tell men de status on de Livingstons," Terror demanded into the phone. His eyes widened at the information he was receiving. "Majestic must not be allowed to live. 'andle dat and get back 'ere because de locals are becoming restless wit' mem rule and a few examples will be needed," he added before hanging up.

He sat there foreseeing his future. The information he had just received hindered his plans a little, but wouldn't stop anything. He was also saddened a little bit, but the feeling quickly passed as a wicked smile slowly spread across his face.

"Mem beautiful Sasha. It looks like ye chose de wrong mon."

Chapter 21

Majestic was on a rampage. After the death of his mother, all reasoning left him. Terror had violated him in the worst possible way and he would not rest until he held Terrors head in his hands unattached from his body. The thing he felt the most was the failure to his father. He had let the matriarch of their family get murdered in her own home and to him, that was unacceptable. That's why he was dead set on fulfilling his father's wishes to build an army and take back what rightfully belonged to him and his sisters. He had a team, but they didn't have the funds to get anything of consequence done and that was something he was going to get by any means necessary. The Rude Boys were putting the fear of Jah into the citizens of Miami. They were terrorizing Miami with a brand of chaos rarely seen. They were leaving no part of the city untouched. Little River, Opa Locka, Carol City, Overtown and Liberty City were getting used to dreads, machine guns, and machetes because it was home base and the island people took care of their own. Majestic knew the quickest way to generate cash was the drug trade and Miami was the cocaine capital. Since he didn't have a connect to supply him, he would just take the drugs from whoever had them. No prey was too big to go after. Miami beware, a lion was loose.

****

King was getting his hair cut when he felt his phone vibrating on his hip. He looked at the screen and saw that he had five text messages from Lil Trey, Latoya, Christine, Tammy, and Monica. The last three were from his team of female officers he had making moves for him upstate. He knew they only wanted to tell him that they were in the city, so he checked his other two texts. Lil Trey was informing him that Marco had put five stacks on his head, just like he knew he would, but that wasn't something that worried him because he knew that no one in his circle would take the hit and he would deal with that issue before any real gangstas caught wind of it. Now the message from Latoya puzzled him. She was saying that Sophia was looking for him. She had apparently stopped by her office and left a number for him to call. He smirked at the way Latoya was trying him by sending him the number to see if he would call her, but he had no intention of every speaking to his snake ex again. He expected Sophia to look for him once she heard he was out, but to him, she was dead, and he meant it when he said that she and Marco would pay for their betrayal. When the time was right, he would turn the heat up and let people know that the King was back.

****

Jimmy Slim was riding around in his blue BMW 645 coupe, mad that he couldn't find Dior or Bianca. He had woken up in the private room at the executive club with his dick out and his pockets empty. He couldn't remember what had happened, but when he had stumbled out of the room and ran into Tilly, he knew that them bitches had gotten them because his pockets were empty also. Every day since he had been looking for them, but they were nowhere to be found. He had a couple of goons watching their house in case they turned up. In the meantime he was getting money.

He was pulling into the Red Bird mall parking lot when his phone rang. Without checking the caller I.D., he answered. "Hello."

"Why isn't Czar dead yet?" the voice on the other end asked seriously.

At the sound of the voice, Jimmy Slim felt his body tense up. He had been expecting the call, but it still took him by surprise. He took a deep breath and let it out slowly as he found a place to park. "The man is good at running," he answered, trying to effect a cool demeanor, but failing miserable.

"That's because your greedy ass went about the situation the wrong way," the voice said angrily. "You put him on point by showing your hand too soon."

180

"Martinez did that when he missed Czar," Jimmy said nervously.

"You also missed," the voice said coldly.

"The nigga is running," he said angrily. He didn't like being reminded that Czar was still besting him.

"Don't forget your place, Jimmy You need to get rid of Czar soon because you are about to be found out."

"What!" he shouted. "I thought you were going to keep my name out of that shit?" he asked nervously. He already knew what would happen once his name was out.

"I tried, but I underestimated Raul. It seems like he had some connections and he will know that you are a confidential informant soon. We both know what will happen when Martinez finds out, which he inevitably will," the voice said mockingly.

"You set all of this up. You recommended me to Martinez when you already knew I was a C.I., so what do you think he will do to you when he finds that out?" he shot back smugly.

The voice on the other end was silent for a few minutes before responding. "Don't worry about Martinez. I will take care of that end. But you need to handle Czar now. Up the money on his head to a hundred thousand dollars and we'll see how long he can run."

"A hundred stacks?" he repeated, surprised.

"That's what I said. And Jimmy…"

"What's up?" he answered, still thinking about the hundred stacks.

"If you ever even think about threatening me again, you won't have to worry about Martinez," the voice said coldly before hanging up.

Jimmy Slim felt a sense of dread as he hung up the phone but it was replaced by a sense of joy as he thought about the situation he was in. His fifteen minutes might run out sooner than he thought, but he had tasted true power and he wouldn't trade that for anything in the world.

****

"What are we going to do?" Bianca asked seriously because she was becoming crazy. "Sitting in this room is not going to cut it," Bianca added, rolling her eyes.

"We have to kill Jimmy Slim," Czar said as he did push-ups.

"First you need to cut your hair," Dior said, looking at him.

"What?" he asked as he stopped mid push-up.

Dior almost laughed at the look on his face, but she kept her composure because she was serious. "Look, Jimmy has Texas, Louisiana, and Georgia looking for you. So it would be smart to switch it up on him."

Czar thought about what she said as he continued doing push-ups. He had been growing his hair for the past five years and didn't want to cut it, but he understood her logic. He finished his last set and got up off the floor. "Who's gonna cut it? Because I'm not going to a barber shop," he said, first looking at Dior and then Bianca.

"Boy, did you forget that we both have our cosmetology licenses?" Dior asked, placing her hand on her hip with a playful attitude and smirking at him.

"And here I was thinking that all y'all could do was shake ass," he said sarcastically. "Go buy some clippers and let's do this," he added before tossing them a knot of money. He grabbed his guns and walked into the bathroom to take a shower.

"That nigga so full of himself," Dior said as she looked at the closed bathroom door.

"Bitch, stop fronting like you don't like it." Bianca said as she rolled her eyes. She carefully slipped her feet into her flip flops so she wouldn't mess up her freshly-painted toenails. She grabbed her purse and headed for the door. She was ready to go shopping.

Dior just smiled and followed her out of the room. She couldn't deny that she did love everything about Czar.

****

King Killa

Raul was escorted into the attorney-client room, expecting to see his lawyer, but was shocked to see a woman he had never seen before sitting on the other side of the glass. She smiled at him as he sat down.

"Who are you?" he asked as soon as the guards left. He was looking her over and had to admit that she was beautiful, but that still didn't explain what she was doing there to see him.

"A friend of a friend," she said coyly as she pulled some paperwork from her briefcase.

"What friend are you referring to?" he asked with a frown on his face. He didn't like her evasive answer.

"Your father, the infamous Martinez, has a hit out on a man named Czar St. Pierre. Czar isn't the man who snitched you out. It was this man," she said, holding up a picture for him to view.

"Fucking rat!" Raul cursed when he saw who was in the picture.

"My feelings exactly. This man is a contracted confidential informant with the government. Your father is harboring two snakes in his midst. One on the recommendation of the other. Your father is being used as a pawn in a dangerous chess game and he doesn't see it. He has a tendency to have trysts with the women of his rivals. You think hard on what I've told you today and do with it as you will," she said placing the papers back into her briefcase before standing up and to end their meeting.

"Hold on, hold on. Who are you and why should you trust me with this information?" Raul knew his question was absurd, but he was taught to never take anything on face value. It was a hard habit to break.

"I told you that I'm a friend of a friend and I trust you with this information because you're an honorable man. Besides, its beneficial to us both if you do what must be done. You can waste time debating whether or not to trust me but either way I've done my duty. So I will take my leave now because time is money and I have none to waste," she said, grabbing the handle to the door.

"Wait!" Raul called out desperately. "Is my father in danger?" he asked when she turned back to look at him.

"You already know the answer to that question, Raul. It's in your eyes," she said before exiting the room.

Raul stared at the empty booth for a few minutes before everything clicked into place. "Guards!" He yelled. He had to get to a phone and warn his father because he was sleeping with a snake and was about to get bit.

Chapter 22

"Bella, why don't you leave that culero and come be with me?" Martinez asked the woman lying beside him in his king-sized bed as he used his finger to flicker her nipples until they were taut. "You know you love me and I love you. I can treat you better," he added, gasping when she started stroking him to hardness.

"You already know why I can't do that, Carlos," she said, frowning at him. She didn't like the fact that he was pressuring her when the rules were already set. She would not change her objectives for anyone. "We have a good thing going and there's no need for us to mess with it," she added, giving his dick a reassuring squeeze as she smiled at him.

Martinez frowned as he took her hand off of his dick because she was making it hard for him to think. He was tired of the arrangement they had. All they did was have sex and at first he was all right with that, but the older he got, the more he wanted love and it was time to let her know that. "Bella, I love you and want you for more than just sex. I can fuck any woman I desire, but I need something more solid and you can give me that. I'm done playing second fiddle to that cabron you are with now. It's time for you to decide between us." He looked at her and made sure that she knew he was deadly serious.

She looked at his face and was surprised at the intensity in his eyes. She was trying to come up with an answer that would satisfy him but couldn't. Luckily she was saved by the sound of his phone ringing. She breathed a sigh of relief because she needed to get her thoughts together. He really blindsided her with his demands.

"Go ahead and answer your phone, Carlos, because I have to use the ladies room. I'll give you your answer when I get back." She slid out of bed and sashayed to the bathroom.

Martinez sighed and watched her ass jiggle as she walked towards the bathroom. For an older woman, she was still supple and tight and she kept him harder than any young girl. He had held his breath when he made his demands because he knew how fiery and independent she was but he had blindsided her but that was his intention. He had a good feeling about the way she was going to answer. He reached over and answered the phone before the answering machine could click in. "Hello?" He smiled when hearing the operator tell him that he had a collect call from his son. He pressed the necessary buttons and waited for the call to be connected. "Hello, my son."

"Father, we don't have a lot of time. Are you alone?" Raul rushed out.

"Yes, I'm alone," Martinez said cautiously. He lied to his son because he got the feeling that was what his son wanted to hear.

Raul said that he didn't want to talk on the jail phones too much, but he had no choice at the moment.

"What!" Martinez shouted but quieted down immediately when he remembered that he wasn't really alone. He couldn't believe what his son was telling him. He looked over his shoulder and continued talking when he saw that the bathroom door was still closed. "How do you know this to be true?"

""I have my ways. Just trust me for now," Raul said cryptically. He could hear the rage in his father's voice and was satisfied that he was getting through to him. Before this his father had simply dismissed anything he had to say concerning Jimmy Slim.

"Yes, I do trust you, but are you sure?" he asked sorrowfully. He grimaced as the picture his son was painting became clear.

"I'm positive. Eliminate the snake and you will eliminate my case," Raul said seriously.

"It will be handled as soon as we disconnect," Martinez said, just as serious. *And I mean that literally*, he thought sadly.

"Okay, Papa, clean house. Whoever sponsored Jimmy Slim is a snake also," Raul said, thinking about his father's actions over the years and wondering if they were motivated by someone else.

"Will do, don't worry," he said quietly.

"Be safe, Papa," Raul said before hanging up.

Martinez hung up the phone with his mind roiling with the revelations his son had revealed to him. He was angry, but only at himself because he had questioned the move to sponsor Jimmy Slim from the onset. He had always taken Czar as an honorable, trustworthy man, but he let himself be swayed by other sources when he knew better. With a heavy heart he turned around and wasn't at all surprised to find his love standing in the doorway to the bathroom with a gun aimed at his heart. He knew that it was over, but he would go out like the man he was and not the sniveling coward she must think him to be. He looked at the hand holding the gun and saw that it was steady; no nervousness at all. So he knew that he would die whether he tried to make a move or not.

"Did he send you to me?" he asked her. No names were needed. They both knew who he was referring to.

"No one sent me anywhere, Carlos," she said, smirking at him. "You were chosen. I took advantage of your reputation for fucking your rivals' women. It was easy to be honest with you. I manipulated you just like I've been manipulating the men around me all of my life. I'm a Queen and regardless of what the world thinks, the King is not the most powerful piece on the chessboard of life. Sadly, because of your son, your usefulness has run its course." She took a few steps closer to him.

Martinez was livid, but he kept silent as he tried to calculate the chances of him getting to the gun before she shot him.

"If it will make this any easier, your rival will soon follow you into the afterlife." She knew that she was gloating, but she couldn't help it.

Martinez wasn't listening. He was too busy waiting for his chance. When he felt like her attention on him was waning, he lunged.

Boom! Boom! Boom!

She looked down at him and shook her head. "I told you that men are predictable," she said before setting out to erase her presence from his bedroom. On her way out the front door, she was thankful that she had been able to convince Carlos to get rid of his security every time they were together. She hopped into her rental car and erased Carlos Martinez from her mental board as she drove to the airport. He had served his purpose and now she was on to the next.

****

Majestic walked into The Island's Way restaurant he now owned along with his two sisters and saw them preparing to close up for the day. He almost laughed at the way Mega ran towards the storage room when he spotted him. Ever since that first meeting when he put his gun to his head and broke his nose, he had stayed out of his way. Mega was loyal to the family though, so he let him be. He stood there for a few minutes watching the only family he had left deal with the last of the remaining customers before finding a seat in the back of the restaurant to wait until it was empty.

"Mem sorry, sir, but de place is closing," Star said when she reached his table.

"But what if mem de owner?" Majestic asked as he looked over his shoulder and smiled at her.

"Brudda, mem dinna recognize ye." Star said hugging his neck and rubbing her hand over his head. "What 'appened tu ye locks?" she asked.

Mem put dem pon mudda's grave," he said quietly.

"A fitting tribute," she said somberly. "Ye look good though, brudda," she said teasingly as she rubbed his head again.

"Ye tink so?" he asked, smiling before getting serious. "Ye ever 'eard of a mon named Sincere?"

"No," she said thinking. "Should mem know de mon?"

"Our source at de port say 'im a big mon in Miami wit' de drugs. Dey say 'im control most of de east coast."

"Mem don't know mon, but why are ye asking 'bout 'im?" she asked, wondering if her brother was in some kind of trouble.

"'e as a big shipment coming in tonight and we are going to de boat." Majestic looked around to make sure that nobody could overhear them.

"Mem and Sky can be ready in quick fashion," she said, ready to ride.

"No," Majestic said a little too harshly but softened at the look on her face. "Mem need ye ta andle bizness 'ere."

Star saw the look in his eyes and knew what he wasn't saying but was trying to convey with his look. She leaned over and kissed him on the cheek. "We will always 'andle bizness, brudda.

****

Pharaoh was looking over his financial reports with a confused look on his face. If he hadn't been insistent about being directly involved in his business operations he would've never caught it. The reports were being altered. Somebody wanted him to believe that he was making a lot less money than he actually was. Somebody was stealing from him and that somebody could only be one person. He reached over and hit the intercom button for his secretary. "Mya, please find Mr. Riley and send him to me immediately.

****

"I hate to admit it," Dior said, stepping back to admire her handiwork, "but you look better with short hair baby." She was getting turned on by his new look and pissed off at the same time. She wanted some dick but he didn't seem inclined to give her any and she wouldn't let on that he was affecting her - at least not yet - because that's what he wanted. She had to admit, though, that his arrogance turned her on to no end.

"I feel naked without my hair." He stood up to look in the mirror. "I can't lie though, people might not recognize me at first glance," he added, admiring his new Caesar haircut.

"Why even waste time trying to kill Jimmy Slim?" she questioned seriously. "We could go somewhere else and set up shop. Money is not an issue, so all we would have to do is find a connect," she added hopefully.

"Man, you tripping." He turned to look at her, his haircut forgotten.

"All I'm saying is that we could disappear and make it happen somewhere else. Fuck Jimmy Slim," she said softly as he glared at her. "I just feel like it's a waste of time."

"Check this shit out, Dior. I don't run from no man and it's never a waste of time to rid the earth of another traitor. It's no way in hell I'ma let another man, a sucka at that, live off what I built. Suck it up 'cause this soft shit is not you," he added, eyeing her.

"Nigga, fuck you. I'm not soft," she said angrily. She didn't like being called soft, but she knew that her next statement would make her just that. Even then she couldn't help herself. "But Czar, I don't want to lose you," she added looking into his eyes.

Czar saw the love she had for him in her eyes, but he couldn't compromise his character. "No matter if it's New Orleans or Cali, I'll always be me. No violation will go unchecked."

Dior was about to respond to that statement, but was interrupted by Bianca barging into the room.

"Jimmy Slim done upped the money on your head to a hundred bands," she announced somberly. She sat down on one of the beds in the room.

"What!" Dior shouted, shocked at the amount of money Jimmy Slim was using to get Czar out of the picture.

"Word up," Czar said, smirking at them. He broke out into a full smile when he thought about the motivation behind Jimmy Slim's move to put a hundred stacks on his head.

"You act like this shit is nothing to you!" Dior shouted getting upset at his nonchalant attitude. "Niggas' grandmas will try to hit you for a hundred bands." Saddened by the prospect of losing him, she was about to cry and she wouldn't break down in front of him. She went into the bathroom and slammed the door.

"What do you know that we don't?" Bianca asked curiously.

"This move reeks of desperation, B," Czar said as he eyed the bathroom door. He knew that Dior was crying inside, but he made no move to go comfort her. "He knows that I know the truth and can expose him. So now he's trying to get other people to do what he knows he can't do. Kill me."

"Oh, I almost forgot a big drug dealer named Carlos Martinez was found murdered in his home today," Bianca said as she remembered the reports she heard on the radio on her way back to the motel.

"What did you just say?" Czar asked frantically. He wanted to make sure that he heard her correctly.

"Carlos Martinez was found murdered," she repeated as she looked at him curiously. Her eyes got big as the pieces started to fit together. "That was your connect, wasn't it?" she asked excitedly.

Czar ignored her as he tried to process what she had just told him. Martinez dead? It couldn't be true, but she couldn't be lying because she didn't know who Martinez was to him, or used to be to him. At least now he didn't have to kill him. "One less body for me to catch," he mumbled to himself.

"Yeah, and Jimmy Slim gonna be in Miami this weekend too," she said when he wouldn't answer her questions.

"How the fuck you getting all of this information?" Czar asked suspiciously.

"Nigga, I'm a stripper," she said like that should be explanation enough.

Czar was about to ask why Jimmy Slim was going to Miami when it hit him. He needed a connect. A wicked smile formed on his face. "We're going to Miami," he said as a plan formed in his mind.

"Who's going to Miami?"

They both turned to find Dior standing in the bathroom doorway with red puffy eyes staring at them.

"We are," Bianca said giddily.

Dior signed and rolled her eyes at Czar before closing the bathroom door again.

"You know we gotta go shopping, right?" Bianca said seriously.

"Can you find out where he's gonna be staying in Miami?" he asked, ignoring her earlier question. He had murder on his mind.

"Watch me work," she said before pulling out her cellphone. "Give me a few minutes," she added before dialing a number. "Tilly, baby…yes, it's me. I've decided to take you up on your offer. No, no, me and Dior will meet y'all down there. Tell me the name of the hotel. Okay, I'll see you then. My pussy getting wet just thinking about that tongue. Okay, bye, baby." She hung up and smirked at Czar. "They staying at the Mandarian Oriental."

"When that nigga ask you to go to Miami?" he asked suspiciously. He couldn't afford to slip up.

"He called me earlier when I was out. I was gonna send him to voicemail like I had been doing because I knew him and Jimmy had to be mad about that night at the club and were looking for us, but I decided to see what he wanted. He begged to see me bad. He said Jimmy Slim was mad but he wasn't and wanted to see me again. I still thought he was fronting, so I told him I would think about it and hung up. I didn't have any intentions on calling him back until you needed information." She rolled her eyes at him. "My best friend is in love with you and I know that you're a stand-up guy, so miss me with all these suspicious looks and questions," she added bluntly.

"You got that," he said, appreciating her stance. "We'll leave in a couple of hours and well shop in Florida when we get there," he added over his shoulder as he headed towards the bathroom. Without knocking, he walked in and closed the door behind him.

Bianca heard the lock click on the door and sucked her teeth. She grabbed her purse and left the room. She knew how loud Dior got when she was getting fucked and being that it had been awhile for her she would wake the neighbors up. She, for one, didn't want to hear it, especially when she wasn't getting any.

****

Raul looked up when he heard footsteps stop in front of his cell. His heart dropped when he noticed that his unexpected visitor was the religious chaplain standing there with the message of death on his tongue. He slowly stood up and walked to his cell door. "My father is dead," he bluntly stated before the chaplain could open his mouth.

The chaplain was shocked that he already knew of the news he was to deliver but nothing surprised him anymore. "Do you want me to pray with you?" he asked somberly.

Raul, having already receiving confirmation about his father's murder, turned around and walked back to his bunk. He laid down and closed his eyes. He had plans to make and no amount of prayer could help those responsible for the death of his Padre. He opened his eyes when he heard the footsteps of the Chaplain fade away.

"Papa, I promise to avenge your death if it's the last thing I do," he whispered.

Vincent "Vito" Holloway

Chapter 23

"Pharaoh, I just received the message that you wanted to see…" Mr. Riley rushed into the office wondering what was so urgent. His words faltered when he saw Pharaoh had his head of security, Lion, in the office with him. "…me," he finished off when he had regained his composure.

"Have a seat, Riley," Pharaoh said coldly as he indicated the chair across from his desk.

Mr. Riley noticed his tone of voice and wondered what was going on. He started to panic when he thought that he had been found out, but then he calmed down because he knew that he was good at what he did. He did grow a little nervous when Lion came and stood behind him, but he kept his features neutral as he kept his eyes on the man seated in front of him, who was staring at him intently.

"Where's my money, Riley?" Pharaoh asked seriously. He didn't believe beating around the bush when it came to his belongings.

"Wha-what!" Mr. Riley sputtered indignantly. "Your money is exactly where it's supposed to be. I gave you the financial reports the other day and I don't like what you are implying son. I've been loyal to this family for over thirty years and my ethics and loyalty has never been questioned." He tried to stand up, but a hand as big as a Lions paw stopped him from doing so. He sat back down and glared at Pharaoh, but the sweat beads popping up on his face diminished the look.

"Never ever fix your mouth to call me son again." Pharaoh has death in his eyes. "I'm only going to ask you one more time where my money is. Do what's best and tell me where it is," he finished in a voice so cold it made Mr. Riley shiver.

Mr. Riley stared at the boy he had watched grow into a man and saw certain death in his eyes. He quickly made the decision to do what he did best: save his own ass. Pharaoh wanted him to tell him where his money was and he did just that. He told him everything.

"I appreciate your honestly, Riley, and because of that honesty, I'm going to do you a favor," Pharaoh said gently as he stood up. He buttoned his suit jacket as he nodded at Lion.

Mr. Riley caught the move and tried to jump out of his seat, but it was too late. He wasn't quick enough.

Piff! Piff! The silencer barely made any noise at all.

"Give you a quick death." He said as he watched Riley's blood run out of his ruined skull. His anger was palpable. It seemed as if all ties from his old life were being cut. He turned to look at Lion, who stood there impassively awaiting orders. "Clean this up and have my jet ready for takeoff in an hour. We have a trip to make," he instructed before leaving the room.

His secretary Mya looked up when her boss walked past her desk. She had recognized the two soft cough sounds as gunshots fired with a silencer, but that didn't faze her in the least. She knew what type of family she worked for and her loyalty was unquestioned. "Is there anything you need from me, Mr. Carter?" she asked professionally. She was careful to keep her desire for him out of her voice.

"No, Mya," Pharaoh replied softly without so much as a glance in her direction. The information Riley had just told him left him dumbfounded and he needed time to put the pieces together.

The elevator doors opened up and he stepped in but before the door could slide close he stuck his head back out. "On second thought, Mya, find Rah'mel and Chan'nel and inform them to meet me in Miami. Tell them a new Carter is requesting their services," he instructed before allowing the doors to close as he descended towards the underground garage. He knew that he would have to confront his demons sooner rather than later before they destroyed him.

****

Tango was happy to be out of prison, but the Greyhound bus was not how he expected to leave it. He envisioned a bad bitch picking him up in a fly-ass whip, but King had other plans, and since that was his homeboy, he was down for whatever. After King had beaten his appeal and was released, he had started living like royalty in the pen because King had an operation set up so nice that they were both seeing money hand over fist and didn't have to take any risks. Officers Tammy Sanchez, Monica Green, and Sergeant Christine Harris were muling so much dope into the prison for King that the yard was flooded with whatever a person needed, from crack to heroin to powder, pills, and alcohol. In prices, everything tripled from street value and since supply and demand was in full effect, the convicts paid whatever the price was to escape their harsh reality. Before King had left, he had handpicked a group of thoroughbred convicts who were never going home to sell for him and left them in charge of the operation. They had the yard in a chokehold and T.M.C. as Tammy, Monica and Christine were known to the inner circle made sure their people were good on all fronts and they were loyal only to King. If you weren't down on his team, then you were irrelevant. Tango didn't know what King was doing to keep them so loyal, but they did whatever he asked of them. He was seeing thousands of dollars with none of the risk that came with selling drugs. Every week he made sure he had King's money ready for drop off. He always received confirmation from the big homie to let him know that everything was good. Everybody on the team was eating enough to take care of family in the streets, so there was no need for petty jealousies or greed. The set-up was working so well that King was looking to expand into other prisons. He said he had already recruited a couple of females from Riker's Island to move. So things were looking good. The idea was brilliant: let the inmates move the work and they sat back collecting money.

Now that he was out, he was ready to put in some real work. He had placed a dude named Big Burn in charge of the prison so everything would continue to run smoothly on that end. He was 6'4" and 280 pounds and could lift the whole weight pile, so niggas would stay in line and he was completely loyal to King.

The fact that he also had 75 years kept niggas from acting stupid too.

Tango looked around the bus and sighed. He had a few hours before he got to the city and he needed something to do. His eyes locked in on this cutie sitting in the back reading a book. He headed her way to see if he could talk her into the small bathroom in the back and test her brain power.

****

Latoya was lying across the bed in her bedroom reading over some of her clients' files when King walked in and dropped a black duffle bag beside her before kissing her softly on the lips.

"How much is it?" she asked because she already knew that the bag contained money.

"Should be about sixty grand," King said casually as he opened the bag up and dumped it onto the bed.

"You want me to deposit this in my business account?" she asked as she started counting the rubber band stacks. This wasn't the first time he had dropped off bags of money for her to count, so she knew the routine. She also knew not to ask him about his business because the first time she did had resulted in a big fight.

"Please tell me you're not back on the corner like some petty hustler?" She remembered sneering at the bag of money he had dropped at her feet when he walked into the house. "You didn't waste any time, did you?" she asked sarcastically. She crossed her arms over her breasts, ready for a fight.

King didn't respond to her attitude because his word was being questioned and that was something that he wouldn't tolerate, especially from his woman. He walked to the refrigerator, grabbed a bottle of orange juice, and left the brownstone again without so much as a word in her direction.

Latoya stared at the door in disbelief. She couldn't believe that he just left without responding to her questions. She looked down at the duffle bag, rolled her eyes, and left it right where he dropped it.

When King returned home two days later, her whole attitude had changed. He walked into their bedroom to find her in bed with red puffy eyes. He stood there watching her, waiting.

"I'm sorry for questioning you, King, but I'm scared of losing you again." She started to cry again as thoughts of him being locked back up entered her mind.

King climbed into bed and gathered her into his arms. "Ma, I gave you my word I wouldn't pitch the block anymore. I'm doing dirt, but I'm not risking my well-being. My word is my bond and you hurt me when you questioned that. I need you to trust me 100%. Can you do that?" he asked as he wiped her tears.

"Yes," she answered quietly and from that day forth, she never questioned him again.

"You don't have to because we're taking it with us to Miami," King said over his shoulder as he entered the bathroom

"Miami?" Latoya repeated with a confused look on her face. She got up and followed him into the bathroom. "When are we going to Miami?" she asked curiously.

"Damn, can I piss in peace?" he asked playfully as he used the bathroom.

"Boy, please stop with the jokes and answer my question." She folded her arms across her chest. She knew he was playing with her because he was trying to stall her but she was hip to his games.

"You remember my boy Tango that was up north with me?" he asked after he had finished using the bathroom and was washing his hands.

"Yes," she answered as she remembered the man he was referring to. "Oh, he gets out today, right?" she asked as it came back to her.

"Right, and we're going to Miami to live it up for a few days," he said, turning around to wrap his arms around her waist.

"King, I have to work," she said, purring like a cat as he massaged her ass.

"You can't take off?" he whispered as he sucked on her neck.

"No," she said sadly. He could hear the disappointment in her voice. "I have a trial in two days and I need to stay and prepare," she added as her pussy moistened from his manipulations.

"So you don't want me to go?" he asked as he looked into her eyes. He already knew what her answer would be and had planned for it.

"No, you can go," she said, giving him a look to let him know that he wasn't as slick as he thought he was. "But you are gonna have to put this fire out you've started and make sure it stays out until you get back," she added, licking her lips as she grabbed his dick through his pants.

"Just call me the fireman, T." He laughed as he picked her up and carried her to the bed, where he proceeded to make love to her on top of the money.

****

Rah'mel and Chan'nel lived on a farm in the rural area of Guadalupe, Panama. They had no neighbors for miles on either side of them and they preferred the isolation. They lived off of what they themselves could grow. The never visited town unless they needed something essential like gasoline, oil or clothes and only if the ones they owned were too thread bare for Cha'nel to repair. They raised cows, chickens, pigs, goats, llamas and dogs. They had a hundred acres of lush farmland that they cherished and loved. When they were home, they were in their own world and hated to be disturbed. They were avid hunters and took advantage of the wild life that inhabited their lands. Both were expert marksmen and could kill a running jaguar from 300 yards away. They were the picture of an old fashioned couple who lived simply and had no need for the outside world but in reality, that was the illusion they wanted you to see. In truth, they were very wealthy and beyond dangerous. They were the two deadliest people in Panama and probably in the northern hemisphere. Most people would call them mercenaries or guns for hire, but they preferred being called assassins and they had no scruples about who they killed as long as they were adults. They did not condone the killing of children. They considered that sacrilegious, but anybody else were fair game. They didn't need contact with the outside world, but there were a select few who knew how to contact them: the ones who needed someone to disappear and could pay their fees. Outside of that, they minded their business and stayed to themselves unless they were violated which because of well-placed bribes they never were.

Rah'mel was sitting at one of the ponds situated on their land trying to catch some fish for his wife to cook for them, but he was mainly enjoying the solitude. He felt the line on his pole jerk just as his cell phone rang. He steadied his pole as he used his other hand to grab the only indulgence he allowed them to have out of his pocket and answered. After listening to the instructions he was about to decline the job, but decided to accept after doing some quick calculating in his head. He hung up the phone and looked at it with disgust on his face before sliding it into his pocket. He hated modern technology, but in his line of work it was a necessary evil. He gathered up his fishing pole and bait before going to let his wife know about the recent developments.

"We have another job in Miami," he informed her when he reached the house, where she was sitting on the front porch.

"I thought we already had a job in Miami?" she asked with a look of confusion on her face. She knew that it was a rule of theirs to never accept more than one job at a time. So she put her pen down along with her puzzle book and gave him her undivided attention.

"We do, but I figured with the money being offered for this job we could kill two birds with one stone, as the Americans say. Since both are in Miami," Rah'mel said as he returned her stare unflinchingly. He knew that his wife had a sharp mind and he respected her intelligence.

"My husband, whatever you say I'm fine with. I'm ready to kill anyway. I'm bored," she said holding up the puzzle book she was working on before he walked up. She decided to keep her reservations to herself and trust in her husband like she had been doing half of her life.

He laughed unexpectedly at the look on her face. "Me too, baby, me too."

****

Tango got off the Greyhound bus with a smile on his face. The cutie proved to be a genius with the amount of brain she gave him on the ride down to the city. He had gotten her number because she was on her way to North Carolina and he promised to check in on her if he was ever in the Tarheel state. He heard a tap on the window and saw her waving at him as the bus pulled off. She was mouthing for him to call her. He smiled because he knew he would probably never see her again.

"I see you didn't wait long."

Tango spun around and saw King leaning against a smoke grey BMW 645 convertible coupe smirking at him. "Damn, son, you out here eating," he said laughing as he embraced King.

"*We* out here eating, dog, remember that," King said seriously as he retrieved the embrace. "I told you we were going to be on top," he added, smiling.

"No doubt. So when can I get one of these?" he asked as he admired the whip.

"We can go holla at my man in VA before we hit the road," King said like it was no big deal.

"Where we going?" Tango asked as he threw his bags into the back before getting into the passenger seat.

"You thought I was kidding when I said we were going to Miami when you touched?" King asked as they pulled out of the terminal parking lot.

"Bitches better get ready for this fresh out the pen dick, 'cause I'm giving it away to every big butt Latina I see," Tango said, laughing as King let the top down.

King laughed with him as they disappeared into traffic. They had no worries and money on their minds. Life was good...or was it just an illusion?

Vincent "Vito" Holloway

Chapter 24

Sincere stood on the balcony of the condo he owned in a high rise in downtown Miami and thought about his life. He looked down at the clear blue water directly under his feet and admired the beautiful bodies splashing around and laying in the sun. He was rich beyond measure and powerful in his own right. He had politicians, police chiefs, and other local officials in his pocket to do his bidding. He had everything a man could possibly want but his life was meaningless and unfulfilled. He had failed at his once in a lifetime love, the kind of love that made everything in life better, and that would forever haunt him because he felt that it was his fault that he had lost her. It was a rare occasion when he found himself thinking about her because he was so busy but when the memories snuck up on him they hit him hard. His rivals thought that he was cold, calculating, and deadly, but they would have different opinions of him if they could see the unshed tears in his eyes whenever he thought of her.

He looked at the diamond bezel presidential Rolex on his arm and was reminded of his status in life. He had made a deal with the devil and she didn't just wear Prada. She wore Fendi, Gucci, Louis Vuitton, Christian Dior, Hermes, and Versace. He hated her existence because she was a manipulative snake and a cold bitch, but he had to admit that he wouldn't be who he was without her so he tolerated her to a point. On the other hand, he also knew that she held all of the cards being that she never revealed to him who the connect was, but he never worried about it because he was paying next to nothing for the best dope on the east coast. He could've easily gotten another connect on his own, but he knew that he would never find her prices or quality of dope anywhere, so he never rocked the boat, but he also never revealed all of his cards to her. He had a few aces in the hole in case he needed them.

"The staff wanted to know if you would be dining in tonight sir?" she asked politely. She made sure to look in his eyes unlike the other maids, who had a tendency to look down when talking to him.

He was about to answer her until he looked over her shoulder and saw his right hand man Jay Jay walking towards them with a scowl on his face. "I'll let you know in a few, Lita."

"Okay, sir," she replied before turning and brushing past Jay Jay who was stepping out onto the balcony.

Despite his mood, Jay Jay turned and admired her as she walked away. "Damn, she thick," he said when she was out of sight.

"No, you can't have her," Sincere said jokingly. Jay Jay had a habit of fucking anything with a big butt and a smile. It was gonna be his downfall one day.

"Right now she's the least of my worries," he said seriously as he turned to face Sincere.

"Another raid?" Sincere really didn't have to ask because the look on his face said it all.

"The worst one yet." Jay Jay sighed. It was frustrating to him that they were getting hit because they owned the ports and shipping yards but that fact wasn't doing them any good.

"Who has the balls to keep disrespecting me?" Sincere asked, seething mad.

"The Rude Boys." Jay Jay said the name like it was poisonous.

"That group of dread heads I've been hearing about?" Sincere asked. He remembered some of his associates mentioning their name in passing, but since they were staying out of his lane he didn't acknowledge them. But now they had his undivided attention. "Who is in charge of this gang?" He wanted to get to the bottom of the matter and the quickest way to do that was chop the head off of the body.

Jay Jay started smiling for the first time that day as he handed him a stack of photos. "That's him right there," he said pointing to a man in one of the pictures.

Sincere studied the picture and felt a sense of unease settle into the pit of his stomach. There was something eerily familiar about him, but he couldn't put his finger on it. The feeling persisted though. "What's his name?" he asked, never taking his eyes off the picture.

"He goes by Majestic. They say he's cut his dreads off now. The two women with him are his sisters Star and Sky." Jay Jay saw how Sincere was looking at the picture and understood why. He had developed that same feeling when looking at Majestic's face. He couldn't figure out who he was or where he knew him from. In the end it didn't matter because he had to die. "Should I order the hit?" he asked as he shook his head to dislodge the thoughts from his mind.

Sincere was about to give his consent when something stopped him. He couldn't shake the feeling that he knew him from somewhere but he had never seen the man a day in his life. "Nah, let's hold off until after my birthday party. I want to enjoy the rest of the week without worrying about anything except getting older," he joked.

"But I can take him and his sisters out right now with minimal attention," Jay Jay said seriously. He didn't understand his position on this issue. All disrespect must be handled swiftly. *I know he's not going soft on me*, he thought sourly.

"We might not have to kill them," Sincere said thoughtfully as a plan formed in his mind.

"What!" Jay Jay shouted in surprise. These motherfuckas been hitting our shipments and you want to let them live?" He looked at Sincere like he was senile.

"Didn't you say that they were terrorizing the city a few weeks ago and had niggas scared to sell on the blocks, which in turn effects my money?" Sincere asked, looking at him sharply.

"Even more reason to put them in the dirt now," Jay Jay said sarcastically as if the answer was obvious.

"What if I became their connect and put them to work for me?" he asked, watching Jay Jay's reaction.

Jay Jay stared at him as he ran it through his mind. He had never thought of that and it was brilliant.

Sincere smiled because he knew that Jay Jay was seeing the advantages just like he was. "If I started supplying them, we could

Vincent "Vito" Holloway

turn an enemy into an ally - a dangerous one at that." He said making perfect sense.

"I could see that working," Jay Jay said grudgingly." You want me to set up a meeting?"

"Nah, we'll worry about it next week," Sincere said waving him off. "You know where the bitch is?" he asked with a frown on his face.

Jay Jay knew exactly where she was, but before he could answer, she chose that time to make her presence known. They both turned and watched her approach.

"Speaking of the devil," Sincere mumbled under his breath when he saw her. He had to admit that at sixty-five years old, she still put a lot of women to shame with vigorous exercise and a good plastic surgeon. She still had the face and body of a thirty-year-old. Charlene Lloyd had barely changed since they had met that fateful day twenty-five years ago - a day he wished he could forget.

"Sincere, we must talk," she said as she came to a stop in front of them

"What's up, Charlene?" Jay Jay asked as he admired her body in the sundress she was wearing.

She shot him a look of disgust and ignored him. "Well?" she said, tapping her foot impatiently as she looked at Sincere.

"About what?" he asked as he focused on a point over her head. He hated looking at her because she reminded him of his lost love: her daughter Shinah.

"Privately, please," she said before she grabbed his hand and dragged him into the condo Even though he couldn't stand being in her presence, he needed her, so he let himself be dragged along with her.

Jay Jay chuckled at the look of disgust on Sincere's face.

Charlene looked over her shoulder and gave Jay Jay a long look before they disappeared around the corner to the bedrooms.

Jay Jay caught the look, but paid it no mind. "Let me go find out what's up with this maid," he mumbled to himself as he went to get his dick wet.

208

****

A couple of hundred yards from the beach sat a speedboat with a couple who looked like tourists. They looked uncomfortable in their beach attire, but no one was around to notice. They appeared to be fishing, but were in fact doing reconnaissance.

"The target has been sighted," Cha'nel said to her husband after removing the binoculars from her eyes.

Rah'mel reeled in his fishing line and set his rod on the floor of the boat. He nodded at his wife, acknowledging her words as he moved to the wheel of the boat.

"Phase two," he said curtly as he cut the engine on and sped away, slowly at first so they wouldn't attract unwanted attention, but once he hit open water he pushed the throttle.

Cha'nel paid no attention to her husband's abruptness with her as she sat down with her puzzle book. She was so bored. She just wanted to kill.

****

"Girl, we putting these Miami bitches to shame," Bianca said, laughing at the jealous looks they were getting from the women on the beach because their men were following them with their eyes like bees attracted to honey.

"We cornbread fed and these bitches eating salads," Dior said, slapping five with Bianca. They both had on bikinis that left little to the imagination.

"Girl, you are crazy," Bianca said, laughing as they continued up the beach. "I could get used to this," she added wistfully.

"Me too, but Czar not going for it," Dior said. She wanted a change of scenery in her life. Dallas was cool, but it couldn't compare to Miami. "Or at least he not as long as Jimmy Slim's bitch ass still alive," she added, hating him more and more every day.

"Speaking of Czar, ain't that him?" Bianca said, pointing up the beach. "He with some other nigga and they look like they having a good time." she added as she tried to see clearly.

"Where?" Dior asked as she looked where Bianca was pointing. "That look like him, but he stayed at the room to get some rest." She was trying to see their faces.

"I swear that's Czar. Look how he's moving, just like Czar." Bianca was sure she was right.

"Well, we about to go see," Dior said, stomping off. She was pissed off.

There could only be one reason she could come up with for Czar to lie to her and that was to cheat. He had her fucked up if he thought it was going down like that. She had put up with Chrissy because she was there first, but that bitch was dead and she wasn't playing second to nobody again. She wasn't going for the bullshit.

Chapter 25

"Son, this shit is fucking bananas down here," Tango said excitedly as he and King parked at the beach. "And you got two fly-ass New Yorkers riding in nice-ass 'verts so you know the honeys eyeing us." He got out of his brand new money green BMW 645 convertible. It was identical to King's in every way except for the color. They had stopped in Virginia to buy the car and to go shopping for a new wardrobe for Tango.

"Yeah, son, I'm thinking I might want to move down here with my shorty. I could get used to this weather." King leaned against the trunk of his car. He wasn't dressed like a walking billboard for Drug Dealers 'R Us, but if one knew their fashions, then they would recognize the designer labels draping his frame. He had on a pair of Gucci Handsome logo sneakers, all white with the telltale red and green strip on the sides, a pair of white-washed jean shorts by True Religion, a white short-sleeved Ralph Lauren button up shirt with a pair of chrome Gucci sunglasses covering his eyes. His Gucci collection stainless steel white rubber strap watch and two karat diamond earrings in his ears set off the outfit perfectly.

"I could see myself moving down here retiring and getting fat, but I wouldn't bring no chick," Tango said, laughing as he eyed the ladies on the beach wearing next to nothing. "That would be like bringing sand to the beach," he added like even the thought was out of the question.

King laughed at his homeboy's antics, but they were completely different breeds. He guessed that was the reason they clicked the moment they were thrown into a cell together. "Fucking mad different women is cool when you're young, dumb, and full of cum, but dog, it's nothing like having a true Queen on your team who is down for whatever." His thoughts turned to Latoya waiting at home for him.

"Nigga, you only 25 and I'm 26, so you bugging," Tango said before he broke into a huge smile. "Let me find out T got you pussy whipped," he said teasingly.

"Whatever, man," King said before hopping back into his whip." "I'm tired, so I'ma head back to the hotel to take a nap."

"Oh, you gotta check in," Tango said, laughing again. He was so happy to be out of prison it was crazy. In prison one day, on South Beach the next. Ridiculous!

King stuck his middle finger up at Tango as he pulled off, which only made him laugh so much harder.

****

"That nigga saw as well as heard your loud ass, so he took off," Dior said when she saw the car take off.

"I thought you said that wasn't Czar?" Bianca asked, smirking at her.

"I don't think so, but we are about to find out," Dior said, not sure as she once was. "Excuse me."

****

Jay Jay was staring at the picture of Majestic, trying to figure out where he knew the face from but he couldn't put his finger on it. He sighed and put the pictures back into the folder from which they came. He would figure it out sooner or later.

****

Tango had been watching the two thick women with barely there bikinis on as they walked up the beach, so he was surprised when one of them spoke to him.

It must be the car, he thought with a smirk as he studied them. *Both of them bad, but I like the red bone with the red hair and tattoo on her face*, he concluded to himself. "You talking to me?" he asked, pointing at himself.

"Who am I looking at?" Dior spat as she rolled her eyes at his stupid question. She hated stupid questions. She also heard his accent and knew that he was from up North somewhere.

Tango smiled, but he kept silent. He liked her attitude, but she had him fucked up for one of them county niggas. His pimp hand was strong.

"Why your homeboy leave so fast?" she asked, getting straight to the point.

"And you are?" he asked, totally ignoring her question. He could tell that she had something on her mind and he wanted to know what it was but on his terms and definitely on his time.

Bianca saw that he wasn't just going to answer their questions and Dior wasn't helping matters with her attitude. Dior was about to say something else and she knew it would be something smart and sarcastic, so she intervened. "My name is Bianca, but people call me B, and this my best friend Dior." She locked eyes with him.

Tango let his smirk blossom into a full smile because he knew that she knew her friend was going about things all wrong, so she took over the conversation. Dior was the leader, but Bianca was slick in her own right. "My name is Tango." He decided to indulge her.

"Why did Czar leave so fast?" she asked slyly.

"Czar?" he asked with a confused look on his face. "Who the fuck is Czar?" he asked suspiciously.

"That's Dior's boyfriend. He just pulled off in that silver convertible," Bianca said seriously.

"I don't know who this nigga Czar is, but the nigga that just pulled off is my comrade King. We just got here today from New York, and I'm pretty sure he don't know no Czar either."

Bianca just looked at him and smiled.

Tango noticed her expression and it dawned on him that she had gotten the information they were looking for. He burst out laughing and shook his head. "You slick, shorty." He looked her up and down.

Bianca was returning the favor and she had to admit that he had swag. She recognized all of the designer labels he was wearing and felt her pussy get wet. She was a true label whore. "I'm always slick," she said with a smirk.

Tango caught her double meaning and knew that he was gonna fuck her. It was all in her eyes. "Since you tricked me out of the info you were looking for, are you gonna let me get your number?" he asked jokingly.

"No, but you can give me yours." She didn't want him blowing her shit up after she gave him the pussy.

Tango went to the glove compartment and searched for a pen and something to write on. He found a golf pencil and a napkin and wrote down the number to his new cell phone. He handed it to her and said, "Don't have me wasting my time."

"Believe me, if I do call you, it will definitely be worth your time, not a waste." She took the napkin from his hand and walked off with Dior.

Tango watched their asses bouncing in their bikinis and couldn't wait for her to call.

****

Jimmy Slim was in a bind because he had no connect. Ever since Martinez had been found murdered in his home, his hold on the streets was becoming tenuous because he was running out of work, and the only reason niggas fucked with him in the first place was because he had the plug and charged lower than anybody else. Nobody but Czar knew who his connect was so the niggas in the streets didn't know that his connect was dead, and if he had anything to say about it, they never would. That's why he was in Miami with Tilly: to find a connect. After finding out about Martinez, he tossed a couple of hundred thousand dollars in a few duffle bags, hopped in his box Chevy and headed to the Sunshine State.

His other problem was Czar himself. The longer he stayed alive the greater his chances were at getting exposed. He had did what he was told to do and put a hundred grand on his head and he knew that would bring the shooters out but would it be enough? Czar had a reputation for putting his hammer game down and niggas were hesitant to try him head up. He had known Czar for most of his life so he knew the hesitation was justified but he put the money on his head and hopefully he would be dead when he got back home. Right now he had to find a connect.

"How do you plan on finding a connect?" Tilly asked before he sparked up a freshly rolled blunt.

Leave it to this nigga to put the problem on front street, he thought wryly. It was a question he couldn't answer quite yet. At the moment they were riding through Little Haiti just as they had rode through other areas of Miami, Opa Locka, Carol City, and Little River and they were getting the same looks now that they were getting earlier in the day. The looks said, "Who the fuck are you? And we will get you if you slip". Jimmy Slim had noticed these looks and was sure Tilly had too. That's why they hadn't stopped for too long in any one area, just long enough to pump gas, buy some blunts, and get going. The task seemed daunting but he was determined to find a connect.

"We'll hit all the hot spots and let the connect find us," he answered, hoping it would be as easy as he made it seem. "Pass me that blunt," he demanded as he pulled to a stop at a read light.

"I guess the connect just gonna fall out of the sky, huh?" Tilly said sarcastically.

Jimmy Slim wasn't paying any attention to Tilly because his eyes were locked onto a man who had just walked out of a restaurant across the street. He was surrounded by dreads, but the familiar way he moved had his mouth dry and his heart rate up. He figured the man felt him staring because he suddenly turned and stared directly at him. His heart almost stopped when he saw his face. It was Czar. Or was it? It looked like him, but there was something different about him, subtle but different. This man had a low cut. He knew Czar wore cornrows, but he figured that he could've cut his hair. The man was staring at him so hard that the dreads around him turned to see what had captured their boss's attention, and there was no doubt in his mind that he was the boss. You could tell by their quiet deference to him. He knew that they wouldn't hesitate to kill him if the order was given. They were killers. The look in their eyes gave them away. They were cold and bottomless. A million questions were racing through his mind. What was Czar doing in Miami? Was he in Miami? What was he going to do? He broke out in a cold sweat when he saw that the man had a gun in his hand now. He was terrified and his heart felt like it would burst out of his chest.

"Yo, what the fuck is wrong with you?" Tilly asked, looking at Jimmy Slim like he was crazy.

Jimmy Slim continued to ignore Tilly and stare at the man he was sure to be Czar. He almost jumped out of his seat when he heard a horn honk behind him. He looked up and saw that the light was green.

"Pull the fuck off, nigga," Tilly said nervously. He had seen the dreads with their guns out and was now as terrified as Jimmy Slim.

Jimmy Slim pulled off, but he shot a quick glance back at the men and saw that they were following his car with their eyes. He wasn't able to calm down until they disappeared from his rear-view. A connect wasn't so important anymore, especially compared to his life. He had to find out if Czar was in Miami and if he wasn't, then who was that nigga?

Chapter 26

"Right there. Right there...that's my spot!" she screamed out as she tossed her ass back into him.

Jay Jay looked at the woman on all fours underneath him and smirked. From the first moment he met her he couldn't resist her. He looked down at her ass, at how it waved every time he pumped his dick into her, and understood perfectly why he couldn't resist her. "Whose pussy is this?" he asked as he increased his pace.

"You know it's yours, Jason!" she screamed as she gripped his dick with her pussy muscles. "Cum with me, baby!" she yelled as she felt her orgasm building.

When Jay Jay felt her pussy contracting around his dick, he couldn't stop himself from cumming. He pulled out and shot his semen all over her back and ass. He sighed and laid down on the bed. She always put him to sleep after sex.

"Why do you always do that?" she asked indignantly she stood there glaring at him with her hands on her hips.

Jay Jay laid there smirking at her. She acted so prim and proper all the time. He loved treating her like a whore whenever he could. He knew she loved it too. "You like it," he said aloud.

"Whatever, Jason," she said, turning and stomping to the bathroom.

He watched her stomp off and almost laughed aloud. She couldn't fight the smirk he knew was gracing her lips. He knew she loved being fucked rough. He was getting another erection at the sight of his kids sliding down the crack of her ass and the inside of her thighs. He was turned on, but his mind snapped back to business when he saw her step back into the room. "When are we going to finish this?" He didn't have to elaborate because she knew exactly what he was talking about.

"Everything is coming together nicely and soon you will be in a position to do what you want." Her eyes locked onto his erection.

"I'm tired of words. I need results," he said, ignoring the lecherous look in her eyes. "It's been too long already. This nigga needs to go. I don't know why you won't let me just put two in his head and be done with it," he added angrily.

"Tell me what Sincere is doing," she demanded, meeting his eyes briefly before locking back onto his dick.

Jay Jay thought about telling her about the picture to see if she could jog his memory, but decided against it. "He's only worried about his birthday," he replied with a half-truth.

She looked at him for a few seconds as if to gauge his sincerity before going back to his dick. She licked her lips as she walked towards the bed. She got on all fours and crawled over to him. She locked eyes with him and saw his apprehension. "Just trust me," she said before her mouth enveloped his erection.

Jay Jay sighed as her warm, wet mouth surrounded him. That was the crux of his problem. He had never trusted her.

****

Czar heard the door to the room they were renting open and sat up on the bed. He watched Dior and Bianca walk in and laid back down. The last couple of weeks had been tense and he hadn't been getting much sleep. His body was tired and he needed rest before he got caught slipping. He was about to close his eyes again when he looked at the expression on Dior's face. She was upset about something. He looked over at Bianca to see if she would clue him in, but she just smirked and rolled her eyes before walking into the bathroom. He closed his eyes again and waited for her to speak because he knew she wouldn't wait long.

"You know a nigga named Tango?" she asked seriously.

He opened his eyes and saw that she was standing in front of the television with her arms folded across her chest and a frown on her face. He didn't answer right away because he moved on his own time and because he knew that people didn't ask questions without reason so he stayed silent and took the time to peruse her body. He was remembering their sex session before they left Dallas and he couldn't help picturing her shaved pussy with his name tatted right above it.

King Killa

Dior saw the look in his eyes and knew what he was thinking. She was getting wet from thinking about it also but that didn't matter at the moment because she was pissed off. "Answer my question," she demanded.

Czar looked at her like she was crazy but answered her anyway. "No, I don't know a fucking Tango. Nigga sound like a fruit loop with a name like that." He grilled her.

"What about a nigga named King?" she asked, confused. She could tell he was telling the truth and that was baffling to her.

"Who the fuck is King and what's up with the twenty questions?" he asked glaring at her.

"You been here the whole time we've been gone?" she asked, ignoring his look.

"Where else have I been?" Czar asked, looking at her like she was on drugs. "You bugging," he added before closing his eyes again.

She knew he was going to ignore her, but she didn't care because she was satisfied. He had answered her questions, albeit reluctantly, but his answers only seemed to raise more questions - like who was that nigga on the beach? She never got a chance to contemplate that before Bianca came out of the bathroom dressed and looking good.

"We going to Club 305 tonight," she announced, looking at them with a proud look on her face.

"Why?" Dior asked, narrowing her eyes suspiciously. She knew her best friend had something up her sleeve.

"It's supposed to be the hottest club on South Beach and..." she was drawing it out for dramatic effect. "...that's where Tilly and Jimmy Slim going to be tonight," she finished with a smile.

"And that's where them bitch ass niggas gonna die." Czar said seriously as he sat up. He was tired of the cat and mouse games. It was time to end this.

****

Majestic was still standing in front of his family's restaurant, staring in the direction of where that car had disappeared. The fear on the driver's face was on his mind. It was like the man knew him, but he was sure that he had never seen him before because he didn't forget a face. One thing was for sure: now he would never forget his face and if he ever saw him again he would find out exactly where he knew him from right before he stopped his heart from beating. He put that in the back of his mind as he thought about the raid last night. It was too easy, plain and simple. That might sound strange coming from a man who robbed for a living, but they had pulled it off with ease and his people were being lulled into thinking the jobs were easy so they could let their guards down then walk into a trap but that would never happen because he was a lion and lions never let their guards down. He didn't like the way the situation was looking, so far they were getting away relatively unscathed but the safety and protection of his brethren came first, and for that reason alone, he decided to cancel all raids until they got rid of the product they had stored in their warehouses.

"Brudda."

He turned and saw his sister Star beckoning him into the restaurant. Before he pulled the door open to enter, he got the feeling he was being watched again. He turned around and scanned the street for anything suspicious but couldn't find anything out of the ordinary. He knew his father was giving him a warning, so he would take heed and be extra careful. If only he had looked up, he would've seen death staring back at him.

"Come ta di back. Mem wanta talk ta ya," Star said, leading him to the office located at the back of the restaurant. When they entered, they found Sky talking on the telephone. After a couple of more minutes she hung up the phone,

"We found someone ta buy di product from ye," she said to her brother.

"Who?" Majestic asked, wondering who they could've found so fast to buy that much product. He had just told them what he wanted to do that morning. He saw his sisters look at each other nervously.

"E a pale skin," Star said quietly as she waited on his reaction.

Majestic almost laughed at their nervousness. He understood their reactions because by rule, anyone who didn't like black-skinned people were Babylon and pale skins were usually in that category. But he needed to get the product off and all money was green. "E willin ta buy it all?" he asked.

Sky and Star both relaxed when he didn't get mad. Their father had always taught them to be wary when dealing with pale skins and they thought he would refused to deal with him. "'E wan to deal but 'e wan to meet wit' ye ta talk de prices out," Sky said giving him the details.

"Do ye trust 'im?" Majestic asked. If his sisters wanted to deal with him, then he would deal with him.

"'E never dealt shady wit' us," Star said seriously.

"Set de meeting up fa tonight." He put his trust in his only remaining blood relatives.

Sky picked up the phone to do as he asked.

****

Chaka smiled as Majestic turned around and scanned the street. She knew he could feel her watching him and that feeling had him on alert. She could've killed him anytime she wanted, but there was something about him that intrigued her. She was a hunter, and she recognized the hunter in him. Over the last couple of weeks, she had stalked his movements and had a number of opportunities to dispose of him but she had admired the way he conducted the raids his mob went on. A few times they had been on the verge of getting caught and she had taken care of the problem. She was a creature of the night and loved to hunt, especially another hunter. So she sat back and waited because she wanted this kill to be personal. To a certain degree she respected the Lion she recognized inside of him so she was more than a little disappointed that he didn't bother to look up when he was scanning his surroundings.

She was about to remove the binoculars when she saw a familiar form enter into her line of sight. It was a man dressed in old rags, begging the pedestrians for money. To a normal observer, it would appear that he was a poor person begging, but to a seasoned hunter, she knew better. The differences were subtle, but she was trained to recognize those differences. The sharpness and intelligence of the eyes. The fake limp he was using. The way he was watching everything and everyone around him. The last couple of days she had noticed him around, but didn't pay him too much attention other than to catalogue his presence and move on. She didn't believe in coincidences and his appearance today only reinforced that. She recognized the hunter in him and wondered whether Terror had sent back-up to make sure the job got done. The thought enraged her, but just as quickly she extinguished her anger as a new thought fought its way into her consciousness. Did Terror send someone not to clean up after her, but to clean her up? She wouldn't put it past him, and the thought amused her. But if he did, then she would make sure he died with the regret.

She watched the man for a few more minutes then decided it was time to meet her what? Equal, adversary, maker or next victim? The last one seemed the most likely but she never underestimated her opponents she loved the opportunity to test herself. One thing she knew for sure was that one of them was going to die.

****

King was taking a nap in his room when he was awakened by somebody banging on his door. "Who the fuck is this beating on my door like the police?" he questioned as he sat up and looked at this watch.

He couldn't believe he had been resting for two hours. He had come back to his room, checked in with Latoya, and laid down. He was sleeping good too and now somebody was knocking like the

SWAT team. He got up and padded silently over to the door. Without bothering to ask who it was, he snatched the door open. He was about to curse out whoever it was until he saw Tango stranding there with a smirk on his face.

Tango saw the look on his face and burst out laughing. He pushed past him and into the room. He flopped onto the bed and said, "Don't tell me we're in Miami and you in your room taking a nap." He got himself under control and looked at his homeboy in the eyes. "Please tell me it ain't so," he mocked.

"Motherfucker," King said in Spanish, knowing Tango couldn't understand it.

"Oh, you want to switch languages up on me," Tango said, laughing. "Buenos dias to you too, nigga," he added, chuckling.

King tried to stay mad, but Tango's laugh was infections and he started chuckling. "Yo, son, you are a clown." He went into the bathroom to brush his teeth and take a piss.

"Son, you shouldn't have left," Tango said getting animated. "It was so many bitches out there, it was bananas."

"How many of them let you get your dick wet?" King asked after he finished in the bathroom.

"Only two, but the day is still young," Tango said rubbing his hands together like Dr. Evil.

"Only two?" King asked, looking at his right hand man like he was slipping. "Its three o'clock in the afternoon, son," he added jokingly.

"I got plenty of time to add to that. Them hoes go crazy when I tell them I just got out of them modern day plantations," Tango said, smirking.

King shook his head and changed the subject. "What we getting into tonight?" he asked.

"It's whatever, but I heard about this new nightclub on South Beach that's official. We can check that out," Tango said as he checked his watch.

"V.I.P. all the way, son," King said, ready to live it up with his man. "I don't do lines, fam," he added with a cocky smile. He remembered how he felt when he got out of prison and he only did a few years, so he could imagine how Tango was feeling after doing ten years in the bing.

"That's what up. I'll meet you in the lobby at eight o'clock tonight," Tango said getting up and walking to the door. "I got a Latina that's waiting on this New York fly guy," he added before walking out.

King chuckled and grabbed his keys. Since he was up, he wanted to explore Miami. He didn't like being in unfamiliar surroundings.

Chapter 27

Back in New York, Marco pulled to a stop at a red light in Manhattan. He was stressed out because he couldn't figure out what King was planning to do. From all indication, he wasn't going to do anything, but he knew better. He grew up with King and knew firsthand how cunning and ruthless he was. He knew better than to think that King wasn't going to do anything about the betrayal he and Sophia had dealt him. Death before dishonor was King's favorite motto and he took that to heart. He knew King would do something, but he didn't know when or what he would do. He was so stressed out over waiting on King to do something that he had started using cocaine. He was up to snorting a ball of powder a day. Adding that to the stress he was already feeling had turned him into a paranoid madman, but he didn't care because he felt like the powder calmed him down and kept him on point, so he indulged. In reality, he knew he couldn't see King when it came to the gangsta shit, but the powder had him thinking he was super-man and he was ready for whatever, or at least he thought he was.

As he waited for the light to change, he reached into his ash-tray and grabbed the bag of powder he kept there for emergencies. As he was feeding his nose, he looked up and saw a homeless man with a spray bottle and a rag getting ready to clean his windshield. He was about to hit his horn and tell him to get the fuck away, but decided against it and went back to feeding his nose. A few seconds later, a tap on his driver's side window drew his attention. He looked to his left and froze. He found himself staring down the barrel of a gun. He looked up into the dirty face holding the gun and recognized Lil Trey smirking at him. Before the bullets entered his face, he thought about another of King's favorite mottos. The one who has to react is at a disadvantage. I strike first.

Lil Trey dropped the gun in Marco's lap and disappeared into the chaos his gunshots had created.

Vincent "Vito" Holloway

Chapter 28

Chaka stopped in front of a clothing boutique and acted like she was perusing the wares, but she was really checking on the progress of the man tailing her. She smiled when she caught sight of him in the reflection of the glass. He was still playing the role of the destitute man and she had to admit that it was a good disguise - but not good enough to fool someone of her skill. It was time to make the introductions, she thought grimly as she left the window and started moving through the pedestrian traffic crowding the sidewalks. She picked up her pace, knowing it would force her pursuer to speed up and abandon his façade. She suddenly changed directions and crossed the street. She glanced over her shoulder and openly smiled at the man. He had now given up all pretense at secrecy and was trying in vain to keep her in his sights. She spotted the alley she had scouted earlier and turned into it. Now it was about to get fun.

****

Rah'mel knew he had been spotted, but it didn't bother him in the least. In fact he found the chase exhilarating, but he was also angry because the information they had received on the target was obviously incomplete. This woman he was stalking was more than met the eye. He recognized the ability in her and had witnessed it the last couple of days he had trailed her. She was a hunter and he realized that she had made him days ago but filed him away as insignificant. He took solace in the fact that his disguise had worked to a certain degree but that wasn't good enough because he strived for perfection and his prey had made him a failure in his profession. He assuaged his pride with the knowledge that his prey would soon be dead.

He casually walked past the mouth of the alley and out of his peripheral vision, he saw that the alley was empty. He continued on for a few feet then pivoted and entered the alley. He stopped and scanned the alley. His prey was hiding from him and he loved it. He imagined that he smelled her fear as he slowly stalked further into the alley. He looked at the other end of the alley and saw the traffic moving by. An amateur would've run straight through to the other side thinking the prey kept going but he was a professional, the best and he knew without a shadow of a doubt that she were still in the alley. He sensed that she was hiding and that gave him a shot of adrenaline knowing that she feared him enough to hide from him but it wouldn't be enough to save her because she had to die.

He saw a black sedan pull to a stop at the top of the alley and sit idle. When a group of Jamaicans got out of the car with guns in their hands, he knew then that he had walked into a trap. He didn't even have to look over his shoulder to know that there was also a group of Jamaicans at his back. The trap was well set and well thought out. He had walked right into it. The thought of being trapped didn't bother him as much as it would some people. He actually smiled because he knew that they were underestimating him, and that would cost them their lives. He put his hands into the pockets of his dirty coat and felt his smile grow because he knew that they wouldn't be expecting his next move. But a voice up above him wiped the smile from his face just as fast as it appeared.

"Mem wan know why ye are 'unting mem?" Chaka asked from where she was standing on the roof. She looked down at him and smiled as she trained her gun on him.

Rah'mel looked up at her and felt his smile reappear. He had noticed the fire escape on the side of the building but had dismissed it because he hadn't thought that she could've made it up there fast enough. Obviously he had underestimated her once again and this time it looked like it was going to cost him, but the idea of death didn't faze him. He had accepted that death was a hazard in his profession a long time ago. So he was prepared for whatever the outcome was going to be.

"You know one of us has to die," he told her in his heavily-accented voice.

Chaka stared at him with confusion etched onto her face. Here was a man standing below her casually with his hands in his pockets like he didn't have a care in the world, like he didn't have gun-toting Jamaicans on both sides boxing him in, and he was talking like he had a chance to make it out alive. He was too confident for the situation. She looked into his eyes, then at his smile, and it suddenly clicked. She noticed his hands moving, but it was too late. She pulled the trigger on her gun, but he was already moving.

Rah'mel moved so fast it was like he had an extra set of arms. He dived into a roll and came up with two grenades in his hands. He tossed one towards each end of the alley, where the Jamaicans still hadn't reacted fast enough. Before they even landed, he had two pistols in his hands, firing at his prey, but she was on the move also. The grenades went off and the concussions took care of the threats on the ground with him. In ten seconds, he had turned her advantage back into an even playing field, and he hadn't even broken a sweat. Time was of the essence now because he heard the sirens in the distance. He hadn't killed a cop in a long time, but he would. He knew he might die, but he was determined to take his target out before he did He had a perfect kill record and he planned on it staying that way.

He spotted his prey running. It wasn't away from him, like he anticipated, but towards him. His shock at her boldness froze him for a fatal second and before he could bring his guns around, he felt the first bullet enter his stomach right below his bulletproof vest, proving that he was dealing with a professional. He had enough strength left to bring his guns up and get off a few shots, but they were off balance and missed his target. Another bullet hit him in his leg and he buckled, but he kept his balance. Another bullet shattered his kneecap and he finally crumbled to the ground. He managed to hold onto one of his guns, but another bullet hit his wrist, almost cleaving his hand from his arm, and he dropped it. He watched in hatred and admiration as his target somersaulted down to the ground and walked over to him. She stood over him with a look of pity in her eyes and that look had him angrier than his defeat. He spit at her and cursed her in his native Spanish. Death had finally won the battle, but he was ready. He closed his eyes, contented with his fate. His last thought before he took his last breath was of his wife standing over his killer like she was standing over him.

Chaka stood there for a few seconds staring at the body lying at her feet and felt her anger return in force. Somebody had put a contract on her head and she knew what she must do. She turned and climbed back up to the roof as graceful as a spider just as the police and ambulances pulled onto the scene. She didn't like being toyed with and whoever it was would pay. Terror will come, Terror will Reign!

Chapter 29

Lil Trey showed up at the apartment Sophia had shared with Marco, suspicious, wondering why she had called him. Since he had just left Marco's snake ass sitting in traffic with holes in his face a few hours ago, her call made him even more suspicions, but there had been something in her voice that made him come see her. He contemplated turning around and leaving for a few seconds before deciding to satisfy his curiosity. He knocked on the door and waited for her to answer.

"Who is it?"

"It's me."

Sophia opened the door and stood there smiling at him. "What's up, Lil Trey?" she asked before walking away from the door.

Lil Trey walked in and shut the door behind him. His eyes were stuck on Sophia as she walked away from him. She had on a wife beater with no bra and a pair of small shorts that could barely cover her ass. Her feet were bare, showing off her pedicured toes. Her nails were done. Her hair was curled to frame her face, highlighting her beautiful features. She was sexy but she was also grimy, a perfect combination in the gritty streets of New York City. He kept his mind on the matter at hand.

"Why did you call me over here?" he asked, getting right to the point.

"You want something to drink?" she asked as she ignored his question. She looked over her shoulder and smiled as she noticed him staring at her ass as it bounced in her shorts. This is going to be easy, she thought as she walked into the kitchen. She opened the refrigerator and grabbed two sour apple Smirnoffs. She walked back into the living room, handed one to him, and sat down beside him on the couch. She faced him and folded her legs Indian style, giving him a clear view of her goodies.

"Where Marco at?" Lil Trey asked casually as he locked in on her pussy print. The way her pussy lips were outlined told him that she didn't have on any panties. He felt his dick get hard.

She screwed her face up at the mention of Marco. Since King had been out their relationship had disintegrated and she was glad. He wasn't on her level at all and that was a turn off. "Fuck that puto. I haven't seen him in a couple of days," she said truthfully.

Marco was history, thought Trey as he smirked at her response. His eyes were glued to her pussy lips. He decided then that he was going to fuck her - King be damned.

Sophia saw how he was staring at her and spread her legs wider to give him a better view. "You see something you like?" she asked seductively.

Lil Trey heard the tone she used to ask him that question and looked up. When he saw the look on her face, he leaned over and kissed her.

She opened her mouth to him willingly and let her tongue dance with his. She reached for the buttons on his shirt and started taking it off of him. He stepped back and hurriedly undressed. He set his gun on the coffee table and stood before her naked. Sophia felt her eyes grow big because he was hung. Her pussy instantly grew wet.

He grabbed her hand and stood her up. He pulled her wife beater up over her head and tossed it behind him. He attacked her extended brown nipples. His dick grew another inch when she moaned in his ear. He pulled her shorts down to her ankles and helped her step out of them.

Sophia couldn't wait any longer. She had set out to seduce the young boy, but now that it was happening, she found herself wanting to feel him inside of her. She bent over on the couch and poked her ass up in the air.

Lil Trey saw her pretty pink pussy lips and dived in.

"Ooh papi, mierda!" she screamed out when he entered her. "Fuck me…fuck…me… Oooh…my…God…papi. That's my spot." she moaned as she met him thrust for thrust.

"Damn, you got some good pussy." He grunted as he sped his hips up. He couldn't believe that he was fucking her. When he used to see her with King, he used to fantasize about her, but his respect and loyalty to King were absolute and he kept his thoughts to himself. Now he had her naked and bent over the couch listening to her ass cheeks slap against his stomach as he fucked her from the back.

"Trey, I'm cumming. Can you cum with me, papi?" she moaned. "Cum...with...me papi!" she screamed as her orgasm erupted from her pussy.

Lil Trey felt his nuts tighten up and knew that he was about to cum. He took a few more long strokes before pulling out and shooting his sperm all over her ass cheeks and back. "Damn, you got some good panocha." He sighed as he sank onto the couch.

Sophia stood up on shaky legs. She couldn't deny that he had put it on her. She had ulterior motives, but that didn't mean she couldn't enjoy him also. "You want to take a shower with me?" she asked, smiling at him.

Lil Trey stared at her and felt his dick start to rise again but he declined her offer. "Nah, ma, you go ahead. I have to catch my breath before I get another shot at that panocha," he said, smiling at her.

"Okay, but don't keep me waiting too long," she said, walking off to the bathroom. *That was too easy*, she thought smiling to herself.

Lil Trey saw his kids on her ass and back and grabbed his dick. Her pussy was as good as he had fantasized. He could see why King had been in love with her. He waited until hearing the shower cut on before getting dressed. He walked to the bathroom to tell her he was leaving. He listened to her singing and smiled. *I put it down*, he thought smugly. He pulled the curtain back and the sight of her phat ass was almost enough to make him get undressed again and get into the shower with her but he had shit to do.

Sophia felt the cold air hit her body as the curtain was pulled open and smiled. *I got this young boy sprung already*, she thought with a smile as she turned to face him but her smile disappeared when she saw that he was fully dressed. She was about to ask him where he was going, but the question never got the chance to be asked. She tried to scream when she saw him standing there with a gun pointed at her, but the bullets that entered her mouth silenced her forever.

Lil Trey looked at her body lying in the tub with blood pooling around her and shook his head. *What a waste*, he thought. "Fucking conniving whore," he said as he went back into the living room and wiped down anything he might've touched. On his way out of the door, he grabbed the Smirnoff she had offered him when he first got there. *No need to disrespect her hospitality*, he thought sardonically as he opened the front door with the sleeve of his shirt and disappeared back into the streets that raised him.

Chapter 30

"Mike Billy. Long time," Sincere said when he walked into the V.I.P. room on the third level of Club 305.

"Too long," Mike Billy said looking at Sincere with an appraising eye. "Even though your absence has you looking like a million bucks," he added, smirking

"Miami is where we come to retire and get fat," Sincere said, laughing as he patted his stomach. "You're not doing too bad yourself," he added, looking around the lavish V.I.P. room.

"I'm just a country boy trying to make it," Mike Billy said with false modesty in his slow drawl.

Sincere chuckled at Mike Billy's fakeness. He knew that he was a self-serving snake, but he put up with it because he served his purposes and a greedy person was always predictable. "Did you set everything up as I asked?"

"My people at the doors have the picture your people emailed me and when the infamous leader of the Rude Bwoys shows up, he will be directed to the elevator that you just walked out of," Mike Billy said, running down the plan. "The question I want to ask is, do you think he will want to work for you?" Just like everybody else in Miami, he had heard about Majestic and his brutal efficiency at running his gang of ruthless islanders and he couldn't see him being subservient to anybody, especially to the man he had been robbing over the last couple of months. He wouldn't be surprised if he didn't show up at all.

"He would be smart to," Sincere said seriously. "I'm offering him Miami on a silver platter - my silver platter - and I know he will take it."

Mike Billy was quiet for a few minutes as he stared at the look on Sincere's face. "So he has no choice then?" he asked, drawing his own conclusions.

"Oh, he has a choice," Sincere said seriously. "Accept or die."

****

"Man, I can't believe I let you talk me into going out to-night," Jimmy Slim said as he navigated through the foot traffic in the parking lot at Club 305 as he tried to find a place to park.

"Slim, you tripping, man. You act like you scared of this nigga or something," Tilly said as he looked over at Jimmy Slim. "Fuck that nigga Czar. We bust our guns too. So if that was him earlier today, we'll dirt nap his ass. We from the dirty. Already!" he added, getting hyped.

"Already!" Jimmy Slim said, feeding off of his enthusiasm a little bit as he found a parking spot.

"Man, look at all these boppers out here," Tilly said, watching all the breasts and ass walking past the car. "If we can't find a connect here tonight, I don't know where we gon' find one," he added, thinking that the ballers and drug dealers would be out in force tonight.

Jimmy Slim looked out the windshield at all the women walking by with dresses on that left nothing to the imagination and knew that Tilly was right. The big dope boys should be out in force tonight and he planned on connecting with one. But that wasn't what was worrying him though. It was Czar. He had a feeling that was him earlier in Little Haiti and if he was in Miami, he was gonna strike. The question that kept tugging at his consciousness was that if that was Czar then why did he let him drive away instead of slumping him over the steering wheel like he had seen Czar do to so many other niggas? And if that wasn't him, then who was it? These were questions he couldn't answer.

"Let's smoke this blunt before we get in line," he told Tilly. He needed to calm his nerves and orange Kush was the only thing that could do it.

****

"Brudda, calm down," Star said as she noticed Majestic eyeing everyone around them. "Enjoy yerself," she added as they stood in line to get into the club.

King Killa

"Yea 'ave fun, brudda," Sky said, laughing at his suspicious look. "Dis de 'ottest club on South Beach.".

"Mem don't like de big crowd, mon." He was getting the feeling that something wasn't right and he trusted that feeling because he knew it was his father talking to him. He grabbed the lion head pendant around his neck and the feeling only intensified. "Dey not gwan try to take mem guns?" he asked his sister.

"Don't worry, we know de people at de door," Star said reassuringly.

That calmed Majestic down a little bit, but he still had the feeling something wasn't right and as long as that feeling persisted he would stay on point.

They finally made it to the front of the line and the bouncer directed them to an elevator that led to the V.I.P. suites. He got the feeling that the bouncer was specifically looking for him. Maybe he was tripping, but he didn't think so. They piled onto the elevator and waited until it ascended to the floor they were looking for. He kept his hands close to his guns because the closer they got to their destination, the more the feeling intensified until it was almost suffocating him. The elevator doors opened up into a large, lavish V.I.P. room that was surrounded by glass windows that looked out into the club where the people were dancing and enjoying themselves. He ignored his surroundings because his eyes were locked onto the only two occupants in the room besides them. One was the pale skin he assumed they were supposed to meet, but it was the other man sitting with him that drew his attention. This man radiated power, and the way he was looking at him made him feel like the man knew him from somewhere even though he had never seen this man a day in his life. Despite feeling that something wasn't right was like a black cloud hanging over the room, he kept his eyes locked with his. All would be revealed soon enough.

Sky and Star saw the way their brother was staring at the man with the powerful aura and grew confused, but before they could ask him what was wrong, Mike Billy spoke, easing the tension a little bit.

"Welcome," he said cordially as he stood up and walked towards them. "I'm so glad you could make it. Let me make introductions. As you know already, I'm Mike Billy and the man still sitting is the great..." He held out his hands towards him. "Sincere Loyalty," he finished with a chuckle.

Majestic heard the name and everything clicked into place. It was a set-up. Sitting before them was the man they had been raiding over the last couple of months. He should've listened to his instinct and now they would probably die, but they were going to kill as many as they could before they left earth. He pulled his pistols out and he didn't have to look at his sisters to know that they were doing the exact same thing.

"Whoa, whoa!" Mike Billy threw his hands in the air and backed up. "What's going on?" He asked with a look of abject terror on his face.

Nobody paid him any attention as they kept their guns pointed at him and the man calling himself Sincere, who despite four guns pointed his way was smiling, like he expected this exact outcome.

"So we finally meet?" Sincere finally asked as he downgraded his smile to a smirk.

****

"Son, check these bitches out," Tango said as they walked towards the line outside of the club. "I'm guaranteed to fuck tonight," he added excitedly.

King couldn't front. There were some beautiful women walking around. But he wasn't checking for anything, even though there were a few who might tempt him under the right circumstances. He looked at the line wrapped around the building and knew that there was no way he was standing in it.

"Yo, we going straight to the front to pay these bouncers to let us in V.I.P. We stars, so we should party with the stars." He led the way. He ignored the grumbling and complaining coming from the fronting-ass niggas in line. If they were doing it big like their clothes and jewels indicated, they wouldn't be stuck in no line.

"You think they will let us in with our ratchets?" Tango asked. He did not want to be without his hammer in case something popped off. Everybody knew country boys hated on New York cats.

"Cash rules everything around me. You know that," King said, pulling the bouncer to the side to whisper into his ear. But to his surprise, he didn't have to pay anything before they were escorted to a private elevator and told to go to the third floor.

"Son, they didn't even search us," Tango said as the elevator started moving.

"Yeah, it was like he was waiting on us," King said, replaying the scene in his head.

"Whatever, kid. I'm ready to pop bottles," Tango said as the elevator doors opened up. "What the fuck!" he shouted.

King snapped out of his daze when he heard Tango shout. He looked up to see two females with dreads pointing guns at them, but that wasn't what had him fucked up. "Who the fuck are you?" he asked, not believing what his eyes were seeing.

****

Majestic heard the elevator moving and knew somebody else was coming up. "Sky, Star!" he barked but it was pointless because they were already moving. They both turned and trained their guns on the elevator. When the doors opened up, they both gasped which made him glance over his shoulder to check the scene. What he saw staring back at him made his heart skip a beat.

"What the fuck!" Tango shouted when he saw the guns pointed at them

"Who the fuck are you?" King asked, not believing what his eyes were seeing.

"No, mon," Majestic said as he turned to fully face the elevator. "De question tis, who de fuck are ye?"

"What the hell is going on here?" Mike Billy asked, but he was ignored.

"What the hell?" Sincere mumbled to himself, not believing his eyes. Something wasn't adding up.

****

"Girl, Czar needs to hurry up so we can go in," Bianca said impatiently. "We saw Jimmy Slim and Tilly pull in, so he should've killed them clowns by now," she added jokingly.

Dior wasn't even paying attention to her. She was staring in the direction Czar had disappeared around the back of the club. As soon as Jimmy Slim and Tilly pulled into the club parking lot, Czar had gotten out of the car and started moving. It had been ten minutes now and he hadn't returned yet. She had wanted to go with him but he forbid it and told her to go wait in line with Bianca. They were waiting, but not in line because they didn't want to be noticed looking nervous. They were standing off to the side waiting on him to reappear. She was about to go find him despite his instructions when they heard the gunshots.

"Bye bye, Jimmy Snake and good pussy eating Tilly," Bianca quipped.

****

Jimmy Slim needed two blunts before he calmed down. The car was so cloudy he and Tilly couldn't even see out of the windows. "Let's go," he told Tilly. He opened up his door, but it hit something solid and bounced back against him. "What the fuck?" he mumbled as he looked up. He felt his bladder loosen and barely stopped his bowels from releasing when he saw Czar standing there with a scowl on his face and his two gravediggers pointed directly at him. He started to beg for his life, but he couldn't seem to get his voice to work.

"Your bitch, snake ass thought you was gonna make it, didn't you?" Czar asked with a smirk on his face before he made Jimmy Slim's face unrecognizable with his slugs. He saw Tilly get out of the car, and try to run but he put two slugs into his back, stopping him short. The parking lot was going crazy with people running away from the sound of gunshots. He pulled his hoody up over his head and used the confusion to get back to Dior and Bianca.

"Let's go," Dior said, ready to get away from the murder scene.

"We're going into the club. The police gonna be looking at everybody leaving right now," he said, ignoring her. His hands were still on his guns inside his hoody pockets. "We not standing in no line either," he added as he peeped how long the line was.

"They have a separate V.I.P. line," Dior said anxiously. She was ready to get away from the crowd because it felt like everybody was staring at them.

"Good. Let's go." Czar's eyes constantly moved over the crowd to make sure nobody was paying too much attention to him.

He followed behind Bianca and Dior as they made their way towards the bouncers manning the V.I.P. line. Before they got there, he pulled his hoody down to look less suspicious. When they arrived, the bouncer stared at Czar so long they thought it was going to be a problem, but he didn't ask any question as he led them to the elevator that led to the V.I.P. rooms. He hadn't even searched them.

"That was strange," Dior said when she thought about how the bouncer had acted.

"Girl, what you complaining about?" Bianca asked, making sure her makeup was on point. "We got into V.I.P. for free," she added, smiling.

Czar knew that anything in life was rarely free, but he didn't say anything. He had seen how the bouncer had looked at him and something in the look didn't sit well with him, but his senses were on point, ready for anything. He was just glad to put distance between him and his two bodies, especially with the murder weapons still in his pockets.

He felt the elevator slow to a stop. He couldn't wait to get a drink in his system just to knock the edge off a little bit. The doors opened up and the scene before his eyes made him bring his guns back out.

Dior looked at Czar then at the people in the V.I.P. room and back again. "Oh my God," she whispered.

"This shit is crazy," Bianca said seriously. She couldn't believe her eyes.

King Killa

Chapter 31

Jay Jay was in the security room of Club 305 watching the cameras to make sure everything was good when the door opened up behind him. He looked over his shoulder and saw Charlene walk in. As his eyes took in her outfit, he felt his dick get hard. She had on a short, loose-fitting dress that showed off her curves. The vanilla white color set off her chocolate skin tone perfectly. Her matching vanilla white Jimmy Choo six inch heels accentuated her legs and made his dick that much harder. "I thought you were with Sincere?" he asked with a smirk on his lips.

"He's with Mike Billy and I didn't want to sit through that meeting, so I came to see you," she said, walking over to the camera monitors and feigning interest in what was going on down on the dance floors. She saw his dick get hard when he looked at her and loved teasing him. The power she had over the opposite sex was intoxicating.

"So what did you want to see me about?" he asked as he stared at her ass. The shortness of her dress was teasing him.

Charlene looked over her shoulder and smirked when she saw his eyes glued to her backside. "I don't know, but I figured you might want something to eat." She bent over at the waist to get a closer look at the monitors - or at least that's what she wanted it to look like. She felt her dress rise up above her ass a little with the maneuver, revealing her true intentions. She smiled when she heard his sharp intake of breath. She didn't have on any panties and her pussy was staring him in the face. "So are you hungry?" she asked teasingly as she rolled her hips side to side, permeating the air with her scent.

Jay Jay stared at her pussy lips glistening with her wetness and licked his lips. He had an affinity for eating pussy and she knew that. He almost laughed aloud when he remembered what an older woman told him one time before about country boys: "All y'all are good for is eating cornbread and eating pussy." He took his fingers, spread her lips, and licked her clit since it was staring at him.

243

"Oh my goodness," Charlene moaned, shuddering as pleasure shot through her body. "I love your tongue, Jason," she said, closing her eyes to enjoy the sensations she was feeling. He used his tongue to fuck her pussy as he sucked on her clit. He was soothing with his manipulations because he was so good. In record time he had her on the verge of climax.

"Oh my God, I'm cumming!" she screamed when she felt herself cresting that wave of pleasure. She opened her eyes for a brief second and was about to close them again when movement, a familiar gait on one of the monitors, caught her attention. She tried to focus on what she was seeing, but it was hard to concentrate when she was getting her pussy ate. When realization of what she was seeing hit her at the same time her orgasm shook her body, she screamed not out of pleasure, but horror.

Jay Jay heard her scream and smiled as he sucked up all of her juices. He pulled his dick out and was about to dive in but she suddenly stood up. "What you doing?" he asked, bewildered as he held his dick in his hand.

"It's that time," Charlene said seriously as she smoothed out her dress. On the surface she was calm and collected, but inside her heart was beating out of control.

"Time for what?" Jay Jay asked with a confused look on his face. He put his dick back into his pants because it didn't look like he would get a chance to use it.

Charlene looked at him with a frown on her face.

Realization dawned on him when he finally figured out what she was talking about. "How do you know it's time?" he asked urgently as he wondered what brought on her mood change.

"Just trust me, Jason," she said before she opened the door and walked out.

Jay Jay watched her leave with a frustrated frown on his face because she always left him in the dark with her pat answer to all of his questions. He sighed and followed behind her. He locked the door behind him and thought about the path he had chosen over twenty years ago. However, it turned out it was too late to turn back.

King Killa

****

"What is going on, Mike Billy?" Star asked, staring in bewilderment at the people gathered in front of her. She was trying to keep her gun hand steady, but the shock of what she was seeing was getting to her.

"How in the hell should I know?" he said, just as confused as she was. "I don't know about you, but I'm looking at three people that look exactly alike," he added, stating the obvious. He glanced over at Sincere, but it seemed as if he was in deep thought.

Majestic, King, and Czar were staring at each other in silence. None of them knew what to say about the unexpected turn of events.

"Czar, I didn't know you had any brothers," Dior said as she studied all three of them. She had a hard enough time dealing with one Czar. She couldn't imagine three.

"I don't have any brothers," he responded skeptically. He didn't sound too sure of his answer, so he kept his guns steady.

"King, you know these niggas?" Tango asked curiously. He wasn't as shocked as some of the others.

"Nah, son, but something not right with this picture," he said seriously as he continued to stare at his mirror images. "It can't be a coincidence that we're all here at the same time. Somebody set this shit up."

Majestic kept his peace because he was confused. He had thought that Star and Sky were the only remaining family he had left, but that was obviously not the case. The alternative would mean he was adopted, and that thought didn't sit right with him either.

Sincere was staring at the three men, trying to figure out why they seemed so familiar to him. He studied their features and it finally clicked. "It can't be," he said to himself. It all made sense now. He was about to say something when a door opened up and in walked Charlene followed by Jay Jay looking fearful about something. "So nice of y'all to join us," he said sarcastically.

Charlene stopped in her tracks when she saw that Sincere and Mike Billy weren't alone. Once she realized who was having a Mexican standoff in the room, her mind started racing. She couldn't believe it. It seemed as if all of her well-laid plans were falling apart right before her eyes, but she was the Queen for a reason, and she could improvise. "Let me guess," she said, pointing. "Majestic, King, and Czar," she finished with a smirk on her face.

"Who are you?" King asked with confusion etched onto his face because she knew his name.

Czar and Majestic kept silent. The surprises were not having the same effect anymore. It was obvious a lot more was going to come out of the closet soon. In the meantime, they were just trying to figure out what was going on.

"You wouldn't believe me even if I told you, sweetheart," Charlene said with a sad smile on her face.

Sincere watched her and her actions only confirmed his suspicions, but before he could say anything about it, he heard the elevator moving so he kept silent.

"If another one of y'all walk off that elevator, I'm through," Bianca said, rolling her eyes. Shit was getting too crazy.

Everybody's eyes were on the elevator, but they didn't expect the series of events that unfolded when the doors opened up.

When the doors opened up, out ran a group of men dressed in all black carrying semi-automatic handguns. At the head of the group was a big man with locs that resembled a lion's mane and wild eyes. The expression on his face dared anybody to move. They spread out in a semi-circle and kept their guns trained on the people in the room. Then out of the elevator walked an expensively-dressed man who gave off the aura of power. He had on a black double breasted suit with black wing tips. He carried a pistol in his hand and wore a scowl on his face. His eyes swept over the crowd of people in front of him, but they only registered one face.

Jay Jay saw the man lock onto him and everything fell into place. It was the kid he left alive at his graduation after murdering his parents. His one act of mercy would turn out to be his biggest mistake. He reached for his gun anyway.

Pharaoh saw the man who had changed his life, who had mistakenly left him alive, and felt his rage burn out of control. He saw the man go for his gun and raised his own. He methodically disarmed the man with well-placed shots to his arms and knees. He walked over and kneeled beside the whimpering man who murdered his parents and looked him in his eyes.

"I want you to look into my eyes and remember that the little boy you left alive at your own peril is the cause of your demise," he whispered before placing the barrel of his gun to his temple and putting him out of his misery. He stood up and spit on his corpse. "That was more mercy than you showed my parents," he added bitterly. He briefly closed his eyes and relived the worst day of his life. He could feel a weight lift off of his shoulders now that his parents' murderer was no longer breathing. After reopening his eyes, he blinked a few times as if he was just realizing that he was standing in a room full of people, three of whom looked exactly as he did. He looked at each of their faces and saw the confusion that he was sure was mirroring his own. He noticed that the men he assumed were his brothers were standing back to back with their guns pointed at his men. He thought it would be a good idea to ease the tension in the room.

"Lion, stand down," he ordered. After his men did just that, he turned back to his brothers. "Now what are your names?" he asked curiously.

Czar and Majestic kept silent as they eyed the men in black. They might've lowered their guns, but theirs were still up. King had finally managed to pull his gun out, but he was trying to figure out the situation in front of him. He had been raised as an only child by his parents, who were now dead, but it was obvious he had three identical brothers.

"Pharaoh, meet your brothers: Majestic, Czar and King." Charlene said, trying to improvise and regain control of the situation. Jason's untimely death had set her back, but she was still determined to succeed with her plans.

"Who are you?" Pharaoh asked with a frown on his face. He had almost killed her because she had been standing too close to his parents' murderer, but she wasn't showing too much emotion over his death, so he gave her the benefit of doubt.

Sincere was watching the drama unfold and couldn't believe how blind he had been. He had thought that he was one step ahead of Charlene, but she was more cunning than he gave her credit for.

Charlene had a huge smile plastered on her face because she was still manipulating the board. She was about to answer Pharaoh's question when she heard the elevator start moving again.

"If number five steps off of that elevator, will somebody please shoot me?" Bianca said jokingly.

The elevator doors slid open and out walked a beautiful woman with a serene look on her face.

"Who the fuck are you?" Dior asked with confusion lacing her words. She wished somebody would explain to her what was going on.

"Yeah, who are you?" King asked quietly. He was starting to put the pieces together.

The woman stepped forward and smiled at him.

"Oh shit," Mike Billy said fearfully.

"Shinah," Sincere whispered in disbelief. He had long given up hope of ever seeing her again.

"I'm your mother, baby," she said as she locked eyes with each of her sons. She felt tears well up in her eyes at seeing them healthy and grown, but she blinked them away. There would be time for emotions later. "I promise to explain all later," she told them sincerely. "Can I please borrow this?" she asked King as she reached for his gun.

A confused King reluctantly gave her the pistol. *My mother?* he thought, confused.

"How are you doing, Mother?" Shinah asked, glaring at the woman who gave birth to her.

Charlene looked at her daughter in utter contempt. This was an unforeseen development, but she felt like she could still come out on top. "Nice to see you," she spat.

Shinah smirked as she admired her mother's bravado. Here she was still acting like everything was okay, but she would learn soon enough the error of her ways. "Please have a seat. We have a lot to discuss later," she said sweetly before raising the gun she was holding and shooting her mother in her right kneecap.

"Ahhh! You dirty little bitch!" Charlene screamed as she clutched her bleeding leg. She seemed not to care that she still didn't have on any panties. "I'ma kill you, you little bitch!" she continued to scream.

Shinah walked over and wrapped her hair around her fist. Then she leaned down and whispered something into her mother's ear. Whatever she said made Charlene shut her mouth and whimper in silence. She turned to her boys, who were staring at her like she was Assata Shukar. "As you now know, this is your grandmother," Shinah told them before turning and locking eyes with Mike Billy.

He remembered vividly all of the degrading things he did to Shinah, sometimes against her will. Hell, he even dreamed about them sometimes. But now his dreams had turned into a nightmare as she stood there glaring at him with a gun in her hand. He started to explain that he had grown up, but she cut him off.

"Me and you will definitely have a conversation that's long overdue," she told him coldly.

Mike Billy didn't know whether to be happy for the respite or dread the conclusion of the conversation she was referring to.

Sincere was watching everything unfold and wondered how the love of his life and Mike Billy even knew each other, but that was on the periphery of his mind as he stared at the woman who had run out of his life. He watched as she raised the gun she was carrying and pointed it directly at his face. His heart felt like it was breaking all over again.

"My dear sons," Shinah said with a strained voice. She didn't expect to still love him after wanting him dead for the past twenty plus years, but seeing him and the love swimming in his eyes for her almost broke her resolve. She shook her head because she had to avenge the one person who loved her beyond anything on earth, the person Sincere murdered for her mother: her father. "I want you to meet your father," she whispered before her finger tightened on the trigger.

"Shinah, don't."

She heard the voice, but couldn't believe her ears. She turned and saw him walk into the room looking exactly as she remembered him. With nerveless fingers, she dropped the gun and ran to him with tears running down her face. She jumped into his arms and hugged him. "Daddy," she whispered through her tears.

Bianca and Dior looked at each other and wondered what the hell was going to happen next.

The End of the Beginning

Cha'nel stared down at the grave of her companion - her friend, her confidante, her husband Rah'mel - and wished she could cry. She had made arrangements for his body to be transported and buried on their land because she wanted his final resting place to be the sanctuary they shared together. Seeing him hooked up to all of those machines killed something inside of her. When the doctor told her that there was no chance of him recovering, she kissed him one last time before disappearing from the hospital. The rage she felt over what happened to him grew with each passing day and would not abate until the one who did him harm was dead. She knew death was a part of their profession, but she couldn't accept his, at least not without avenging him first. She wouldn't be able to live without him, not because she couldn't, but because she felt like she didn't deserve to be enjoying life while he laid in the cold earth. From that day forth, she had only one mission in life, and that was to avenge her husband's death. Nothing else mattered. As long as she accomplished that, she would be able to die in peace. She would join him wherever he was as soon as she killed the woman calling herself Chaka.

"I'm coming, baby. I promise," she said in halting English. She had vowed to herself to never speak Spanish again in memory of him. She laid the flowers she was holding onto his grave and walked away. Not once did she look back. She had a body to catch.

****

Terror walked into the house he shared with his family in Windsor. He had just gotten back from meeting with Jamaican politicians Seaga and Manley in Annoto Bay. He had to pay the customary bribes or "gifts" to make sure the authorities were in his pocket. He was in a celebratory mood and wanted to take his family out to dinner in new Kingston.

"Anyel, Marley, Anyella, Nika!" he called out as he walked through the house. He had a beautiful, loyal wife, two gorgeous daughters, and a son who would one day take over his reign. He walked into the living room and stopped cold. He tilted his head back and let out a primal roar. Hanging from his ceiling fan were the heads of his family. He pulled his gun out and checked the house. After finding it empty, he went outside and searched the grounds. He was so blinded by rage that he didn't know what he was doing. He was moving off instinct. After finding the grounds empty, he went back into the house and whipped out his cell phone.

"Find Chaka and bring de bitch ta mem. Scour de island. Mem don't care 'ow ye do it, but find de bitch." He hung up and stared at the words written on the wall in what he assumed was his family's blood.

Death before dishonor!

Terror will come. Terror
will reign!

"Find 'er before she finds mem," he said quietly as he sank to his knees and cried.

To Be Continued…
King Killa 2
Coming Soon

King Killa

Lock Down Publications and Ca$h Presents assisted publishing packages.

BASIC PACKAGE $499
Editing
Cover Design
Formatting

UPGRADED PACKAGE $800
Typing
Editing
Cover Design
Formatting

ADVANCE PACKAGE $1,200
Typing
Editing
Cover Design
Formatting
Copyright registration
Proofreading
Upload book to Amazon

LDP SUPREME PACKAGE $1,500
Typing
Editing
Cover Design
Formatting
Copyright registration
Proofreading
Set up Amazon account
Upload book to Amazon
Advertise on LDP Amazon and Facebook page

***Other services available upon request. Additional charges may apply

Lock Down Publications
P.O. Box 944
Stockbridge, GA 30281-9998
Phone # 470 303-9761

Submission Guideline

Submit the first three chapters of your completed manuscript to ldpsubmissions@gmail.com, subject line: Your book's title. The manuscript must be in a .doc file and sent as an attachment. Document should be in Times New Roman, double spaced and in size 12 font. Also, provide your synopsis and full contact information. If sending multiple submissions, they must each be in a separate email.

Have a story but no way to send it electronically? You can still submit to LDP/Ca$h Presents. Send in the first three chapters, written or typed, of your completed manuscript to:

**LDP: Submissions Dept
Po Box 944
Stockbridge, Ga 30281**

DO NOT send original manuscript. Must be a duplicate.

Provide your synopsis and a cover letter containing your full contact information.

Thanks for considering LDP and Ca$h Presents.

NEW RELEASES

THE PLUG OF LIL MEXICO by CHRIS GREEN
THE STREETS STAINED MY SOUL 3 by MARCELLUS
ALLEN
KING OF THE TRENCHES 2 by GHOST & TRANAY ADAMS
MOB TIES 5 by SAYNOMORE
KING KILLA by VINCENT "VITTO" HOLLOWAY

KINGPIN KILLAZ IV

STREET KINGS III

PAID IN BLOOD III

CARTEL KILLAZ IV

DOPE GODS III

Hood Rich

SINS OF A HUSTLA II

ASAD

RICH $AVAGE II

MONEY IN THE GRAVE II

By Martell Troublesome Bolden

YAYO V

Bred In The Game 2

S. Allen

CREAM III

By Yolanda Moore

SON OF A DOPE FIEND III

HEAVEN GOT A GHETTO II

By Renta

LOYALTY AIN'T PROMISED III

By Keith Williams

I'M NOTHING WITHOUT HIS LOVE II

SINS OF A THUG II

TO THE THUG I LOVED BEFORE II

By Monet Dragun

QUIET MONEY IV

EXTENDED CLIP III

THUG LIFE IV

By **Trai'Quan**

THE STREETS MADE ME IV

King Killa

By **Larry D. Wright**

IF YOU CROSS ME ONCE II

By **Anthony Fields**

THE STREETS WILL NEVER CLOSE II

By **K'ajji**

HARD AND RUTHLESS III

THE BILLIONAIRE BENTLEYS II

Von Diesel

KILLA KOUNTY II

By Khufu

MONEY GAME III

By Smoove Dolla

JACK BOYZ VERSUS DOPE BOYZ

By Romell Tukes

MURDA WAS THE CASE II

Elijah R. Freeman

THE STREETS NEVER LET GO II

By Robert Baptiste

AN UNFORESEEN LOVE III

By **Meesha**

KING OF THE TRENCHES III
by **GHOST & TRANAY ADAMS**

MONEY MAFIA II

LOYAL TO THE SOIL II

By **Jibril Williams**

QUEEN OF THE ZOO II

By **Black Migo**

THE BRICK MAN IV

By King Rio

VICIOUS LOYALTY II

Vincent "Vito" Holloway

By Kingpen
A GANGSTA'S PAIN II
By J-Blunt
CONFESSIONS OF A JACKBOY III
By Nicholas Lock
GRIMEY WAYS II
By Ray Vinci
KING KILLA II
By Vincent "Vitto" Holloway

Available Now

RESTRAINING ORDER **I & II**
By **CA$H & Coffee**
LOVE KNOWS NO BOUNDARIES **I II & III**
By **Coffee**
RAISED AS A GOON I, II, III & IV
BRED BY THE SLUMS I, II, III
BLAST FOR ME I & II
ROTTEN TO THE CORE I II III
A BRONX TALE I, II, III
DUFFLE BAG CARTEL I II III IV V VI
HEARTLESS GOON I II III IV V
A SAVAGE DOPEBOY I II
DRUG LORDS I II III
CUTTHROAT MAFIA I II
KING OF THE TRENCHES

King Killa

Vincent "Vito" Holloway

By **Meesha**
A GANGSTER'S CODE I &, II III
A GANGSTER'S SYN I II III
THE SAVAGE LIFE I II III
CHAINED TO THE STREETS I II III
BLOOD ON THE MONEY I II III
A GANGSTA'S PAIN
By **J-Blunt**
PUSH IT TO THE LIMIT
By **Bre' Hayes**
BLOOD OF A BOSS **I, II, III, IV, V**
SHADOWS OF THE GAME
TRAP BASTARD
By **Askari**
THE STREETS BLEED MURDER **I, II & III**
THE HEART OF A GANGSTA I II& III
By **Jerry Jackson**
CUM FOR ME I II III IV V VI VII VIII
An **LDP Erotica Collaboration**
BRIDE OF A HUSTLA **I II & II**
THE FETTI GIRLS **I, II& III**
CORRUPTED BY A GANGSTA I, II III, IV
BLINDED BY HIS LOVE
THE PRICE YOU PAY FOR LOVE I, II ,III
DOPE GIRL MAGIC I II III
By **Destiny Skai**
WHEN A GOOD GIRL GOES BAD
By **Adrienne**
THE COST OF LOYALTY I II III
By **Kweli**

King Killa

A GANGSTER'S REVENGE **I II III & IV**

THE BOSS MAN'S DAUGHTERS I II III IV V

A SAVAGE LOVE **I & II**

BAE BELONGS TO ME I II

A HUSTLER'S DECEIT I, II, III

WHAT BAD BITCHES DO I, II, III

SOUL OF A MONSTER I II III

KILL ZONE

A DOPE BOY'S QUEEN I II III

By **Aryanna**

A KINGPIN'S AMBITON

A KINGPIN'S AMBITION **II**

I MURDER FOR THE DOUGH

By **Ambitious**

TRUE SAVAGE I II III IV V VI VII

DOPE BOY MAGIC I, II, III

MIDNIGHT CARTEL I II III

CITY OF KINGZ I II

NIGHTMARE ON SILENT AVE

THE PLUG OF LIL MEXICO II

By **Chris Green**

A DOPEBOY'S PRAYER

By **Eddie "Wolf" Lee**

THE KING CARTEL **I, II & III**

By **Frank Gresham**

THESE NIGGAS AIN'T LOYAL **I, II & III**

By **Nikki Tee**

GANGSTA SHYT **I II &III**

By **CATO**

Vincent "Vito" Holloway

THE ULTIMATE BETRAYAL
By **Phoenix**
BOSS'N UP **I , II & III**
By **Royal Nicole**
I LOVE YOU TO DEATH
By **Destiny J**
I RIDE FOR MY HITTA
I STILL RIDE FOR MY HITTA
By **Misty Holt**
LOVE & CHASIN' PAPER
By **Qay Crockett**
TO DIE IN VAIN
SINS OF A HUSTLA
By **ASAD**
BROOKLYN HUSTLAZ
By **Boogsy Morina**
BROOKLYN ON LOCK I & II
By **Sonovia**
GANGSTA CITY
By **Teddy Duke**
A DRUG KING AND HIS DIAMOND I & II III
A DOPEMAN'S RICHES
HER MAN, MINE'S TOO I, II
CASH MONEY HO'S
THE WIFEY I USED TO BE I II
By Nicole Goosby
TRAPHOUSE KING **I II & III**
KINGPIN KILLAZ I II III
STREET KINGS I II
PAID IN BLOOD **I II**

King Killa

CARTEL KILLAZ I II III
DOPE GODS I II
By **Hood Rich**
LIPSTICK KILLAH **I, II, III**
CRIME OF PASSION I II & III
FRIEND OR FOE I II III
By **Mimi**
STEADY MOBBN' **I, II, III**
THE STREETS STAINED MY SOUL I II III
By **Marcellus Allen**
WHO SHOT YA **I, II, III**
SON OF A DOPE FIEND I II
HEAVEN GOT A GHETTO
Renta
GORILLAZ IN THE BAY **I II III IV**
TEARS OF A GANGSTA I II
3X KRAZY I II
STRAIGHT BEAST MODE
DE'KARI
TRIGGADALE I II III
MURDAROBER WAS THE CASE
Elijah R. Freeman
GOD BLESS THE TRAPPERS I, II, III
THESE SCANDALOUS STREETS I, II, III
FEAR MY GANGSTA I, II, III IV, V
THESE STREETS DON'T LOVE NOBODY I, II
BURY ME A G I, II, III, IV, V
A GANGSTA'S EMPIRE I, II, III, IV
THE DOPEMAN'S BODYGAURD I II
THE REALEST KILLAZ I II III

Vincent "Vito" Holloway

THE LAST OF THE OGS I II III
Tranay Adams
THE STREETS ARE CALLING
Duquie Wilson
MARRIED TO A BOSS I II III
By Destiny Skai & Chris Green
KINGZ OF THE GAME I II III IV V VI
Playa Ray
SLAUGHTER GANG I II III
RUTHLESS HEART I II III
By Willie Slaughter
FUK SHYT
By Blakk Diamond
DON'T F#CK WITH MY HEART I II
By Linnea
ADDICTED TO THE DRAMA I II III
IN THE ARM OF HIS BOSS II
By Jamila
YAYO I II III IV
A SHOOTER'S AMBITION I II
BRED IN THE GAME
By S. Allen
TRAP GOD I II III
RICH $AVAGE
MONEY IN THE GRAVE I II
By Martell Troublesome Bolden
FOREVER GANGSTA
GLOCKS ON SATIN SHEETS I II
By Adrian Dulan
TOE TAGZ I II III

King Killa

LEVELS TO THIS SHYT I II
By Ah'Million
KINGPIN DREAMS I II III
By Paper Boi Rari
CONFESSIONS OF A GANGSTA I II III IV
CONFESSIONS OF A JACKBOY I II
By Nicholas Lock
I'M NOTHING WITHOUT HIS LOVE
SINS OF A THUG
TO THE THUG I LOVED BEFORE
A GANGSTA SAVED XMAS
By Monet Dragun
CAUGHT UP IN THE LIFE I II III
THE STREETS NEVER LET GO
By Robert Baptiste
NEW TO THE GAME I II III
MONEY, MURDER & MEMORIES I II III
By **Malik D. Rice**
LIFE OF A SAVAGE I II III
A GANGSTA'S QUR'AN I II III
MURDA SEASON I II III
GANGLAND CARTEL I II III
CHI'RAQ GANGSTAS I II III
KILLERS ON ELM STREET I II III
JACK BOYZ N DA BRONX I II III
A DOPEBOY'S DREAM I II III
By **Romell Tukes**
LOYALTY AIN'T PROMISED I II
By Keith Williams
QUIET MONEY I II III

Vincent "Vito" Holloway

THUG LIFE I II III

EXTENDED CLIP I II

By **Trai'Quan**

THE STREETS MADE ME I II III

By **Larry D. Wright**

THE ULTIMATE SACRIFICE I, II, III, IV, V, VI

KHADIFI

IF YOU CROSS ME ONCE

ANGEL I II

IN THE BLINK OF AN EYE

By **Anthony Fields**

THE LIFE OF A HOOD STAR

By Ca$h & Rashia Wilson

THE STREETS WILL NEVER CLOSE

By K'ajji

CREAM I II

By Yolanda Moore

NIGHTMARES OF A HUSTLA I II III

By King Dream

CONCRETE KILLA I II

VICIOUS LOYALTY

By Kingpen

HARD AND RUTHLESS I II

MOB TOWN 251

THE BILLIONAIRE BENTLEYS

By Von Diesel

GHOST MOB

Stilloan Robinson

MOB TIES I II III IV V

By SayNoMore

King Killa

BODYMORE MURDERLAND I II III
By Delmont Player
FOR THE LOVE OF A BOSS
By C. D. Blue
MOBBED UP I II III IV
THE BRICK MAN I II III
By King Rio
KILLA KOUNTY
By Khufu
MONEY GAME I II
By Smoove Dolla
A GANGSTA'S KARMA I II
By FLAME
KING OF THE TRENCHES I II
by **GHOST & TRANAY ADAMS**
QUEEN OF THE ZOO
By **Black Migo**
GRIMEY WAYS
By Ray Vinci
XMAS WITH AN ATL SHOOTER
By Ca$h & Destiny Skai
KING KILLA
By Vincent "Vitto" Holloway

BOOKS BY LDP'S CEO, CA$H

TRUST IN NO MAN

TRUST IN NO MAN 2

TRUST IN NO MAN 3

BONDED BY BLOOD

SHORTY GOT A THUG

THUGS CRY

THUGS CRY 2

THUGS CRY 3

TRUST NO BITCH

TRUST NO BITCH 2

TRUST NO BITCH 3

TIL MY CASKET DROPS

RESTRAINING ORDER

RESTRAINING ORDER 2

IN LOVE WITH A CONVICT

LIFE OF A HOOD STAR

XMAS WITH AN ATL SHOOTER

King Killa